NUCLEAR WINTER I

FIRST STRIKE

BOBBY AKART

THANK YOU

Thank you for reading FIRST STRIKE, book one in the Nuclear Winter Series by Author Bobby Akart.

Join Bobby Akart's mailing list to learn about upcoming releases, deals, contests, and appearances. Follow this link to: BobbyAkart.com

Or, visit his dedicated feature page on Amazon at Amazon.com/BobbyAkart

PRAISE FOR AUTHOR BOBBY AKART

"Bobby Akart is the master of nail biting, edge of your seat fiction based on fact."
~ Amazon Review of New Madrid Earthquake

"Author Bobby Akart has the acumen to be able to weave fact-based fiction into a very believable story full of intrigue, suspense, and action."
~ Amazon Review of Odessa Rising

"He takes you on a ride that becomes a roller-coaster."
~ Amazon Review of Odessa Reborn

"As with any of the best novels, this book really captures your attention and makes it hard to put down at the end of the day."
~ Early review of Nuclear Winter First Strike

"There are no accolades I can give Bobby Akart that haven't been said numerous times. His fact-based, heavily researched stories are the stuff of nightmares. He is truly one of the greatest authors I have ever read."

NUCLEAR WINTER I

FIRST STRIKE

by
Bobby Akart

OTHER WORKS BY AMAZON CHARTS TOP 25 AUTHOR BOBBY AKART

Nuclear Winter
First Strike
Armageddon
Whiteout
Desolation

New Madrid (a standalone, disaster thriller)

Odessa (a Gunner Fox trilogy)
Odessa Reborn
Odessa Rising
Odessa Strikes

The Virus Hunters
Virus Hunters I
Virus Hunters II
Virus Hunters III

The Geostorm Series
The Shift

The Pulse
The Collapse
The Flood
The Tempest
The Pioneers

The Asteroid Series (A Gunner Fox trilogy)
Discovery
Diversion
Destruction

The Doomsday Series
Apocalypse
Haven
Anarchy
Minutemen
Civil War

The Yellowstone Series
Hellfire
Inferno
Fallout
Survival

The Lone Star Series
Axis of Evil
Beyond Borders
Lines in the Sand
Texas Strong
Fifth Column
Suicide Six

The Pandemic Series
Beginnings
The Innocents

Level 6
Quietus

The Blackout Series
36 Hours
Zero Hour
Turning Point
Shiloh Ranch
Hornet's Nest
Devil's Homecoming

The Boston Brahmin Series
The Loyal Nine
Cyber Attack
Martial Law
False Flag
The Mechanics
Choose Freedom
Patriot's Farewell (standalone novel)
Black Friday (standalone novel)
Seeds of Liberty (Companion Guide)

The Prepping for Tomorrow Series
Cyber Warfare
EMP: Electromagnetic Pulse
Economic Collapse

Copyright Information

ACKNOWLEDGMENTS

Creating a novel that is both informative and entertaining requires a tremendous team effort. Writing is the easy part.

For their efforts in making the Nuclear Winter series a reality, I would like to thank Hristo Argirov Kovatliev for his incredible artistic talents in creating my cover art. He and Dani collaborate (and conspire) to create the most incredible cover art in the publishing business. A huge hug of appreciation goes out to Pauline Nolet, the *Professor*, for her editorial prowess and patience in correcting this writer's same tics after fifty-plus novels. Thank you, Drew Avera, a United States Navy veteran, who has brought his talented formatting skills from a writer's perspective to create multiple formats for reading my novels. Welcome back Kevin Pierce, the beloved voice of the apocalypse, who will bring my words to life in audio format.

Now, for the serious stuff. Accurately portraying the aftermath of nuclear war required countless hours of never-ending research and interviews of some of the brightest minds in the world of planetary science.

Once again, as I immersed myself in the science and history, source material and research flooded my inbox from around the globe. Without the assistance of many individuals and organizations, this story could not be told. Please allow me a moment to acknowledge a few of those individuals whom, without their tireless efforts and patience, the *Nuclear Winter* series could not have been written.

Many thanks to the preeminent researchers and engineers at the National Center for Atmospheric Research in Boulder, Colorado. Between responses to my inquiries and the volumes of scientific publications provided, I was able to grasp the catastrophic effect a regional nuclear war would have upon the Earth and its atmosphere. They impressed upon me the danger of inundating our air with the results of these massive nuclear detonations. It would result in a climatic event akin to the eruption of the Yellowstone Supervolcano.

A shout-out must go to Brian Toon, professor of atmospheric and oceanic sciences at the University of Colorado – Boulder. He has been a tireless advocate warning all who'll listen of the consequences of nuclear winter. This quote had a profound effect on me and led to the writing of the Nuclear Winter series—*It could potentially end global civilization as we know it.* In other words, TEOTWAWKI.

At Rutgers University, Distinguished Professor and acclaimed climatologist, Alan Robock, has been studying the potential threat of nuclear winter with a particular focus on the human impact. The incredibly fast cooling of the planet would trigger global famine and mass starvation. His models of fires and firestorms in the aftermath of a nuclear war provided me detailed estimates of the extent of wildfires as well as the timeframes associated with the smoke and soot lofted into the atmosphere.

Now, to the special friends and acquaintances who helped make my characters realistic. Admittedly, my exposure to teenagers is non-existent. Yet, from time-to-time, I have teen characters who speak a different language, sort of. In order to add a sense of realism to their dialogue, I call upon a number of resources to enlighten me on their own unique vocabulary.

Thank you to Pam and Tim Johnson who reached out to their teenage grandson, Simon Andrews. He's credited with a number of phrases in the Nuclear Winter series including—Yeet! Dear reader, this interesting term will be explained within First Strike, book one.

Thank you to Jessica Devenny, referred to me via Pam Johnson and her bestie, Betty. Jessica's sons, Jacob and Parker, also helped to fill my *teenspeak* dictionary.

Also, Dani's followers on Instagram were up to the task. Instagram is one of the few social media networks where the vast majority of your interactions are positive compared to Facebook and the downright nasty Twitter platform. When called upon, hundreds of terms and phrases were offered. Thanks to you all!

The cigar selections in Nuclear Winter First Strike were suggested by my friend Brad Levy. Brad has read all of my novels, twice, in most cases. He always looks forward to his day on the lanai, enjoying a fine cigar and a good book. Thank you, my friend!

Finally, as always, a special thank you to my team of loyal friends who've always supported my work and provided me valuable insight from a reader's perspective—Denise Keef, Joe Carey, Shirley Nicholson, Bennita Barnett, Karl Hughey, and Brian Alderman.

For the Nuclear Winter series, several avid readers volunteered to make my writing *more better*: Martin McDonell, Cody McDonell, Leslie Bryant, Tim Coppess, Caryl Lynne Honea, Mike Neubecker, Pete Steffens, and Kelly Trone.

Thanks, y'all, and Choose Freedom!

ABOUT THE AUTHOR, BOBBY AKART

Author Bobby Akart has been ranked by Amazon as #25 on the Amazon Charts list of most popular, bestselling authors. He has achieved recognition as the #1 bestselling Horror Author, #1 bestselling Science Fiction Author, #5 bestselling Action & Adventure Author, #7 bestselling Historical Fiction Author and #10 on Amazon's bestselling Thriller Author list.

Mr. Akart has delivered up-all-night thrillers to readers in 245 countries and territories worldwide. He has sold over one million books in all formats, which includes over forty international bestsellers, in nearly fifty fiction and nonfiction genres.

His novel *Yellowstone: Hellfire* reached the Top 25 on the Amazon bestsellers list and earned him multiple Kindle All-Star awards for most pages read in a month and most pages read as an author. The Yellowstone series vaulted him to the #25 bestselling author on Amazon Charts, and the #1 bestselling science fiction author.

Since its release in November 2020, his standalone novel, New Madrid Earthquake, has been ranked #1 on Amazon Charts in multiple countries as a natural disaster thriller.

Mr. Akart is a graduate of the University of Tennessee after pursuing a dual major in economics and political science. He went on to obtain his master's degree in business administration and his doctorate degree in law at Tennessee.

Mr. Akart has provided his readers a diverse range of topics that are both informative and entertaining. His attention to detail and impeccable research has allowed him to capture the imagination of his readers through his fictional works and bring them valuable knowledge through his nonfiction books.

SIGN UP for Bobby Akart's mailing list to learn of special offers, view bonus content, and be the first to receive news about new releases.

Visit www.BobbyAkart.com for details.

DEDICATIONS

With the love and support of my wife, Dani, together with the unconditional love of Bullie and Boom, the princesses of the palace, I'm able to tell you these stories. It would be impossible for me to write without them in my heart.

Freedom and security are precious gifts that we, as Americans, should never take for granted. I would like to thank the men and women, past and present, of the United States Armed Forces for willingly making sacrifices each day to provide us that freedom and security. Also, a not of thanks to their families who endure countless sleepless nights as their loved ones are deployed around he world.

They are the sheepdogs who live to protect the flock. They bravely and unselfishly confront the wolves who threaten our country, our freedoms, and their brothers in arms from those who would bring destruction to our door.

Choose Freedom!

AUTHOR'S INTRODUCTION

February, 2021

Since scientific discoveries in the late 1930s made nuclear weapons a possibility, the world began to realize they posed an enormous threat to humanity. In 1942, with the secretive research effort in the U.S. known as the Manhattan Project, a race toward nuclear supremacy began. Since their very first use in World War II, different leaders and organizations have been trying to prevent proliferation to additional countries. Despite their efforts, more nation-states than ever before have obtained nuclear weapons.

Following pioneering research from scientists in the early 1980s, the world was introduced to the concept of nuclear winter. Researchers had known that a large nuclear war could cause severe global environmental effects, including dramatic cooling of surface temperatures, declines in precipitation, and increased ultraviolet radiation.

The term nuclear winter was coined specifically to refer to atmospheric cooling that resulted in winter-like temperatures occurring year-round. Regardless of whether extreme cold temperatures were reached, there would be severe consequences for humanity. But how severe would those consequences be? And what should the world be doing about it?

To the first question, the short answer is nobody knows with absolute certainty. The total human impacts of nuclear winter are both uncertain and under-studied. The aftereffects of the twin atomic bombs dropped on Japan to end World War II were not analyzed in depth. More research on the impacts would be very helpful, but treaties have limited nuclear weapons testing. Therefore research, other than theoretical conclusions, has been limited.

As to the question of what the world should be doing about it, all nations agree non-proliferation is a start. However, there are still more than sufficient nuclear weapons capable of being launched to bring the world to the brink of Armageddon.

Today, nuclear winter is not a hot topic among the world's leaders. When the Cold War ended, so did attention to the catastrophic threat of nuclear winter. That started to change in 2007 with a new line of nuclear winter research that used advanced climate models developed for the study of global warming.

Relative to the 1980s research, the new research found that the smoke from nuclear firestorms would travel higher into the atmosphere causing nuclear winter to last longer than previously thought. This research also found dangerous effects from smaller nuclear exchanges, such as an India-Pakistan nuclear war detonating *only* one hundred total nuclear warheads.

Some new research has also examined the human impacts of nuclear winter. Researchers simulated agricultural crop growth in the aftermath of a hundred-weapon India-Pakistan nuclear war. The results were startling. The scenario could cause agriculture productivity to decline by around twenty to sixty percent for several years after the exchange.

The studies looked at major staple crops in China and the United States, two of the largest food producers. Other countries and other crops would likely face similar declines. Following such crop declines, severe global famine could ensue. One study estimated the total extent of the famine by comparing crop declines to global malnourishment data. When food becomes scarce, the poor and malnourished are typically hit the hardest. This study estimated two billion people would be at risk of starvation. And this is from the hundred-weapon India-Pakistan nuclear war scenario. A larger nuclear exchange involving the U.S., China, or Russia would have more severe impacts because the payloads are much larger.

This is where the recent research stops. To the best of my knowledge there have been no current studies examining the secondary effects of famines, such as disease outbreaks and violent conflicts due to societal collapse.

There is also a need to examine the human impacts of ultraviolet radiation. That would include an increased medical burden due to skin cancer and other diseases. It would also include further losses to the agriculture ecosystems because the ultraviolet radiation harms plants and animals. At this time, we can only make educated guesses about what these impacts would be, informed in part by research surrounding enormous volcanic eruptions.

A note on the impact on humanity, we can look to society's reaction to recent political events. Imagine what U.S. cities would look like if the triggering event for protests and riots was based on lack of food. The social unrest would quickly spread into suburban areas as the have-nots would search for sustenance from those who might have it.

When analyzing the risk of nuclear winter, one question is of paramount importance: Would there be long-term or even permanent harm to human civilization? Research shows nuclear winter would last ten years or more. Would the world ever be able to come back from the devasting loss of billions of lives?

Carl Sagan was one of the first people to recognize this point in a commentary he wrote on nuclear winter for Foreign Affairs magazine. Sagan believed nuclear winter could cause human extinction in which case all members of future generations would be lost. He argued that this made nuclear winter vastly more important than the direct effects of nuclear war which could, in his words, *kill only hundreds of millions of people.*

Sagan was, however, right that human extinction would cause permanent harm to human civilization. It is debatable whether nuclear winter could cause human extinction. Rutgers professor Alan Robock, a respected nuclear winter researcher, believes it is unlikely. He commented, "Especially in Australia and New Zealand, humans would have a better chance to survive."

Why Australia and New Zealand? A nuclear war would presumably occur mainly or entirely in the northern hemisphere. The southern hemisphere would still experience environmental disruption, but it would not be as severe. Australia and New Zealand further benefit from being surrounded by water which further softens the effect.

This is hardly a cheerful thought as it leaves open the chance of human extinction, at least for those of us north of the equator. Given all the uncertainty and the limited available research, it is impossible to rule out the possibility of human extinction. In any event, the possibility should not be dismissed.

Even if people survive, there could still be permanent harm to humanity. Small patches of survivors would be extremely vulnerable to subsequent disasters. They certainly could not keep up the massively complex civilization we enjoy today. In addition to the medical impact, the destruction of the power grid, the heartbeat of most nations, would likely occur due to the electromagnetic pulse generated by the nuclear detonations. It would take many years to rebuild the critical infrastructure ruined by the blasts.

It would be a long and uncertain rebuilding process and survivors might never get civilization back to where it is now. More importantly, they might never get civilization to where we now stand poised to take it in the future. Our potentially bright future could be forever dimmed, permanently.

Nuclear winter is a very large and serious risk. In some ways, it doesn't change nuclear weapons policy all that much. Everyone already knew that nuclear war would be highly catastrophic. The prospect of a prolonged nuclear winter means that nuclear war is even more catastrophic. That only reinforces policies that have long been in place, from deterrence to disarmament. Indeed, military officials have sometimes reacted to nuclear winter by saying that it just makes their nuclear deterrence policies that much more effective. Disarmament advocates similarly cite nuclear winter as justifying their policy goals. But the basic structure of the policy debate unchanged.

In other ways, nuclear winter changes nuclear weapons policy quite dramatically. Because of nuclear winter, noncombatant states may be severely harmed by nuclear war. Nuclear winter gives every country great incentive to reduce tensions and de-escalate conflicts between nuclear-capable states.

Nation-states that are stockpiling nuclear weapons should also take notice. Indeed, the biggest policy implication of nuclear winter could be that it puts the interests of nuclear-capable nations in greater alignment. Because of nuclear winter, a nuclear war between any two major nuclear weapon states could severely harm each of the others. According to intelligence sources, there are nine total nuclear-armed states with Iran prepared to breakthrough as the tenth. This multiplies the risk of being harmed by nuclear attacks while only marginally increasing the benefits of nuclear deterrence. By shifting the balance of harms versus benefits, nuclear winter can promote nuclear disarmament.

Additional policy implications come from the risk of permanent harm to human civilization. If society takes this risk seriously, then it should go to great lengths to reduce the risk. It could stockpile food to avoid nuclear famine, or develop new agricultural paradigms that can function during nuclear winter.

And it could certainly ratchet up its efforts to improve relations between nuclear weapon states. These are things that we can do right now even while we await more detailed research on nuclear winter risk.

Against that backdrop, I hope you'll be entertained and informed by this fictional account of the world thrust into Nuclear Winter. God help us if it ever comes to pass.

REAL-WORLD NEWS EXCERPTS

U.S. EXPLODES TEST H-BOMB; EYEWITNESS TELLS BLAST FURY

~ *Los Angeles Examiner, November 5, 1952*

The blast expanded in seconds to a blinding white fireball more than three miles across (the Hiroshima fireball had measured little more than one-tenth of a mile) and rose over the horizon like a dark sun. The crews of the task force, thirty miles away, felt a swell of heat as if someone had opened a hot oven, heat that persisted long enough to seem menacing. "You would swear that the whole world was on fire," one sailor wrote home.

Swirling and boiling, glowing purplish with gamma-ionized light, the expanding fireball began to rise, becoming a burning mushroom cloud balanced on a wide, dirty stem with a curtain of water around its base that slowly fell back into the sea.

The wings of the B-36 orbiting fifteen miles from ground zero at forty thousand feet heated to ninety-three degrees almost instantly.

In a minute and a half, the enlarging fireball cloud reached

57,000 feet; in two and a half minutes, when the shock wave arrived at the Estes, the cloud passed 100,000 feet.

The shock wave announced itself with a sharp report followed by a long thunder of broken rumbling.

RUSSIANS SPEED UP CUBA BASES, U.S. PREPARING FURTHER ACTION

~ The St. Louis Globe-Democrat, October 28, 1962

Nuclear missiles near full operational capability.

The White House said late Friday that a nuclear missile build-up in Cuba is continuing at a rapid pace, "apparently ... directed to achieving full operational capability as soon as possible."

The statement was clearly aimed at warning the Soviets the United States is able to keep watch on their activity in Cuba.

It described the scene at missile sites indicating the Russians had not slowed their attempt to establish ballistic missile launching platforms, despite President Kennedy's declaration that existence of those sites has brought on the crisis.

INDIA SETS OFF NUCLEAR DEVICE

~ NY Times, May 19, 1974

India conducted today her first successful test of a powerful nuclear device.

The surprise announcement means that India is the sixth nation to have exploded a nuclear device. The others are the United States, the Soviet Union, Britain, France and China.

A brief Government statement said that India's Atomic Energy Commission had carried out "a peaceful 'nuclear explosion' experiment." The underground blast took place "at a depth of more than 100 meters," or about 330 feet, the statement said.

In exploding the device, India was entirely within her rights in international law, Government officials said.

NORTH KOREA WITHDRAWS FROM NUCLEAR TREATY

~ *UK Guardian, January 10, 2003*

The North Korean nuclear-weapons crisis intensified today as Pyongyang announced it is withdrawing from the 1968 Nuclear Nonproliferation Treaty.

Under the treaty, North Korea was barred from making nuclear weapons, but said it was pulling out of it today with immediate effect, blaming US aggression for its decision.

North Korea warned the United States against taking retaliatory military action, saying it would "finally lead to the third world war". However, the regime routinely issues such inflammatory comments.

The North Korean government said in a statement carried on KCNA, its official news agency: "We can no longer remain bound to the Nonproliferation Treaty, allowing the country's security and the dignity of our nation to be infringed upon."

NORTH KOREA ALLEGEDLY HELPING IRAN BUILD NUCLEAR WEAPONS

~ *The Independent, May 29, 2015*

An Iranian dissident group said Thursday a delegation of North Korean nuclear weapons experts was in Iran in April visiting a heavily guarded secret military site, presumed to be a nuclear weapons development facility.

The National Council of Resistance of Iran (NCRI), which exposed the existence of a key Iranian nuclear weapons facility in 2002 and significant, illicit Iranian nuclear weapons developments since then, said this was the third visit to Iran in 2015 by a North Korean delegation.

Also, citing confidential information from sources inside Iran's Islamic Revolutionary Guard Corps, research and aerospace agencies, said in a statement another group of North Korean nuclear weapons experts is slated to return to Iran in June.

Iran's hardline government has repeatedly said it is pursuing a nuclear program for peaceful purposes. But the deputy director of NCRI's Washington-based U.S. office said the group has uncovered what he called a "big, big, red flag".

During North Korea's third nuclear weapons test in February 2013, according to NCRI, Iran's top nuclear experts traveled to Pyongyang to observe the trial.

EPIGRAPH

No war really comes unexpectedly. The drums are beating long
before a single shot is fired.
~ Margaret Case Harriman, Author

It is an unfortunate fact that we can secure peace only by preparing
for war.
~ U.S. President John F. Kennedy

If we don't end war, war will end us.
~ H. G. Wells, English Writer

The survivors of a nuclear holocaust will envy the dead.
~ Nikita Khrushchev, First Secretary of the Soviet Union

After great trouble for humanity, a greater one is prepared
The Great Mover renews the ages:
Rain, blood, milk, famine, steel and plague,
In the heavens fire seen, a long spark running.
~ Nostradamus, Century II, Quatrain 46

Except for fools and madmen, everyone knows that nuclear war
would be an unprecedented human catastrophe.
~ Carl Sagan, Planetary Scientist and Author

Death and the strong force of fate are waiting.
There will come a dawn or sunset or high noon
When a man will take my life in battle, too.
~ Homer, The Iliad

Alea iacta est.
The die has been cast.
~ A Roman General to Julius Caesar as he prepared to lead his army
across the Rubicon River

NUCLEAR WINTER I
FIRST STRIKE

And God said, "Let there be light," and there was light.

Until there wasn't.
And so it begins ...

PROLOGUE

Early October
Isfahan, Iran

For more than a decade, he'd been simply referred to as Agent L, short for *Lightning*. His true identity had exploded along with the Ford Explorer he'd been driving as several pursuit vehicles chased him out of Algeria following the assassination of a Libyan target. Those in pursuit reported seeing the fireball, together with the driver's side door sailing through the air until it crashed into a storefront forty feet away. The oily black cloud of smoke spewed out of the carcass of the Explorer, the flames hungrily devouring anything flammable.

The pursuers reveled in their victory as they verily confirmed that the famed Mossad agent had been forever dispatched to the Gates of Hell. Israel privately mourned the loss of its prized operative, who'd led a team with no name designation on many operations on behalf of the Jerusalem government. Their own satellite reconnaissance confirmed no one could have survived the blast.

There was no memorial service for Agent L. His code name was retired forever, along with his moniker—Lightning. He was presumed dead by everyone.

Yet here he was leaning against a stucco wall on the streets of Isfahan, a city of two million, located in central Iran. Isfahan, a word meaning *half the world*, was the cultural center of Iran. Its elaborate mosques, adorned with ancient mosaic tiles and remarkably well-preserved calligraphy, added to the beautiful hardscapes found throughout the city.

Isfahan was also the location of the Islamic Republic's largest nuclear assembly and production plant. Over Israel's continued objections, appeasement policies from Western governments resulted in Iran's nuclear weapons program proliferating. That, coupled with technological assistance from Russia and North Korea, resulted in the rogue nation pulling even with their sworn enemy to the west—Israel.

Israel had made it known for decades that Iran was approaching a red line, a line in the sand that couldn't be crossed. Now, Iran, with its ninety nuclear warheads, was on par with the Israelis. At the United Nations, the Israeli prime minister made his feelings on the burgeoning Iranian nuclear arsenal loud and clear. Enough was enough.

That was three weeks ago. Agent L, who lived in a Greek villa overlooking the Mediterranean, had received a packet of materials and an offer. A lucrative offer. Payable in an incredible amount of untraceable bitcoin. His employers never revealed their true identity. But for a seasoned intelligence operative like himself, all indicators pointed in a single direction. A nation he'd done work for in the past. One whose offers bore a marked resemblance to this one.

Only, this was the largest compensation package he'd ever been presented. The task was a difficult one, to be sure, but not beyond his capabilities. He would have to go it alone, which was his preference. The result when, not if, he was successful would be a tremendous ancillary benefit to the nation he loved.

A throng of pedestrians shuffled their way along the sidewalks of a small road that led to the nuclear enrichment facility on the outskirts of the city. Nearby, an annual arts fair had commenced that morning, complete with musicians vying for patrons' attention and vendors who were hawking everything from balloons for the kids to delectable treats for adults.

The afternoon was blustery and warm for early October. A balmy breeze that swept down the dirt-covered streets of the ancient city reminded him of Tel Aviv, where he was born. He shielded his eyes from the sun to watch the tops of the decrepit palms rustling as though they were applauding the performers nearby.

Agent L glanced over his shoulder as a flatbed loaded with crates bound by heavy-duty straps lumbered along the rough road toward him. The driver, who was partially blinded by the sun, seemed to be having a rough time choosing the appropriate gear as he prepared to leave the city limits. He revved the engine, and the truck's exhaust spewed out a black trail of diesel as it trundled past him.

Just ahead, by prearrangement, a cart led by the most stubborn donkey in Isfahan awaited the truck's approach. Just a moment before the truck's arrival, a man led the cart into the roadway. The driver blared his horn in anger and swerved to the left, careening onto the sidewalk. Several pedestrians stepped back from the truck's path in time to avoid being run down.

"Moron!" the driver exclaimed through his open window. "Move that ass. And yours, too!"

Agent L didn't hesitate. He rushed across the street during the chaos and easily closed on the rear bumper of the truck within seconds. While all eyes, including the driver's, were on the braying donkey, Agent L deftly climbed up the back of the truck, hurled himself over the steel gate, and rolled between the crates until he was hidden.

Now he would hold his breath until the driver arrived at his appointed destination—the Isfahan Nuclear Technology Center, or INTC.

Built with Chinese assistance and opened in 1984, the facility at Isfahan was Iran's largest nuclear research complex, employing nearly three thousand scientists. In the past year, United States and Israeli intelligence had confirmed that the INTC had become the center of Iran's secret nuclear weapons program. It operated three Chinese-made nuclear reactors. Its conversion facility, fuel production plant, and zirconium cladding plants were state of the art. The Chinese, through their proxy North Korea, had spared no expense in helping Iran become a nuclear powerhouse once the U.S.-imposed sanctions had been lifted years ago.

Agent L had been hired to deal the program a setback.

The security detail manning the walled perimeter of the complex was heavily armed. They wore light windbreakers to ward off the pelting sand stirred up by the October winds, customary for that time of year.

In addition to the perimeter guards, several other armed personnel could be seen wandering through the inner compound. These men were assigned to the top-level scientists who operated the facility. They were members of the Ministry of Intelligence and were not to be trifled with. Agent L had lost a partner to their assassins years ago.

The truck pulled into the loading dock area surrounded by a simple chain-link fence. If the intelligence he was given was correct, and it always was from this particular employer, the driver would park the truck and leave it for others to unload the next day. One crate on the flatbed truck would be specially identified for Agent L to view its markings with his night-vision optics. Everything he needed was contained inside.

He trusted this employer, as they'd never let him down. Naturally, he was uneasy when he learned he'd have to enter the INTC compound with nothing more than two sidearms, a knife and several Japanese *shurikens*, also known as throwing stars. With these minimal weapons, he could clandestinely manage to eliminate a single target or two. However, he couldn't fight an army of security personnel when it came time to extract. An extraction that he considered near impossible, making him wonder if it was by design.

As darkness set in, he continued to surveil his surroundings. The addition of the personal bodyguards accompanying the scientists around the compound resulted in complications for the former MOSSAD operative.

Once complete darkness had set in, he located the specially marked crate and quietly pried it open with his knife. As promised, the interior contained a Galil rifle, the Israeli version of the AK-47. Weighing just over eight pounds, this battle rifle was capable of firing six hundred fifty 5.56-millimeter rounds per minute. He was provided six fifty-round magazines to complement the two hundred rounds of ammunition for his sidearm.

Agent L quickly checked the rifle and then donned the black combat vest found in the crate. The loadout would be heavy, but necessary. He secured the additional magazines in the pouches and took another few minutes to look around the compound before he moved on to the next phase of the operation.

Every light in the compound's main entrance glowed bright, the expansive grounds fully illuminated and designed to eliminate potential hiding places. The utility yard where he was located was dimly lit by comparison, yet bright enough for him to be observed by the perimeter guards at the two towers near that side of the complex.

He tried to locate and count as many hostiles manning the fenced area as possible. His intelligence did not indicate what time the shift would change, so he had to be mindful of that plus the time for his attack. The number of armed personnel were a testament to the importance of the work being performed at Isfahan. The ten-foot-high walls surrounding the complex added to the sense of invulnerability to outside observers.

Invulnerable to most, except Agent L.

Comfortable that he wouldn't be disturbed, he turned his attention back to the contents of the crate. Again using his night-vision optics, he undertook the arduous task of assembling a complex piece of machinery, a technological wonder that combined artificial intelligence with a deadly weapon.

While constantly checking his surroundings, Agent L assembled the components of the weapon, carefully checking his progress against the plans written in his native Hebrew. Methodically, he pieced the weapon together. He constantly checked his watch to ensure he wasn't approaching go time. The instruction materials he'd received were adamant that he meet his employer's timetable. There were certain preparations that had to be made, and there was no margin for error once he'd placed the weapon in position.

Once it was fully assembled, Agent L shook his head from side to side in wonderment. The weapon reminded him of something out of an American big-screen movie. He'd often said if a moviemaker could imagine it, then it could be done.

He hoisted the device onto his shoulder and stealthily climbed over the steel gate at the back of the truck. Once he was on the ground, he raced across the utility yard with the seventy-pound device weighing heavily on his back.

Agent L slid in between the dumpsters until he had a clear view of the compound's entrance and the lush area of grass surrounded by beautifully maintained plant material. The oasis created for visitors and workers alike stood in stark contrast to the dirt-covered surroundings.

Using a small bolt cutter supplied in the crate, he cut a hole in the chain-link fence, moving slowly to avoid attracting attention. He prepared the weapon according to the instructions provided, and then he flipped down the cover of a small control panel located on the mount. He powered on the display in dark mode and entered the code provided in his materials. Then he held his breath and squinted as he watched the display for instructions. His handlers responded with a message on the screen, requesting adjustments, which he promptly complied with. Then a green light illuminated.

Check. Now he was on his own.

Agent L glanced at his watch. It was approaching the time for Salaat Fajr, the morning Shia Muslim prayer.

Quietly. Reverently. The scientists who operated the nuclear facility at Isfahan made their way into the courtyard with their prayer blankets. Among the men who would kneel that morning was Mohsen Farouk, the mastermind of the covert Iranian program to develop and then proliferate the nation's nuclear arsenal. He would be joined by everyone within his team. The best of the best who'd gathered in Isfahan to assess North Korea's technological advances using low-Earth orbiting satellites as a means to launch nuclear warheads.

To be sure, dropping a bomb on the facility at this hour would more than accomplish his employer's purposes. However, bombs left breadcrumbs, trails of evidence of where they came from, easily allowing fingers of blame to be pointed. Operatives like him were ghosts, before and after death.

Agent L retreated from the weapon, slightly concerned about a malfunction or a case of mistaken identity. He scanned the perimeter and confirmed his plan to extract himself from the compound when the time came. He checked his watch. It was 5:03. The grassy area was filled with INTC personnel, men only, kneeling on their prayer blankets.

He studied his digital watch.

5:04. Sunrise.

From a satellite high above the planet, artificial intelligence pulled the trigger on the computer-controlled machine gun. The powerful 7.62-millimeter rounds poured out of the drum magazines affixed to the bottom of the weapon. The laser sights, powered by the AI, scanned the courtyard full of those in prayer, searching for movement. Any quiver or flinch or deep breath created a target for the weapon, which immediately locked on and riddled the body with bullets.

Agent L was astonished at the speed and accuracy of the killing. No human being, including a trained killer like himself, could accomplish the slaughter of over a hundred people in mere seconds.

The incredible killing machine then turned its sights on the security personnel manning the perimeter.

One by one, the targets were eliminated with ease. The electronically controlled gun turret swept back and forth, alternating between the armed guards on the perimeter wall and the security personnel racing through the front entrance to lend an assist. Shouting and screams of agony filled the air as the weapon spent hundreds of rounds, killing everyone.

Agent L heard sirens in the distance. Helicopters could be heard inbound. He scooped up his rifle and ran to the rear of the utility yard, where he climbed the chain-link fence at the point where it adjoined the perimeter wall. He ran along the top of the wall until he reached the northernmost side of the compound, relieved that the building stood between him and the most destructive automatic weapon he'd ever witnessed.

As dust rose into the morning sky from the vehicles approaching the facility, Agent L paused to look toward the rising sun in the east. He was certain his employers—in Beijing—would be pleased with the results.

PART I

ONE WEEK IN OCTOBER

Day one, Friday, October 18

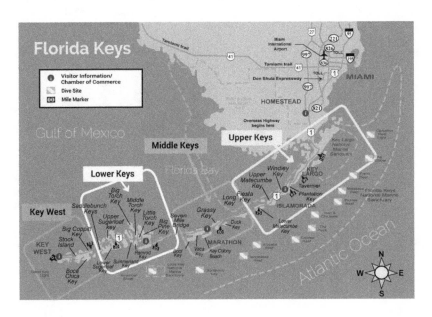

CHAPTER ONE

Friday, October 18
Driftwood Key
Florida Keys, USA

Hank Albright looked out across the turquoise waters of the Gulf of Mexico. Off in the distance, storm clouds were brewing, causing the points of the waves to lance up and down. The miniature pinpricks at their crests were white against the backdrop of the bluish-green gulf. It was never ending. A perpetual motion machine of energy coming ashore, teeming with life and creatures and an entire world he'd spent his life admiring.

He'd always been drawn to the water. He had been born on Driftwood Key in the Albright family home, which had been there since the early days following the connection of the string of islands to the mainland via the Flagler Railroad. The original *Conchs*, as those early settlers were called at the turn of the twentieth century, were dependent on the pristine waters for survival.

Albrights, Russells, Pinders, and Parkers shared a common background. Their forefathers were American Tories who fled the Thirteen Colonies at the end of the Revolution to a new home in the Bahamas. They became fishermen and sailors. They discovered the bounty beneath the pristine Caribbean waters and made a life for themselves.

Their descendants ultimately found their way to the Florida Keys when transportation generated commerce and trade routes to a burgeoning American economy. They brought their trade and craft with them and harvested the sea of the large mollusks known as conch.

The Albrights were pioneers in their own right. In a way, the Florida Keys was somewhat of a wilderness at the time the Flagler Railroad was built. Like their counterparts who'd traveled to the west on the mainland, the new settlers built towns, established local governments, and created businesses to sustain themselves. Today, the one-hundred-twenty-five-mile-long chain of islands that begins just south of Miami and stretches to within ninety miles of Cuba is known for its sun, sand, surf, and tourism.

Hank, despite having lived his entire fifty-one years on Driftwood Key, never tired of the deep scent of saltwater, the moist tropical air, and the mild subtropical climate. Certainly, hurricanes were a factor, but Driftwood Key and the buildings that dotted its landscape had withstood the worst of what Mother Nature had to offer. Thus far, anyway.

He slid his hands into the pockets of his white linen pants. Hank didn't have a uniform per se, but if he did, white linen pants topped with a Tommy Bahama camp shirt would be it. No shoes required. He looked and dressed the part of a retired islander with sun-kissed skin, bleach-blond hair, and a slightly weathered face courtesy of years of exposure to the sun and salty sea.

Hank, however, was not retired. He operated the Driftwood Key Inn, a property on the National Register of Historic Places, built by the Albright family in the early 1920s. The inn, which was more of a village, actually, was situated on a twenty-eight-acre island in the heart of the Middle Keys just west of Marathon.

Driftwood Key was unique in that it was not located directly on State Road A1A, a north-south Florida highway that runs along the

Atlantic Ocean from Key West to Fernandina Beach at the Georgia border. Many a crooner had belted out a song about A1A, providing imagery of swaying palm trees and margaritas to music lovers.

The Albright property was an anomaly in the Keys. It was only accessible by a private bridge that connected it to the much larger Vaca Key. It was exclusive as room rates go, yet all-inclusive, meaning it was an expensive property to visit, but its guests were provided everything they needed for their stay.

Throughout Driftwood Key were nineteen self-catered cottages complete with kitchens and all the amenities. Food was delivered to the guests daily by the inn's staff or, at their option, they could have dinner with Hank and other guests in the main house.

The private beach and stunning freshwater swimming pool were surrounded by native palm trees and vegetation. The mature growth, coupled with the ever-present breezes off the gulf, allowed guests to completely block out any sound or light emanating from the other keys.

Hank loved his home and business. He understood why people were drawn to the warm, maritime climate of the southernmost part of the U.S. Who could argue with a beachfront umbrella, toes in the sand, and a cold drink in hand? Most couldn't and were willing to spend their entire budget on a multi-thousand-dollar stay at the Driftwood Key Inn.

Hank mindlessly kicked at the sand that morning as he spoke to his wife, a daily ritual since she'd died of breast cancer eight years ago. He still missed her, and coming out to the beach with the break of dawn was his way of keeping her close to his heart. The sadness and despair over her loss had passed years ago. There were constant memories of her throughout Driftwood Key. A random flower garden planted here. A secluded hammock hung there. These reminders didn't torture Hank. They allowed him to hold her close to his heart.

"Good morning, Mr. Hank!" a voice cheerily announced.

Hank turned to greet Jimmy Free, the youngest son of Sonny and Phoebe, who had worked for the Albright family since they were young. The entire staff at the inn referred to him as Mr. Hank. Early on, he tried to force them to call him Hank. Heck, he'd grown up with most of them, and attaching the word *mister* to his name didn't seem right. Nonetheless, out of respect, once he took over the inn's operations, they began to refer to him as Mr. Albright. Hank pitched a fit, and finally a compromise was struck. It was agreed that he would be henceforth referred to as Mr. Hank.

Jimmy, like the rest of his family, who'd worked on Driftwood Key for generations, was of Seminole Indian descent. Their ancestors had immigrated to southern Florida in the late eighteenth century and had been employed by merchants after the railroad was built. The Frees were one of the largest Seminole families in the Keys. Jimmy's aunt, Lindsey Free, was the mayor of Monroe County.

"Good morning, Jimmy," Hank greeted heartily. He genuinely liked the young man who'd just taken over the water sports activities at Driftwood Key. Jimmy was one of the many young men who grew up involved in all manners of water activities, from fishing to diving to beach games. His zest for life was addictive, which made him a favorite of the inn's guests.

He handed Hank a red Solo cup with a straw protruding out of it. "Mom asked me to bring this to you."

Hank took the cup and looked at the concoction. It was adorned with a pineapple slice.

"It's a little early for cocktails, don't you think?"

"Said no one ever," replied Jimmy with a toothy grin. The young man's joke was surprising in light of the fact Jimmy had never had a drink in his life as far as Hank knew.

He shrugged and took a tentative sip. His eyebrows rose, and he nodded his head with approval. He sucked it down in earnest the second time around.

He raised the cup in the air. "Hell yeah. I approve. What is it?"

"It's a new breakfast smoothie Mom's trying out. She added flax seed, papaya, banana, and protein powder. Hella good, right?"

Hank laughed as he took another sip. The icy-cold drink gave him a mild attack of brain freeze.

"Hella good," he repeated Jimmy's words.

Jimmy began to unpack his scuba bag containing fins, mask and a snorkel, although he rarely used it. He was capable of holding his breath under water for nearly ten minutes, five times the average person.

"I'm gonna empty out the lobster traps and then get everything set up for the backgammon tournament." The inn had set up dozens of traps around the island to catch Caribbean spiny lobster. Jimmy also liked to dive near the reefs and catch them by hand.

"Fins up, Jimmy!"

The young man provided Hank a thumbs-up and began to jog down the beach. Hank turned toward the main house just as the sun was peeking through the palm trees on the east side of the island. It was gonna be another glorious day in paradise.

CHAPTER TWO

Friday, October 18
Driftwood Key

Hank turned up the smoothie and made sure to consume every drop. He would encourage Phoebe to make this a part of his daily routine if she had time. Hank rarely stopped for breakfast in the morning unless some of the Albright family stayed overnight or a notable guest happened to be in residence.

He bounded up the broad, sand-covered steps leading to the porch of the main house. The sand covered part of the porch, a wood deck covered with an upper balcony and kept cool with numerous ceiling fans that also served to shoo away mosquitos during the summer months. Hank glanced to his left and greeted the man who truly kept the inn running smoothly.

"Whadya say, old man?" he said with a laugh.

"Not as much as you, old man, but *my words of wisdom* are worth listening to," Sonny Free shot back.

Since they were boys, the two men had grown up together as brothers just as close as Hank was to his actual brother, Mike. Hank enjoyed all things water, and Sonny had spent much of his time understanding the unique ecosystem of the Florida Keys. While in high school together, they were in an American literature class that taught Ernest Hemingway's works, including *The Old Man and The Sea*. Sonny referred to Hank as the old man in the sea, and Sonny was playfully called the old man on the land. The nicknames had been used between the two men for thirty-five years.

Sonny noticed the empty cup in Hank's hand. "I see you got a serving of my missus's new concoction. Could you taste the secret ingredient?"

Hank was puzzled because he thought he could identify the fruit and even the hint of vanilla from the protein powder. "Which one?"

"Conch, naturally."

"Really. I swear I couldn't taste it." Conch, which didn't have a strong flavor, usually left a bit of a salty aftertaste. Its rubbery texture must've been obliterated in the blender. "Why would she add conch?"

Sonny laughed and adopted his best Jamaican-islander accent. "Because, mon, it makes you strong, if you know what I mean." Sonny made a fist and rammed it into his hand several times.

Hank shook his head and rolled his eyes. His friends, family, and pretty much anybody who knew him personally had encouraged him to make lady friends. Perhaps, they suggested, find time to go on a date. Or, at worst, enter into one of those *friends with benefits* relationships.

He wasn't interested. Nobody could ever replace his wife, and he was certain he'd constantly be comparing his new relationship to the one he'd had with her. Yet it was human nature to have companionship, and he supposed it was inevitable that the right person would come along at some point. In the meantime, he had Driftwood Key and all that came with it.

"Yeah, yeah. Whatever. Say, Sonny, you wanna install the thatch roof on the new massage gazebo today? We're gonna have a full house this weekend, and I'd like to set up a second spa area for the guests."

"Sounds like a plan. After lunch? It won't take long."

"I'll find you," replied Hank as he entered the open foyer.

Most times of the year, the windows and doors to the main house remained open. Some seasons were buggier than others, and of course, inclement weather caused the staff to batten down the hatches, as they say. Occasionally, a wild critter native to the Florida Keys would find itself inside. Many years ago, the Albrights had eliminated the Key Largo cotton mouse population. By taking away its preferred prey, the ringneck snakes that inhabited the other keys were no longer around either. Once in a while, a curious marsh rabbit would find its way inside the house or even a wayward sanderling. They were allowed to mill about inside until at some point they'd get hungry and move on. This was life for Hank and every living being that inhabited Driftwood Key. They were like family.

The main house, as Hank called it for lack of a better term, was more of a gathering place for guests as well as the center of the inn's administration functions. His bedroom was upstairs, overlooking the gulf-side beach, while family guest rooms were located on the south side of the building, facing the Atlantic. Downstairs, Hank had an office, as did Laura, his reservationist who doubled as a front desk clerk. The formal dining room of the home had been expanded to accommodate up to forty guests. Coupled with a gathering room that included a bar and seating, the main floor was both functional for the business as well as an entertainment hub for guests.

There was one part of the main house off-limits to everyone except a select few. The kitchen. This was Phoebe Free's domain. She was the ruler of the roost. Phoebe was the chef. Head of procurement. Matron of the housekeeping crew. In essence, she was the *grande dame* of Driftwood Key. And Hank liked it.

There were a lot of aspects of the inn's operations that he enjoyed. He was always inserting himself in Sonny's activities. He led more fishing charters than the boat captain he'd hired to perform the task. Evenings were a genuine pleasure, as he was able to get to know folks from all around the world. Conversations were lively. Drinks were enjoyed. Most nights, Hank went to bed with the pride of another successful day under his belt.

He entered the kitchen. "Phoebe! You've done it again. This smoothie was fabulous."

"Well, I'm glad you approve, Mr. Hank. I thought this would be a better start to your day than eggs, sausage, bacon, biscuits, cholesterol, fat, and artery-clogging goodies."

"You know I don't eat that very often," said Hank. Only a couple of times a week, anyway. His father had died of congestive heart failure, and everyone who loved Hank vowed to save him from the same fate. "By the way, the secret ingredient is really not necessary."

Phoebe turned her body slightly to conceal the kitchen counter where she'd been working. She blushed as she sneakily slid an emptied conch shell and its contents behind her back.

"Whatsoever do you mean, Mr. Hank?" she tried to say with a straight face.

"Sonny ratted you out. I couldn't taste it, but I know what you're up to."

Phoebe scowled and glanced toward the open window that overlooked the front porch. If she'd caught a glimpse of her husband, she might've slung a butcher knife at him. "My ingredients and recipes are none of your concern, Mr. Hank. It's just, well, Laura said a nice group of ladies, sisters actually, are coming in for the week today, and I just thought ..." Her voice trailed off before she revealed her true intentions.

Hank set the cup and straw in the sink and rinsed off his hands. He dried them on a dish towel and folded it as he addressed Phoebe. "I know about the reservation, and I know nothing about the guests except they are all female."

"One is a VIP," added Phoebe. "I've been planning several special meals for the week."

"We get lots of VIPs. I don't need to be devouring conch just because one of them is female."

"Not true, Mr. Hank. You've forgotten your father's words. Eyes wide open."

Hank laughed. "He was talking about something totally different. It had nothing to do with you fixing me up with a lady friend."

Phoebe pouted and then furrowed her brow. "Okay, fine. But you will drink these smoothies every day. Please?" Her tone of voice begged just enough that he couldn't say no. Plus, it had been really good.

Hank wrapped his left arm around her shoulder and gave her a hug. "Thanks for taking care of me."

She nodded and patted him on the chest in a motherly sort of way. She was three years younger than Hank, but Phoebe had assumed the role of lady of the house after his wife passed. She eagerly took care of him as if it had been a solemn promise she'd made to the Albright family.

CHAPTER THREE

Peter Albright knew an attack was imminent the moment the shouts of Abu Dhabi police assigned to the conference security detail reached a fever pitch. But that moment was almost too late. Even as the implication of their warnings registered in his brain, and the logical conclusion calculated, the blast of a car bomb ripped through the Abu Dhabi National Exhibition Centre in the United Arab Emirates.

Peter, the oldest son of Hank Albright, was a pool reporter traveling with the U.S. secretary of state. It was one of the worst jobs in journalism unless you loved to travel. Starting from the bottom, you might be assigned to vice presidents, or the second ladies of vice presidents. Dutifully following them to unexciting locales like Dayton, Ohio, or Fresno, California. Then, with luck, you might get elevated to the president's entourage, complete with Secret Service companions and Air Force One amenities.

Peter hadn't achieved that level of experience yet. However, the opportunity to follow Carolyn Sanders, the secretary of state, around the world, was a good one. And she was a frequent flyer to be sure. There wasn't a conference she didn't want to attend. Every event of national importance to America's allies was worthy of her presence. Her appearances rarely made news, as she enjoyed her role as a figurehead for the Washington administration and not a politician trying to make a name for herself. The president seemed to enjoy surrounding himself with, as Peter called them, underachievers.

In any event, he was prepared to pay his dues. Despite the fact his primary employer, the *Washington Times*, paid his salary, Peter ended up doing work for a whole lot of news organizations that didn't pay him one plug nickel. Most often, he'd end up writing a lot of vacuous nonsense, like:

Pool Report #1

SOS greets local officials as she arrives at something-or-other airport. The ambassador sneezes. SOS says, "Gesundheit." Ambassador's aide sneers and shakes head in disgust. Nation is at odds over trade agreement with Germany. SOS waves at people who lined up outside the fence surrounding the tarmac. They are waving American flags and cheering. Everyone scrambles for motorcade vehicles, and entourage pulls away at 10:11 a.m.

It was gripping, scintillating stuff like that. And he had to do it over and over and over again, even when there was even less to say than the faux pas associated with an innocent sneeze.

Today was different.

The bomb blast was sudden and violent. It came without any warning other than the last-second shouting. Peter acted on reflex, diving behind the large sectional sofa in the middle of the conference center lobby. He scrambled on all fours until he could wedge himself under a marble sofa table to shield his body from flying glass and debris.

His duck-and-cover instincts had been developed in press

rooms, not on the field of battle. He'd never experienced anything like a bomb blast, but he'd learned to dodge the verbal assaults of DC politicians looking to make an example of a reporter who questioned the veracity of their statements.

From beneath the marble tabletop, Peter turned his head toward the source of the blast, the circle driveway along the front entry. Once a hundred-foot-wide, thirty-foot-tall section of ornate etched glass, it was now broken into a million pieces, with shards of the panes peppering the attendees of the conference.

Peter checked his exposed skin. For a second, he was relieved. He'd avoided the debris from the blast. He glanced behind him. A woman was dying from a piece of glass that had pierced her neck and severed her jugular. Her once pristine white suit was now being splattered with various shades of crimson.

Mayhem reigned in the lobby. Cries for help. Screams of agony. Moans of pain. The roar of human devastation was deafening.

Then came the gunfire.

Shrieks filled the air as hysterical attendees were frightened to the next level of horror. Peter understood their fear because he sensed there was more to come. The bombs were detonated, and then they were done. However, automatic weapons could go on and on until a good guy with a gun kills the bad guy.

Bullets ricocheted throughout the building. Peter set his jaw in determination. He had no intention of dying under the marble console table. He crawled past the now-dead woman in white along the back of the half-moon sectional. He tried his best to keep the sofa between him and the front entry, the source of the rapid gunfire.

He scanned the lobby. Besides the banks of elevators, there was a hallway that most likely led to the conference center's administrative offices. All the events were to take place on the third floor overlooking the marina below and the Persian Gulf in the distance. He calculated the distance he'd need to cross in the open to make it to the double doors leading down the hallway.

Thirty yards. He could make it.

He listened, waiting for a lull in the gun battle. Maybe the Abu Dhabi police would give an all clear. Or maybe if he waited for just the right time, he'd run out of time.

Peter sprang to his feet and raced along the back of the sofa in a low crouch. He'd made it several paces without being shot when he crashed hard into one of the gunmen. They rolled over and over in a tangle of arms and legs.

The man was as surprised to be knocked down as Peter was to have engaged the killer. Peter's will to live gave him the edge he needed to grab the man's weapon and shoot several rounds into his legs.

Then three things happened all at once.

The killer screamed in agony and shouted, *"Allahu Akbar!" God is most great!* He reached inside his vest and retrieved a grenade. Just as he reached for the safety pin to reveal the striker, Peter shot him in the face. He'd killed someone for the first time.

Well, actually four things. Peter cursed repeatedly. The kind of profanity that someone hurled when both angry and scared.

He gripped the Uzi and pushed himself against the back of the sofa with the heels of his feet. His head and eyes darted in all directions, the barrel of the small rifle following his movements.

To his left, a man tried to run for the same hallway Peter intended to escape through. It didn't end well. A burst of staccato gunfire erupted and struck him several times in the back. His body was slammed to the marble floor, falling like a glass brushed off the edge of a table. Only, instead of shattering, it just hit the floor with a thud, twitching as it fought for its last breath.

The man's eyes were open, staring at Peter. They were behaving like any human would when the realization came that they no longer had a functioning circulatory system. Peter had just seen three people die, three more than he'd seen in his lifetime. He physically shook himself to force his mind to focus.

He couldn't run. The dead man twelve feet away from him proved that. He wasn't prepared to cower behind the sofa. Another detonation would kill him. Gunfire and the subsequent bullets would rip through the cushions, and he'd suffer the same fate as so many others. He needed a distraction.

Peter had an idea. When he and his best friend growing up, Jimmy Free, used to play hide-and-seek on the grounds of Driftwood Key, Peter would often use coconuts to throw Jimmy off his trail when he was getting too close. He wondered what kind of confusion could be garnered from tossing the terrorist's grenade.

Gripping the rifle in one hand, he scrambled over to the dead man and carefully pulled the grenade from his left hand. It was shaped like a large Meyer's lemon not unlike those grown on the key. Even the color was similar.

He held his breath to listen as sporadic gunfire continued. Then he heard the roar of a truck approaching. Was it the police or military? Was it another bomb? He dared not stick his head above the sofa.

Bullets whizzed over his head and pelted the reception table where attendees had been standing moments ago. A woman screamed. And then she was silenced. The gunmen began shouting in Arabic. He couldn't understand what they were saying, but their tone was clear. Orders were given and then acknowledged. The terrorists were sweeping the enormous lobby in search of targets.

It was now or never. Peter glanced to his right and then to his left. The path to the hallway was unobstructed. To his right, a piano together with the mangled instruments of a string quartet—two violins, a viola, and a cello—lay beside their deceased musical ensemble.

Peter studied the grenade. He didn't know if it exploded after a certain amount of time or upon impact. He was sure he could work it. Or at least, he hoped he could. If it didn't explode, he knew he'd be dead seconds after his plan was discovered.

He held the striker lever firmly against the serrated, cast-iron body of the grenade. He set his jaw, pulled the safety pin out with his teeth like he'd seen in the movies, and slung the grenade halfway to where the piano rested on three legs.

The cast iron hit the marble surface with a clank and then rolled against the body of the once beautiful pianist.

"*Qunbula—!*" The man was shouting grenade in Arabic, but the second word in the phrase never left his mouth. The explosion rocked the interior of the lobby. The blast eviscerated the already dead young woman's body and sent the piano flying several feet into the air before it exploded, sending keys and strings in all directions.

Peter didn't watch the result. Like the North Vietnamese tossing a grenade into a Quonset hut without regard to the outcome, Peter bolted across the lobby, zigzagging toward the double doors. Bullets skipped along the marble floor on both sides of him and stitched the doors as he approached. Still gripping the Uzi, he crashed hard through the doors.

He never looked back to see if he was being pursued. With gun in hand, he ran as far away as he could, dashed down another hallway until he found a rear entrance to the building, and emerged in a parking lot at the precise moment the UAE Presidential Guard prepared to enter the building.

Peter dropped the weapon. He raised his arms high over his head and shouted the only words he thought might save him.

"I'm an American!"

CHAPTER FOUR

Friday, October 18
Driftwood Key

"Our compliments to the chef!" exclaimed one of the women who'd arrived late that afternoon with her three sisters in tow. She was the oldest of the group and clearly the leader of the pack.

Hank beamed. Phoebe had never served a bad meal, but a resounding compliment always swelled him with pride. Earlier, his project with Sonny had run into a snag, causing him to work on the roof a little longer than he'd hoped to. While he was in the shower cleaning up for the evening meal, the four sisters had arrived, so he'd missed his usual opportunity to greet them. Over dinner and drinks, he was the center of attention as he relayed the history of Driftwood Key and the rest of the archipelago, the only one connected to the continental U.S.

As they waited for dessert, he got to know the sisters at the insistence of Phoebe and pretty much everyone else on the staff. Unsurprisingly, the oldest sister, who was married, took control of the conversation.

"Of course, the baby in the family happens to be the most

famous of us all," she began with a nod and a smile toward her youngest sister at the end of the table. The woman, who was in her late forties, was not familiar to Hank, so he was intrigued.

"Hush, Maggie," the woman protested. "I'm not famous. Besides, I bet Mr. Albright meets lots of famous people based upon the photographs on the wall."

Hank shrugged. "We've had a few." He was being modest. Over the nearly hundred years of its existence, the Driftwood Key Inn had hosted notables from Hollywood to Washington.

The youngest sister continued. "I'd be willing to bet Hank doesn't even know who I am unless he was busy on Google before we arrived."

Hank laughed at the reference to Google. It seemed to be common practice for people to dig around online to learn all they could about the people they came into contact with, completely incognizant of the fact that others were doing the same to them.

He raised his hand and smiled. "Sorry, I'm not a fan of googling people. In the Keys, we have too many pirates, if you know what I mean."

Everyone, including an elderly couple who'd arrived that day, laughed. It was Friday night and the first night of Fantasy Fest in Key West, the annual two-week-long celebration of Halloween. Most of the guests had made the forty-five-mile drive to the southernmost point in the U.S. to join in the festivities that evening.

"See, Maggie," she said with a sneer at her meddling oldest sister. The woman nervously fiddled with her ring finger that no longer held a ring. She made eye contact with Hank. "I'm Erin Bergman."

Hank nodded and feigned recognition although he had no idea who she was. "Nice to meet you, Erin."

"She's the secretary of agriculture," pointed out her proud sister.

"Oh, of course. Um, I saw you folks listed a Tallahassee address on—"

The overbearing sister interrupted Hank. "No. That was before. Erin is the new United States secretary of agriculture."

"Okay, sis," Erin interjected. She appeared embarrassed by her sister's actions. "We don't need to bother Mr. Albright with my résumé."

"Hank, please."

"Yes, of course."

Hank studied Erin. She was markedly different from her sisters, especially her oldest one. She had softer features and was more reserved. The conversations at dinner had been dominated by the others. He wasn't sure if she was shy, unusual for a politician, or perhaps she was dealing with things in her personal life. Hank, despite his continuous protestations to anyone who suggested he find a female companion, suddenly found himself checking for a wedding ring on his new acquaintance.

"Erin, accept my apologies. I don't really follow politics. I mean, I do when they raise my taxes but otherwise, um, not really. Well, I do vote. Most of the time, anyway." Hank found himself suddenly nervous. He was usually a very confident host around strangers. This was different.

"I totally understand," Erin said. "Face it, most Americans have no idea who their secretary of agriculture is unless they're mad at me or want something."

The elderly couple roared in laughter at her statement. Somehow, it must've struck a nerve with them on a personal level. Hank allowed them to enjoy their laugh, which also managed to force a smile on Erin.

Her oldest sister continued with Erin's résumé. "After serving as Florida's Ag secretary and transportation secretary before that, she was only the second woman to be confirmed to the U.S. post. And, I might add, the first from Florida."

Erin locked eyes with Hank and grimaced. She was embarrassed by the attention. Fortunately for her, she was rescued by Phoebe, who was presenting her signature dessert.

"Honored guests," she began, causing Hank to cringe. She'd never started like that, making him wonder if she was in cahoots with big sister. "May I present the house specialty dessert—the 1920s Albright key lime pie."

Two members of the inn's waitstaff hustled around the table, setting out dessert plates and forks. A third wheeled in a cart holding two delectable key lime pies topped with meringue. She carefully made the first cut with an olivewood-handled pie knife that had been a staple of the inn's kitchen for nearly forty years. It, like the inn, had withstood the test of time.

Hank explained the name. "Years ago, my grandmother presented my mom with her cookbook. It was a rite of passage that many families experience in the Keys, not unlike the presentation of the family Bible from father to son.

"Her recipe for key lime pie had always been a family favorite, and therefore it was passed down from generation to generation. I must say, Phoebe has perfected it."

"It's because of one special secret ingredient," she interjected.

Hank's eyes grew wide. He'd never heard of a secret ingredient, and he immediately assumed she was referring to conch. *My god*, he thought to himself, *Phoebe has gone off the rails and is putting conch in every damn thing.*

Phoebe began to laugh and patted her boss on the shoulder. She lowered her voice as if she could read his mind. "Relax, Mr. Hank. It's not what you think." She made eye contact with the dinner guests before explaining the family recipe. "The recipe is not unlike many others. You know, eggs, condensed milk, sugar, and, naturally, key limes. But here's the difference. We grow them right here on Driftwood Key, so they have that Florida sun-kissed taste."

The elderly man asked, "Well, you folks are known for key lime this and that, am I right? Why would that be a special ingredient?"

Erin raised her hand. "Phoebe, may I take that one?"

"Certainly, honored guest," Phoebe responded with a smile. She slid her left foot over to kick Hank's ankle.

Erin continued. "Many people don't know that the majority of key limes, which are more aromatic and juicier than regular limes, are grown in Mexico because of old trade agreements. Orange growers have faced the same uneven playing field. Part of what I hope to accomplish in Washington is to ease the burden on Florida's agricultural growers by leveling the playing field with Mexico."

Phoebe finished distributing the slices of pie and stood back as everyone tasted it. Nearly everyone closed their eyes to savor the flavor.

"Oh. My. God," said the oldest sister in single-word sentences. She quickly shoved a second bite into her mouth before the first one was completely consumed. "One word. Heavenly."

Hank chuckled. "That it is. Because we grow the limes here on the key, we can pick them while they're still green. Phoebe is an expert in determining when the perfect level of ripeness occurs. She says the secret ingredient is the fact that we grow them here. In actuality, it's the love and attention she gives to picking just the right ones."

Erin laughed. "Hey, Phoebe. It sounds to me like a good time to ask for a raise."

"Yes, Mr. Hank. How about it?"

Hank was about to answer when Erin's phone began to vibrate and emit a text tone that resembled an emergency warning. She quickly pulled it out of her shorts pocket and studied the display.

"I'm sorry. I need to make a phone call."

A look of concern came over her sister's face. "Is everything okay?"

"There's been a terrorist attack in Abu Dhabi."

CHAPTER FIVE

Friday, October 18
Curry Hammock State Park
Fat Deer Key, Florida

Marty Kantor was a drifter. He had no roots. He had no sense of purpose. He had no soul. There was no way out of the downward spiral he'd succumbed to the day he'd tried his first joint as a teen. Drug experimentation was the first stage toward full-blown addiction, and the readily available hallucinogenic had been a logical place to start.

Soon, the high wasn't good enough, and he turned to Google. His mom, a functioning alcoholic and manic-depressive, had a treasure trove of goodies to choose from in her medicine cabinet. Kantor researched them all and began taking a few here and there. The highs and lows were glorious.

His mom was too oblivious to notice the missing pills until she tried to get refills and the pharmacy refused to accommodate her. So Kantor mastered the art of *placeboing*, if that was even a word. Perhaps it was, not that it mattered. It was one he made up, but at least he understood it. Kantor learned how to empty the contents of his mom's medicine capsules and replace it with a placebo, usually baking starch or flour. He'd ingest the drugs, and she'd get to swallow a baker's secret ingredient of no medicinal use.

Initially, she didn't notice the difference until she began to descend into madness. Her meds weren't working; she'd complained to the pharmacist and then her doctor. When the doctor fired her as a patient for all intents and purposes, she'd try to find another one. However, government regulations made sure her medical records followed her everywhere. Soon, she became desperate to keep her mind sane and sought alternative ways to self-medicate.

This new program worked well for Kantor. Mom would score some heavy shit like crystal meth or even heroin. After she partied with *Christy* and the *Dragon*, her dutiful son would rob her of the remaining drugs and use them himself.

Then, one day, the Kantor party came to an end. At least in Miami, anyway. His dear mother unexpectedly became the dearly departed Mrs. Kantor. This sucked for Kantor because he still had a life to live, sort of. For a while, he toughed it out with his mother's dead body lying in a heap on the far side of her bed against a wall.

You see, he had to keep her alive, ostensibly, so he could collect the myriad of government checks that came her way. Kantor cashed them at a liquor store, begrudgingly paying the required twenty percent *you-ain't-the-payee* fee. He'd immediately roll right around the corner to pick up some more crystal meth. Now he was partying hearty with *Christy*.

This worked for Kantor for a month or so. He'd score a diamond of the dangerous drug, get his high, and try to function. Jobs were plentiful, as the economy was roaring, so warm bodies were in high demand. He'd work for a while, cash a paycheck or two, and then increase his drug intake.

Marty Kantor decided to move on when his dead mom began to stink so bad that he couldn't mask the smell with bonus hits on the meth pipe. He really didn't have anywhere to go, but he'd always heard the Florida Keys were a party place. Since partying was all he knew, he loaded up dearly departed Mom's Chevy Lumina with anything of use and headed south.

Kantor made it all the way to Key West before the Lumina crapped out. It was a piece of shit anyway, but it had enough gas to get him to his destination. No matter, Kantor convinced himself. He wasn't goin' back to Hialeah anyway. He got settled into his new digs, the backseat of the Lumina.

He tried to party the old way, scoring crystal meth and sailing out to sea in his demented mind. He soon realized Key West was a different kind of party town. It wasn't full of dope dealers on every corner. There weren't opportunities to trade sexual favors for a few bucks. The place wasn't full of pawnshops to exchange stolen valuables for a few bucks. They ran a clean operation down there, and that sucked for him.

Kantor had to change his approach to life, so he made an effort to clean up. He shoplifted a pair of shorts and a polo shirt from a local boutique. He ripped off a bicycle from the cruise ship docks. He found a drunk college kid on the beach and pilfered his flip-flops.

All in one day.

That night, he snuck into a hotel room while the housekeeping team wasn't looking. He hid in a closet until they were gone. He took a shower, dressed, and studied himself in the mirror. He'd lost a ton of weight. Every tweaker did.

He pushed his shoulders back and tried to stand straight with confidence. The skin sores on his chest revealed themselves through his polo shirt, so he returned to his customary slouch.

He smiled and said to his mirrored self, "Hello, sir. I'm Marty Kantor. I'd like a job." His smile revealed his decaying teeth and gums indicative of meth mouth. Kantor quickly closed his mouth and scowled at himself. This was never gonna work.

Plan A, finding a job that could support his habit, wasn't a viable option. So he moved on to plan B. He recalled a saying from when he first discovered puberty and began to show an interest in girls.

They're all hot at 3:00 a.m., referring to women in a bar at closing time.

Plan B was simple. Try to stay presentable and search for unsuspecting women, or men, in the dark recesses of the local bars at the end of the night. Key West was a party town, and it was full of inebriated something or others interested in a sexual encounter for the night. Marty Kantor was just the guy for the job, although the crystal meth had taken its toll on his manhood, a fact he considered irrelevant. He just wanted their valuables. Cash, credit, or payment in jewelry was all acceptable.

That night, Kantor went to work. He found the perfect bar, well off the beaten path of Duval Street, where the parrothead revelers tended to congregate. His head was in a good place that night, and he easily hooked up with a woman, or at least he thought she was.

The two shared a bottle of vodka and jumped in the target's car. Kantor didn't care where they were going because he was getting drunk. They shared a joint. They laughed about stupid shit. They drove and drove up A1A until his new friend suddenly slowed the car and pulled down a sandy road into Curry Hammock State Park. That was when the whole dynamic of plan B changed.

One minute, Marty Kantor thought he had the upper hand and was ready to make bank from this unsuspecting loser. His mind raced as he thought of the diamond-shaped crystals ready to take him away to another dimension. The next minute, he found his head forced down into the woman's crotch—only, it wasn't a woman.

Kantor had had enough. He tried to pull away from the guy dressed as a woman. He even threw up the contents of his mostly empty stomach as a defensive mechanism. This prevented him from committing the sexual act.

It also ended his life with a swift, brutal blow.

The man, dressed as a woman, thrust a knife into the base of Kantor's skull and twisted and twisted before pulling it out. By the time he was done with the meth-head-turned-grifter, the body was unrecognizable.

Human scum. Detective Mike Albright of the Monroe County Sheriff's Department studied the crime scene from a distance. He'd trudged through the wetlands and slopes surrounded by the stands of hardwoods that covered the island. The evidence trail was a hundred yards long, and the low-lying palmettos still showed blood splatter. There were body parts everywhere. Some were missing, either to the wildlife that inhabited the hammocks or because the killer had decided to take them as trophies.

It didn't look like any body he'd seen before. The corpse was naked. The upper body had been stabbed dozens of times. Appendages had been sawed off, including the man's genitals. Even its hair was gone, with only a few patches of bloody scalp remaining. What the brutal murderer had done to the victim's face was unimaginable. The crime was sadistic.

Mike knelt down over the corpse and studied what remained. Where would the medical examiner even start? Did it really matter what the precise cause of death was? He supposed it would in the event the perp decided to go to trial. He tried to imagine what a jury, many of whom might be friends or casual acquaintances of the Albright family, would think of the photographs the forensic team was taking.

The ME approached him. "Mike, the killer has escalated his rage. The MO on this victim is the same as the other except for the obvious increase in body mutilation post-mortem."

"Any sign of the murder weapon?"

"Part of it," the ME replied. He handed Mike a Ziploc evidence bag with the handle of a knife inside. "It appears to be spring-assisted. The handle is roughly three and a half inches long. Perfectly legal."

"What about the blade?" asked Mike.

The medical examiner shrugged and turned toward the body. "In there somewhere, I suspect. I'll get to work this afternoon and let you know what I find."

Mike grimaced as he thanked the ME. He'd seen enough. The forensics team would do their level best to gather evidence, but most likely, since this was the second murder in the last two weeks, the Florida Department of Law Enforcement, FDLE, would get involved.

The Florida Keys wasn't exactly the murder capital of the world. It wasn't even a murderous county. They were few and far between. Most cases that Mike investigated related to assaults, robberies, and the occasional rape.

These killings were disgusting. Demented. Psychotic. Unlike anything he'd seen or heard about in his lifetime. And they were becoming more brutal.

CHAPTER SIX

Friday, October 18
Havana Jack's Oceanside Restaurant & Bar
Marathon, Florida

Mike balanced his empty glass on the edge of the teak bar, waiting for the bartender to refill it with Jack Daniel's and a few cubes of ice. The young man had been preoccupied with a group of pretty girls sitting at the other end of the U-shaped outdoor bar overlooking the Atlantic. They were knocking back pineapple-looking drinks full of rum and juice and all kinds of sweet things skewered by an extra-long toothpick. Of course, a tiny paper umbrella had been plunged into the pineapple slice adorning the rim of the glass.

Typical, he thought to himself.

Mike wanted a quiet moment to gather his thoughts, and he hoped Havana Jack's might give him a place of respite. Mike was not much of a drinker. None of the Albrights were. Hank had gone through a period of escape after his wife died but eventually returned to nothing more than a social drink with his guests in the evening.

For Mike, however, today was different. A special occasion, if you will. He'd worked all day at the grisly murder scene, and technically, this was the end of his tour. A Jack on the rocks or three just might help him cope with what he'd just seen in the hammocks.

A female voice entered his solemn consciousness. "Can I buy you a drink, sailor?" Cliché, but real. It was also familiar.

To confirm it wasn't all in his head, he felt the woman run her fingers across his broad shoulders, briefly touching the nape of his neck, causing the tiny hairs to rise in response.

More familiar.

He closed his eyes and took a deep breath as he inhaled her scent.

Even more familiar.

Not perfumy. Salt water.

"How'd you know I was here?" he asked without taking his eyes away from the last swig of bourbon.

She set her phone next to his on the bar, drawing his eyes to study its display. On the map, there were two red dots blinking nearly on top of one another.

"I used the *where's my husband* app," she replied as she hoisted herself onto a barstool.

Jessica Albright, Mike's wife of fifteen years, leaned over and kissed him on the cheek, savoring the slightly scruffy feel of his five-o'clock shadow on her lips.

With Jessica's arrival, the bartender managed to pull himself away from the vacationing college girls to take her drink order.

"I'll have a Tanqueray and tonic with a splash of Nellie & Joe's," she said, pointing at the yellow plastic bottle with the green flip-top. The Florida-bottled lime juice was an essential ingredient in many recipes and a favorite complement to a gin and tonic.

Mike pushed his empty glass toward the bartender. "I'll have another, and don't be a stranger next time. Okay?" His demeanor was slightly surly.

"Um, yes, sir," the young man replied sheepishly.

Mike and Jessica sat in silence until the bartender returned with their drinks and a mango wood bowl full of fortune cookies.

Mike leaned back on his stool and glanced at Jessica before addressing the young man. He pointed at the bowl of cellophane-wrapped treats usually found in Chinese restaurants.

"Seriously?" he asked.

"Um, yes, sir. The Sysco salesman dropped off a case this morning. I guess China Garden ordered way too many or something like that. He gave it to us for nothing." He reached for the bowl to remove it from the bar, but Mike raised his hand.

"Nah. Leave it. It fits right in with the screwy day I'm havin'."

They each took a sip of their drink and opened a fortune cookie.

"Me first," said Jessica as she broke open the packaging and cracked the fortune cookie in two. "'Luck helps those who help themselves.' I like it. Time to play the Mega Millions Powerball game."

Mike smiled as his wife tried to drag him out of his melancholy mood. She knew they both thought the lottery was a way to tax the poor. He opened his fortune cookie and read it.

"Your life is a dashing and bold adventure," he read aloud. He shook his head. "No thanks." He slid the small piece of paper in front of Jessica and took hers instead.

She immediately protested. "Hey! Fortune cookies don't work like that. You can't just pick and choose your good fortune."

"I need luck, and you like adventure. Sounds like a fair trade to me."

"Mike, you can't trade fortunes."

"Why not?"

"Um. Well, it's against the rules or the laws of good fortune or something."

Mike started to laugh and immediately felt better. He reached over and squeezed her hand before kissing her on the lips.

"Why can't you just let me be miserable?" he asked jokingly.

"Because, Detective Albright, that's not who you are," she replied. "I heard about it on the radio. Was it that bad?"

Jess also worked for the Monroe County Sheriff's Department as a member of their WET team, an acronym for Water Emergency Team. She was a trained scuba diver as well as a paramedic.

Mike nodded. "Much worse than the first one, Jess. I just don't understand people."

"Same MO?" she asked, hoping that by talking about it, Mike would feel better.

"Yeah. Vic was a young male. Stabbed to death. The first murder weapon was a butcher knife. This time, the killer used a spring-assisted knife."

"Like a switchblade?"

"Sort of, but shorter by law. The max length is three and a half inches, I think."

Mike and Jessica had met in 2017 when he was investigating several brutal murders in the Middle Keys. In the spring of that year, a woman lost control during her birthday party and went on a bloody rampage, stabbing her boyfriend to death. The couple's four children were in the house at the time. A month later, a man was arrested for stabbing his friend to death after the victim made unwanted sexual advances in a trailer they shared. In late summer that year, a man got into a dispute with his landlord over an eviction notice. Four lethal stab wounds later, the landlord was dead, and the killer had dumped the body in the brackish water off the Upper Keys. Jessica's team had recovered the corpse, and Mike had been assigned to investigate the murder.

A murder a year was the norm, and they almost always involved a domestic dispute or an argument between transients. Because of the significant tourism levels in the Florida Keys, the crime rate was twenty percent higher than the rest of the country. While the rate of violent crime was much lower than the state's, property crime was nearly thirty percent higher.

The two continued to talk about the murders, which Mike was prepared to identify as the work of a serial killer. Jessica asked a logical question. "What's your gut tell you?"

Mike sat back again and glanced over at the television, which was airing CNN. It was the top of the hour, and as was their custom, the breaking news graphic was displayed on the screen. There was always breaking news of some kind as far as cable news networks were concerned.

"In a way, they resemble a crime of passion. Well, at least the first one did. Killing someone with a knife is very personal. The vic and the killer are necessarily in close proximity to one another. The killer can feel the life of their victim being extinguished.

"What bothers me the most by this second murder is the escalation in the attack. Jess, it was sadistic. Angry. It makes me want to gather up all of our family and hide on Driftwood Key where the monsters can't get us."

Jessica nodded. "I'll be honest. I was worried for Lacey when she moved to California with Owen. I look at that place as a cesspool. Did you know many of the nation's serial killers began in California? After what I've seen here, maybe she's better off out there?"

"Maybe," replied Mike in a soft tone of voice. His eyes suddenly became affixed on the television when the chyron read *Secretary Sanders unharmed*. The video footage of the carnage caused him to jump off his barstool and scream at the bartender, "Hey, turn that up!"

"Mike, what is it?" asked Jessica.

He turned back to her abruptly and replied, "Peter is over there."

CHAPTER SEVEN

Friday, October 18
McDowell Residence
Hayward, California

"Tucker McDowell! Let's go!" shouted his mom, Lacey, from the bottom of the stairs. "Do you wanna walk to school?"

Her son had the perfect solution, at least in his mind. "Just leave the keys to the Bronco. I'll drive myself."

Lacey shook her head and rolled her eyes. She turned around to check the time on the grandfather clock in the foyer.

"Not a chance for two reasons! One, you're fifteen and only have a learner's permit!" Lacey paused. She couldn't think of reason number two right off the top of her head. She went with the old standby used often by her mother. "And because I said so!"

"You don't have to yell, Mom," Tucker said calmly as he stepped off the stairs into the foyer.

Startled, Lacey swung around to address her son. "Where did you come from?"

"Duh, upstairs," he replied sarcastically, pointing his thumb over his shoulder. "Are you ready?"

He's just like his father, she thought to herself. *Why couldn't I have had a sweet adorable little girl? Because they grow up to hate their mothers, that's why.*

"Jesus!" she exclaimed as she tried to stop the debate raging in her head.

"Okay. Okay. I'm sorry. I was just pullin' your chain. I'm ready."

Lacey took a deep breath. "No, I wasn't yelling at you. I was only—"

"Yelling at Jesus," Tucker interrupted. "You know, Mom, prayer works best in silence sometimes."

Lacey playfully swatted at her son, who easily dodged the blow. "Come on, kiddo. You know this is a big day for your dad. I wanna get there early, that's all."

"Who's opening the store for you?"

"Carlos is coming in. I should be there to relieve him by two." She swept her key fob off the foyer table and picked up her handbag, which waited for deployment in a chair. It was rare for her to carry one, opting for a shoulder-sling backpack most of the time.

They made their way to the car when Tucker commented, "You look really nice, Mom. I'm sure the muckety-mucks will be impressed."

Lacey appreciated the comment from her son. "Thanks, honey. As long as your dad is proud and confident during the presentation, that's all that matters."

"Do you think he'll get the job?"

Owen McDowell was a marketing executive with Yahoo in Sunnyvale, California. The tech giant had just hired its fifth chief executive officer in the last nine years. The new CEO, an accountant and marketing executive by training, intended to bolster Yahoo's presence in the lucrative online display advertising market by competing with Google AdWords.

Yahoo had been experiencing declining sales and market share for years until Owen used his formidable technical skills and marketing intuition to give the brand a makeover. Over time, Yahoo had failed to generate a brand identity geared toward the younger generation of users. Owen had instituted a number of marketing programs that yielded inroads into Google's market share.

Today, he was making a pitch to corporate executives focusing on the Yahoo! portal as a starting and ending point for users' web visits. He'd led the charge on a more privacy-oriented search function, much like upstart DuckDuckGo, which differed significantly from the overly intrusive Google search engine.

"We've got our fingers crossed, son," Lacey replied. The two headed toward Hayward High School, which was only a few miles from their home. The sprawling campus taught nearly two thousand students. Tucker had just begun his junior year and was an above-average student.

A few minutes later, Tucker was off to class, and Lacey gave herself one last look in the mirror before she headed for Sunnyvale. She turned on the radio to listen for a traffic report.

The Nimitz Expressway was bumper-to-bumper. "No surprise there," she quipped as she considered her alternatives. She decided on the Bayfront Expressway over San Francisco Bay into East Palo Alto. As she drove, her mind wandered to her husband.

They'd met at the University of Miami. Owen had been a graduate student pursuing his master's in science in the management of technology curriculum. Lacey had been a junior when she and a group friends went scuba diving at John Pennekamp Coral Reef State Park near Key Largo. Owen and some of his guy friends were on the same dive, and the group got together for beers that night at Snapper's. They immediately hit it off and began to date.

Three years later, the two were married, and Tucker was on the way. Owen had accepted a lower-level management position at Yahoo but quickly impressed his superiors. Lacey, who graduated with a business management degree because she hoped to run the Driftwood Key Inn someday, opened up a boutique store in Hayward called Jefferson Outfitters.

The family enjoyed all things outdoors, including hiking, camping, skiing, and various water sports. Owen's salary was easily able to sustain their household while Jefferson Outfitters, which more than broke even, provided Jessica an outlet to pursue her dreams of working in the outdoors while managing a business.

She waited at the security entrance to the campus of Yahoo's corporate headquarters. The architecture of the buildings was unique. They were made of precast concrete, glass, and metal with Yahoo's signature bright yellow and purple accents. The abundant green space and outdoor seating made for a casual, relaxed work atmosphere.

Lacey parked the car and checked herself once again. She was glad they were relaxed, she thought to herself. She was a nervous wreck. This opportunity meant a lot to Owen and would have a profound effect on their financial future.

She walked with confidence along the sidewalks traversing the artificial turf that had been installed to replace the grass that used to lie there. The turf, made of one hundred percent recyclable materials, was a testament to Yahoo's interest in preserving the environment. It was, however, often used against them in the corporate shareholder meetings by those who thought the company should focus more on profits and less on environmental issues. Regardless, Lacey thought the artificial turf was pretty, and hey, you never had to mow it.

Her phone indicated a text message had come through. She rifled through her bag and saw that it was from Owen. She quickly checked her watch to see if she was late. She wasn't.

Owen: I see you.

Lacey searched the campus for her husband. She texted him back.

Lacey: Show yourself, creeper. Or I'll call the law!

Owen: Behind you.

Lacey swung around, and there was her husband, dressed in his best power suit, standing with one hand in his pocket. He was wickedly handsome, and she loved him more than life.

PART II

ONE WEEK IN OCTOBER

Day two, Saturday, October 19

CHAPTER EIGHT

Saturday, October 19
Oval Office
The White House
Washington, DC

President Carter Helton was the son of a coal miner who'd labored for decades in Greene County, Pennsylvania, where coal was still king. President Helton's father wanted a better life for his five kids. He was the oldest of the five and was the first member of the Helton family to attend a university. His grades had earned him a partial scholarship to Slippery Rock University, and his excellent work ethic, along with his father's savings, propelled him to Penn State, where he got his law degree.

In addition to being book smart, he was a streetwise individual who possessed the gift of gab, an almost perfect trifecta for becoming a politician. He rose through the ranks of Pennsylvania politics, from the local level in his hometown of Waynesburg, to the State House in Harrisburg.

He paid his dues. Made the right friends. Rubbed elbows with the rich and powerful. Now here he was, well into his first year as president and rushing down the hallways of the West Wing, his security team and a handful of staffers in tow. His new administration was being tested, and the pressure was enormous.

"Good morning, Mr. President," said one staffer nonchalantly as she struggled to keep up with the boss. "Sir, they've changed the meeting to the Roosevelt Room."

As President Helton continued down the hallway, he addressed the young woman. "Who's here?"

"All of them, sir," she replied, referring to the top brass of the Pentagon.

The meeting in response to the Abu Dhabi terrorist attack had been delayed several hours at the president's request. He wanted the best possible intelligence available to make a decision. He was not interested in supposition laced with agenda-setting motives. He'd learned in his first hundred days in office that those permanent residents of the DC political apparatus had their own opinion of how the government should be run. Presidents came and went.

Just as he strode past the chief of staff's suite, Harrison Chandler, former congressman from Pennsylvania and longtime friend, dashed out with his computer tablet stuck in his left armpit.

"Good morning, Mr. President," he greeted. "We've got a full house."

"So I've heard. Is there anything new to add since they delivered the PDB early this morning?"

From the moment he'd been declared president-elect by the media, President Helton was made privy to the same tools given to the former president, such as intelligence reporting and analysis. Known as the President's Daily Brief, the binder created was in essence a toolkit of information that overlapped with that of the president.

Producing and presenting the daily brief was the responsibility of the director of National Intelligence, whose office was tasked with fusing intelligence from the Central Intelligence Agency, the Defense Intelligence Agency, the National Security Agency, the

Federal Bureau of Investigation, and other members of the U.S. intelligence community.

President Helton asked that economic issues be included in the PDB, as the nation was in the throes of an economic and trade war with China. He believed gaining insight into the capabilities and intentions of America's global competitors was every bit as important as keeping an eye on hot spots around the globe, such as the Middle East.

The recent mass assassination of the Iranian nuclear scientists and yesterday's terrorist attack in Abu Dhabi had brought tensions in the Middle East to their highest level in decades. The media was demanding answers from the president's communications team. His White House spokesman had held them off thus far, but many were already looking at the president as weak and indecisive because of the delayed response.

Chandler filled the president in on what to expect. "Here are the highlights. Yemeni rebels. Funded by Iran. Their target was the Israeli delegation, but they came in a little heavy-handed and killed a lot of innocents unrelated to the peace conference."

"A little heavy-handed, Harrison? That's an interesting choice of words."

"Well, sir, I think you'll hear from the Pentagon and intelligence heads that their plan was ill conceived. If their goal was to gain revenge for the attack on the nuclear facility at Isfahan, they could've sent in a suicide bomber or two. Instead, they destroyed the entrance to the conference center and randomly murdered anyone in their path. It was senseless."

President Helton sighed as he reached the open doors to the Roosevelt Room. "Aren't they all?" he asked without expecting a response.

The windowless Roosevelt Room served as a daily meeting location for the White House staff and the president's briefings. It had been upgraded a decade ago to include a wall of televisions and a large screen for multimedia presentations. President Helton often used this platform to conduct video conferences with foreign leaders.

As he entered, the members of the national security team and the White House communications director were getting settled into their seats. As the president entered, they all shot back up in unison out of respect.

"Good morning and thank you for coming in at this early hour," said the president. He noticed the puzzled looks on their faces. "Well, sorry. I realize it's been a long night for you all. Thank you for your efforts. Please sit down and tell me where we stand."

The Joint Chiefs and the CIA director joined the director of National Intelligence in laying out the facts. Since the attack on their nuclear facility, the rhetoric out of Tehran had escalated daily. The terrorist attack had been undertaken by their proxy, the Houthi Shiite rebels in Yemen, who'd acted on behalf of the Tehran government for many years. They were just one of half a dozen well-funded groups throughout the Middle East who waged war on Western and Israeli interests.

"All right, before we address the issue of our response, especially in light of the American delegation being there, including my secretary of state, what are we doing to bolster our presence in the Persian Gulf?"

The chairman of the Joint Chiefs replied, "Sir, the *Nimitz* Carrier Strike Group had been operating off the coast of Somalia as we pulled troops and assets out of that country and redistributed them into Northern Africa following the Isfahan incident.

"As you know, the *Nimitz* was long overdue for a return to port in Bremerton, Washington, after a thirteen-month deployment. However, its skipper has assured us his people are ready to go where their Commander-in-Chief sees fit."

"Please thank Admiral Kirk for me." Rear Admiral David Kirk, a Hershey, Pennsylvania, native, had recently been named the new commander of the massive aircraft carrier and the flotilla of ships that surround it. "What do you have in mind for the *Nimitz*?"

"Mr. President, after the attack on the nuclear facility, we began the process of redeploying the *Nimitz* to the region. They will be entering the Straits of Hormuz within forty-eight hours. However, sir, we might need to rethink deploying the *Nimitz* into the Persian Gulf."

"Why is that?"

"If the conflict between Iran and Israel escalates further into a hot war, the relatively small and nearly landlocked body of water is an anti-ship missile engagement zone. It's rife with other potential threats that are difficult for the carrier strike group to counter, like small-boat swarm attacks, naval mines, and the Iranian's nontraditional submarine operations."

Days after President Helton's inauguration, the Iranian Navy towed a refurbished mock aircraft carrier into the Strait of Hormuz, which links the Persian Gulf to the Gulf of Oman. The movement of the heavily modified barge designed in the likeness of an American flattop aircraft carrier immediately drew the attention of U.S. intelligence.

Satellite imagery revealed the mock carrier being towed into the center of the strait one day, and the next day, a large crosshair had been painted on its top deck. On day three, several fast boats operated by Iran's Islamic Revolutionary Guard were filmed swarming the faux carrier, firing surface-to-surface missiles at the bow. The explosion, most likely generated by fuel containers stored in the front of the barge, could be seen throughout the coastal areas of the Persian Gulf and by astronauts aboard the International Space Station.

It was clearly viewed as a provocation and a message to the first-year president that Tehran was not to be trifled with. After years of being kept in check with sanctions, they were prepared to flex their muscles, apparently.

The president furrowed his brow. The *Nimitz* Carrier Strike Group would've been seen as an effective deterrent to any military action by the Iranians. "What do you suggest we do in the meantime?"

"Sir, we have an Ohio-class submarine, the USS *Georgia*, in the region. We can send her into the Persian Gulf, you know, high profile, to send a message. The Iranians have nothing to counteract a vessel like the *Georgia*, which is packed with Tomahawk cruise missiles and our special operations forces."

"When could it arrive?"

"By tomorrow afternoon, sir."

"Do it, General. Let them know we mean business."

CHAPTER NINE

Saturday, October 19
Holiday Inn Abu Dhabi

Peter Albright stood at the window of his upper-level hotel room in the Holiday Inn Abu Dhabi. He had a bird's-eye of the activity taking place around the National Exhibition Centre, where the terrorist attack had taken place. Large crowds had gathered around the Embassy of Iran, just across Al Maarid Street at the back of the conference location. Likewise, a contingent of U.S. military vehicles had gathered around the U.S. embassy a mere block away.

Peter had just hung up with a friend and college classmate at the University of Miami who worked as a member of the Department of Defense communications team inside the Pentagon. The two had dated while in college, but there was nothing serious other than the usual kids-just-left-home-time-to-play relationship. They still got together for the occasional drink or dinner, followed by a noncommittal sleepover. It worked for both of the young DC professionals, who were trying to advance their careers rather than seeking to settle down.

Jenna Alan loved government. Her father had been a local

politician with designs on higher office before a heart attack struck him while Jenna was obtaining her degree in broadcast journalism. In recent months, she'd been assigned press briefing duty and frequently took to the podium when her boss was traveling with the secretary of defense. Unlike Peter, who didn't have that inside connection with the secretary of state, Jenna was always in the know when it came to the Pentagon's inner workings.

She'd told Peter about the redeployment of the *Nimitz* strike group and the USS *Georgia* toward the Persian Gulf. The drums of war were beginning to beat louder, Peter had thought to himself as he listened to her detail the Pentagon's moves, off the record, of course. The two had a very trusting relationship, allowing them to share information without fear of reading about it online later that day.

Like a good soldier, Peter had filed his press pool report soon after he'd been evacuated from the conference center. Unable to sleep, he'd ordered dinner and half a dozen Heinekens to relieve the stress. He sent out a text message blast to family and friends, letting them know he was safe. Then he sat down to write the best news article for the *Washington Times* he'd ever produced. He was the only journalist who'd witnessed the attack firsthand and lived to tell about it.

During his extensive self-edits, he chose to remove the details related to his killing of a terrorist and the use of the grenade to escape. He feared bringing unnecessary heat on his family. By midmorning in the States, his reporting was being cited and shared by every news agency in the country. He'd already received several requests to appear on camera for interviews as soon as he returned home.

The other big story of the news day was the president's anticipated response. Peter knew the secretary of state and her team were never in imminent danger. Per the schedule, which was widely disseminated, she and the Israeli delegation had been having a preconference meeting on the top floor of the center. This fact struck Peter as odd, in that the terrorists could've easily deployed rocket-propelled grenade launchers to fire upon the upper levels. Either they weren't prepared, or they were amateurs. That was not for him to speculate, so he didn't in his reporting.

The world media began to immediately theorize whether Iran would take their retaliation against Israel to another level—the use of nuclear weapons. Despite the nuclear nonproliferation agreement entered into with Iran more than a decade prior, the rogue nation continued to develop enriched uranium. Quickly, with the help of North Korea and Russia, Iran had amassed nearly a hundred nuclear warheads, to put it on par with Israel in the region.

The nuclear silos dotting the mountains and desert region along the Iraqi border in western Iran were barely a thousand miles from the Israeli targets of Jerusalem and Tel Aviv. An Iranian nuclear warhead affixed to a cruise missile could strike Israel about twenty minutes after launch.

President Helton ran on a platform of stopping the nuclear proliferation in the Middle East. He used especially strong words against North Korea, who was the primary supplier of technology and materials to the Tehran government. The DPRK's actions had just been a continuation of their open defiance of the international community as it related to the nuclear arms race in South Asia and the Middle East.

As a result, the Pentagon was strongly urging the president to resume nuclear testing. Jenna had told Peter about a faction within the Department of Defense that wanted to abandon the current zero-yield standard, the prohibition of test explosions that produce a nuclear chain reaction of any kind. Congress had refused to provide the Pentagon funding for the testing, so they sought an end-run of the budgetary process by asking the new president to reallocate discretionary monies within the budget. Thus far, President Helton, who was decidedly anti-nuke, had resisted.

The other policy issue, as Peter saw it from the perspective of the State Department, was whether the countries like Iran, North Korea, and even Pakistan would see the president's inaction as a sign of weakness. Publicly, the secretary of state did her level best to talk tough to America's adversaries, warning them against the use of ballistic missiles in any conflict.

The continual war of words between America and her adversaries often reminded Peter of something his father, Hank, had told him when he was young. *Words are cheap, but at times, they're all you can afford. Words will just be words until you act on them.*

He closed his eyes for a moment and envisioned what that would look like.

CHAPTER TEN

Saturday, October 19
Driftwood Key

Hank Albright operated a hotel and resort. He was not a cruise director responsible for keeping his guests entertained. Ordinarily, those who enjoyed the environs of Driftwood Key found plenty of things to do without keeping their eyes focused on the television while drinking coffee. He understood their insatiable desire to be in-the-know. He had been like that once until he had an awakening one day. He realized there was nothing he, on an individual basis, could do about newsworthy events. Unless they affected him or the inn, it was just clutter in his brain. This sense of independence from the outside world probably kept him off Prozac or from swimming in the bottom of a bottle of rum.

Because it was Saturday, many of the guests chose to avoid Key West because a cruise ship was in port. The citizens of Key West had passed a referendum limiting the number of passengers who could disembark a cruise ship at any given time to fifteen hundred. Most major cruise lines such as Royal Caribbean, Carnival, and

Norwegian didn't operate ships small enough to pull into Key West. Boutique cruise operators like Oceania and Crystal were regulars.

He got with Jimmy and immediately organized a backgammon tournament for those who didn't already have plans. They set up lounge chairs under umbrellas near the thatched-roof tiki bar. Hank offered some prizes in the form of Driftwood Key swag like tee shirts, caps, and novelties. It was all in fun and designed to take their minds off world events.

Erin Bergman's sisters had all gathered around the media room and enjoyed coffee with a variety of pastries prepared by Phoebe. Hank periodically peered out the windows toward the stairs leading up to the main house in search of Erin, who'd abruptly left during dessert the night before. He was beginning to wonder if she had been forced to leave without notice.

Her older sister picked up on Hank's demeanor and pulled him aside. "Erin has to be available for a conference call this morning. She hasn't been called back to Washington. You know, in case you were wondering."

Hank blushed. He guessed his concern was obvious. "I know things must be stressful in the White House. I'm sure they'd recall her if necessary, right?"

The sister nodded. "Fortunately, she'd be out of the loop on national security matters."

Hank thanked her for the update, and after the news story switched to the punditry portion of the programming, everyone gladly escaped the main house and descended across the pristine Bermuda grass lawn until they reached the white sand beach.

Hank had called in the steel drum band early that day so the atmosphere could be upbeat and festive. After mimosas were offered and good-luck toasts were shared by all, the backgammon tournament began.

Backgammon is a two-player game during which the goal is to move your checker-like pieces along a board consisting of twenty-four points, or spaces. With each roll of the dice, pieces are moved until they are in your home board and can then be taken off. Whoever removes their pieces first wins.

It's a game that requires strategy but one that doesn't require one hundred percent focus. It had been a favorite of sailors who were more interested in soaking in the rum than winning the game, although it was also a favorite of gamblers.

Once everyone was settled in, Hank wandered toward the long dock that stretched into the Gulf. The water was calm that morning, and the fish that fed off the barnacles attached to the piers would be in full view. He squinted his eyes and noticed a woman standing at the end of the dock under the thatched roof. She was wearing a white linen coverup that blew slightly with the breeze, as did the American and Conch Republic flags flanking the pier.

He shoved his hands into his pockets, glanced around, and moseyed onto the dock. A minute later, he'd joined Erin, who was deep in thought.

"Am I interrupting?" he asked politely.

Somewhat startled, she looked down at herself shyly and pulled her bathing suit coverup across her body. She smiled at Hank and replied, "No, not at all. Actually, my little brain needed a break from thinking."

Hank joined her side and laughed. "Somehow, I doubt your brain is little."

"Well, let's just say it's too small for all the crap swirling around in there."

Hank paused before he continued. He pointed toward a stingray that casually swam by the dock. The cow-nosed, mystical creature was oblivious to its admirers as it searched for its next meal.

"Don't you wish you could be that guy?" he asked jokingly.

"Not a care in the world," she replied. She let out a deep sigh.

"Let me know if I'm overstepping, Erin, but is it worse than what the media is letting on?"

"In some respects, yes. In others, no. The media tends to overdramatize things to keep viewers' eyes glued to the screen. It's what they don't know that is concerning."

"Oh?" asked Hank.

Erin leaned forward and placed her elbows on the deck railing as the stingray swam out of sight. She fiddled with her hands.

"International politics are complicated. Over the last hundred years, America's adversaries have changed. The Nazis and Japanese were a clearly defined enemy until they were defeated. Then the Soviet Union tried to take advantage of the power vacuum. They were soon joined by China as the communists began to have a greater influence around the world.

"Today, you have nations like North Korea, Iran, and Pakistan that have deadly nuclear capabilities. They cannot be trusted and are in all respects unpredictable. One always thought—at least as it relates to the U.S., China and Russia, the so-called nuclear powerhouses—that cooler heads would prevail."

Hank interjected, "We've always seemed to respect the concept of mutually assured destruction, right?"

Erin hesitated. "Yes, once upon a time, anyway. Nuclear capabilities have changed over the last thirty years. Quick, precision strikes are now available to all the major powers. We no longer have to launch ballistic missiles from silos in the Northern Rockies. We have ships and submarines that can do it as well. Hell, our intelligence agencies believe both Iran and North Korea have nuclear warheads sailing over our heads, attached to satellites. The Pentagon refers to them as the Axis of Evil."

Hank leaned forward and looked toward the incredibly blue skies. "Really?"

"Really," she replied before shifting the conversation. "Here's the thing, Hank. And please understand, this is just my opinion as an American with more knowledge than the political outsiders. Iran and Israel have been staring each other down for longer than you and I have been alive. Despite the provocation, our government has never believed that Israel would be the first to pull the nuclear trigger in the Middle East. Iran, however, is another matter."

"Are they that stupid? And how do they justify it? Israel has completely denied any involvement in that killing spree a couple of weeks ago."

Erin chuckled. "Nobody believes that, especially the Iranians. The Israeli government has demanded that Iran stop its nuclear weapons program before they actually had them. Now, the speed of their proliferation is mind-boggling. I don't blame the Israelis for taking action."

"Well, it seems all they did was kick the hornet's nest. You know, when you stir up a hornet's nest, you're gonna get stung."

Erin took a deep breath and exhaled. "The question is how big of a stinger will they use?"

CHAPTER ELEVEN

Saturday, October 19
Key West, Florida

The Monroe County Sheriff's Department had a dozen detectives, and only one, Mike, was assigned to homicides full time. When you averaged one to two murders a year, a lot of warm bodies weren't required to investigate murders on a regular basis. The county had one cold case from more than ten years ago, and Mike had reached nothing but dead ends in trying to solve it. Most of his time was spent looking at accidental deaths in order to rule them out as homicides. The current cases were handled much differently.

"Okay. Okay. Please settle down, everyone," said Mike as the complete detective contingent for the sheriff's department gathered in the large conference room at the administration building in Key West. "We're joined today by a couple of familiar faces for those who were involved in the cruise ship slaying a few years ago. Rodriguez and Lively with the Forensic Science Program within the FDLE have come down to lend an assist."

The detectives acknowledged the two scientists, and Mike returned to the lectern. He'd powered up the wall-mounted monitors that flanked him. The second victim's image filled the screens. He explained what he knew so far.

"Dade county provided us this mug shot of Mr. Marty Kantor during a slightly better time. Through some pretty good detective work by uniformed deputies, one of the severed fingers was found in the hammocks. Kantor was apparently a heavy meth user and an infrequent visitor of the dentist, so dental records weren't much help. However, the discovery of an abandoned car together with the single print enabled us to make the positive ID."

"The mother's car?" asked one of the detectives who'd reviewed the file.

"Yes. Mrs. Kantor apparently died of a drug overdose in her home many weeks ago. I drove up to Hialeah to join Dade County detectives as they entered the Kantor home. We found her decaying body wrapped in her bedding on the floor. I suspect Marty was collecting his mother's welfare checks to buy drugs."

Another detective raised his hand. "Any indication of why he came to the Keys? Key West, in particular?"

"Unknown," replied Mike. "We're going to assign some of you to liaison with Dade County to canvass Kantor's neighborhood in Hialeah. You'll also be responsible for scouring the internet, social media sites, etc."

"He doesn't look like an Instagram influencer," quipped one of the detectives, drawing a laugh. Mike wasn't amused. Granted, Kantor was likely a piece of crap. However, he was a human being and a murder victim.

"You never know what leads a person to be the victim of a brutal murder," he said in a disdainful tone. "He is now our second vic in as many weeks, and the MOs are closely matched other than the actual murder weapon. The coroner was able to extract the knife blade from his sternum. It's part of a spring-assisted knife made by SOG. I did a little checking and found it is sold in Walmart. We'll need someone to run down that lead."

"Are we going to publish his image in the paper? See if anyone recognizes him?"

"Yes, tomorrow. In the meantime, we're gonna hit the streets in the area where his car was found. Try hotels and hostels. Bars and restaurants. Public places first before we go door to door. We don't have the manpower to hit all possible locations at once, and if we truly have a serial killer on our hands, he might be planning to kill again in the next week or so."

"Just as Fantasy Fest ramps up," lamented one of the detectives.

Fantasy Fest was by far the wildest gathering of partiers in the Florida Keys. The last two weeks of October attracted thousands of revelers for a hedonistic warm-up to Halloween. Originally developed to draw travelers during the slower tourist period between Labor Day and Christmas, Fantasy Fest drew over a hundred thousand people from around the world. Events included the Royal Coronation Ball where two locals are crowned Conch King and Queen, a street fair, pet masquerade contests, and the selection of the Fantasy Fest drag queen.

"Here's why we have to hit the streets running," said Mike. "Fantasy Fest will bring more and more people into the Keys who weren't here at the time of the first two murders. It expands the number of people we have to question unnecessarily. It also gives the murderer lots of options to choose from for his next vic."

"What about a profiler?"

Mike bristled at the question and the subtle insinuation. Despite the fact that he'd been the lead homicide detective for the MCSD for more than a decade, obviously some within the ranks didn't think he was up to the task.

"Let's gather some evidence and hunt down these leads. That will help this department and any others who are called upon to help. If there's nothing else, you all have your assignments. Let's find this guy before he kills again."

CHAPTER TWELVE

Peter lived in a modest condominium in Falls Church, Virginia, about ten miles from the Harry S. Truman Building, where the State Department was located. The *Washington Times* offices were another ten miles past the Capitol grounds in northeast Washington. He went there once in a while, mainly during those rare periods of time that the secretary of state remained in DC.

Peter wasn't interested in living inside the beltway like many of his counterparts. He grew up in the quiet and serenity of Driftwood Key. There was nothing comparable in the area unless he could find a place that happened to be on the Potomac River, which he wouldn't be able to afford.

He didn't need a fancy place to hang his hat. He was rarely home thanks to being attached to one of the most prolific travelers to occupy the leadership position in the State Department in many administrations. His place was small but quiet. His refrigerator remained empty except for a handful of condiments and lots of

Hurricane Reef beer that he ordered online from their brewery near Miami. It was a little taste of the Keys to go with his dinner of choice, a BBQ chicken pizza made by California Pizza Kitchen.

When he found his way to the local Harris Teeter, his shopping cart screamed *bachelor*. Red Bull. Pretzels. Several bottles of Jack Daniel's Honey Barbecue sauce and a few frozen pizzas from California Pizza Kitchen to dip into it. If he was gonna be in town for more than a couple of days, he'd splurge on a box of Entenmann's doughnuts.

With his horrific eating habits, Peter could've easily packed on the pounds. However, he was fortunate to have his father's genetics and his mother's love for running. Every morning, without fail, Peter would strap on his Asics running shoes and pound the pavement. He'd set his Apple AirPods in place and pick out a couple of podcasts to listen to. Or he'd select the playlist full of beach songs performed by his favorite country music performers.

Considering the strain placed on his body from traveling coupled with a diet that was more college frat boy than adult journalist, Peter remained well-toned and healthy.

He was exhausted and looked forward to crashing in his own bed for a change. He'd popped open a beer and mindlessly surfed through the cable news channels to see footage of the aftermath of the terrorist attacks. A couple of the networks had created graphics quoting him and even used his picture to put a face with the quotes. It was a proud moment for him, although he couldn't relish it. He was genuinely glad to be alive.

Once his pizza was ready, he cut it up and poured a small mound of barbecue sauce in the middle of the plate. It was a routine he'd repeated a hundred times during his years in Washington. To some, it might exhibit loneliness. One could easily feel sorry for the young man who'd devoted his life to journalism. For Peter, eating was the least important part of his daily life. He enjoyed being in the thick of international affairs, even if it was as a reporter looking from the outside in.

He was on his third slice when his landline phone rang in the kitchen. Upon his return, he'd checked his voicemails and found numerous messages from television and radio producers hoping to interview him the next day. He didn't take the time to write them down. The late evening call was unexpected, but most likely a persistent producer. He'd reward them with the first opportunity to score an exclusive.

Peter rose from the couch and headed to the kitchen. As he did, his personal cell phone rang. Then, almost simultaneously, the secure phone assigned to him as a member of the State Department's embed press pool chirped as well. His tiny condo was filled with a variety of ringing sounds, the most annoying of which was the landline. It, however, was the least important.

Peter raced back around the couch and grabbed the secure cell from State.

"Hello."

"Peter, it's Jenna."

"Hey. Um, wait. How'd you get this number?"

"It doesn't matter. Listen—"

Peter's eyes caught a glimpse of the television. He started shouting, "*Oh shit, oh shit, oh shit.*"

"Peter! Peter!" Jenna's voice was coming through the phone's receiver.

"Yeah, I'm here. I see it on the news."

"Listen to me," she continued.

Peter turned his focus back to his longtime friend. She spoke for a moment, and then he pulled the phone away from his ear. He muttered the only words he could seem to grasp at the moment.

"*Oh shit.*"

CHAPTER THIRTEEN

Saturday, October 19
Driftwood Key

After a long day, Mike and Jessica reached out to Hank by phone. He said he had a bungalow available if they'd like to come have a few mojitos and crash for the night. The childless-by-choice couple readily accepted and were treated to a hearty meal by Phoebe. The rest of the evening was spent on the beach, listening to the bongo drums and the steel drum band while a small bonfire shot flames into the sky near the water's edge.

Hank was a social cigar smoker. On those rare occasions he was able to dig his toes in the sand and consume an adult beverage, he enjoyed lighting up his favorite cigar—the Island Jim. The torpedo-shaped smoke had been his father's favorite, and Hank had acquired a taste for them when he used to sneak them out of the humidor as a teen. Shaped like a #2 pencil, the label featured the cartoonish image of a man who seemingly spent his entire life on the beach. Hank liked it for its rich, chocolatey flavor.

"Here's the thing, Hank," began Mike. "We don't have enough warm bodies to beat the streets. Monroe County is not geared up for a murder investigation like this one. Miami-Dade has offered assistance, and of course, the FDLE is chomping at the bit to join in."

Mike, who rarely smoked cigars, always enjoyed one when he was hanging out with his older brother. He'd always looked up to Hank as a kid and tried his best to *hang with the big dogs*, as his mother put it, when he was growing up. Seven years younger, Mike emulated many of Hank's mannerisms and traits although the two men differed in career paths. Mike always wanted to be a cop, and Hank always wanted to be Island Jim. Hank kept a box of Rocky Patel cigars in the humidor for Mike. The Edge, as the cigar was called, was much milder than most smokes. It provided a nice, robust flavor without the strong knockout punch that most cigars hit the casual smoker with.

Hank took a long draw on his cigar and allowed the smoke rings to float into the night until they joined the flames from the bonfire.

"So let 'em," said Hank as he sipped on a mojito. The Driftwood Key Inn was known for several signature traits or amenities. In addition to being the only resort on its own private island, guests raved about their signature cocktail, the mojito.

The Florida Keys, thanks to Jimmy Buffett and his Margaritaville restaurant in Key West, was often associated with margaritas. Margaritas, a tequila-infused lime drink, was first introduced near Tijuana, Mexico, in the late 1930s. Associating it with island living was a direct result of Buffett, his music, and extensive branding.

Since the Florida Keys were first inhabited, and probably because of their close proximity to Cuba, the mojito cocktail had been the drink of choice. Originally a medicinal drink used to curb disease in Havana, it was created with bootleg rum mixed with readily available mint, lime juice, and sugar cane syrup.

The Albright family, like the other early settlers of the Florida Keys, had imbibed in the tart yet tasty drink since the turn of the nineteenth century. At the Driftwood Key Inn, they followed the recipe used by most, except the Albrights insisted on using key limes grown on the property and white rum made by Havana Club, a Cuban rum now available because the embargo against the nation had been lifted.

While Hank and Jessica enjoyed their mojitos, Mike, always the exception, sipped a Jack Black on the rocks.

Hank turned to Jessica. "How about you? Anything exciting on the water today?"

As part of the Water Emergency Team, Jessica had to respond to all manner of emergencies, from people who'd been injured to divers in distress.

"You know, it's hard to compare what I do to Mike. I've watched him tackle these murder cases and take them on personally as if he were a family member of the dead person. I don't have that kind of excitement.

"Today, I had to respond to a family on the water who thought their father was having a heart attack or a stroke. We raced out there only to find out he was toasted inside and out. It was nothing more than pickled innards and dehydration."

Hank nodded his understanding of where she was coming from. "These people are here to have a good time. They wanna drink, get some sun, and do all the things they can't do up in Illinois or Ohio or Vermont. We try to politely warn them, and while they're on our property, Jimmy and the others are able to let them know when they've had too much sun."

The three of them sat quietly for a moment. Mike hoisted himself out of his beach chair to toss a couple more logs on the fire. He spoke to Hank as he returned to his chair.

"So, I was talking to Phoebe while we ate in the kitchen. She tells me that you've met a lady friend."

Hank pulled the bill of his Tommy Bahama Relax hat down over his eyes as he shook his head from side to side. The formerly white hat was stained by years of wear and multiple *washings* in the salty sea.

"Geez, you people are relentless!" exclaimed Hank. "I didn't *meet* a lady friend. She's a guest of the hotel."

"A special guest is what Phoebe told us," added Jessica.

"Phoebe talks too much."

"Tell us about her," said Jessica.

"What's to tell?" Hank asked rhetorically. "She's here with her three sisters for an annual beach vacation. They stay at different places each year, and this year they chose the inn."

"She's a Washington big shot is what Sonny said," interjected Mike.

"Damn. Sonny talks too much as well."

"C'mon, Hank, she is a big deal, right?" asked Mike.

"Nah. Well, yeah. She's secretary of agriculture."

"Come on, Hank," said Jessica. "She's in the president's cabinet. That's pretty damn cool. So you two have hit it off?"

"Yeah, I suppose you could say that. I mean, we're friendly, and she's easy to talk to. Nothing like the politicians and government officials Peter tells us about."

"How is my nephew?" asked Mike. "I got a text saying he wasn't blown up in Abu Dhabi. Odd but good news, I guess."

"A little too close for comfort, Mike. He was more in the thick of it than what was relayed in the news. Peter was lucky, but he made his own luck by some quick thinking."

Hank finished his mojito and glanced over at Jessica's glass to see if she was ready for another one. She noticed his interest and finished off her drink, waving the glass with a smile as she swallowed.

Hank rose and took her glass. "Michael? Ready?"

"Yeah, I'll walk with ya." Hank reached out with his free hand and clasped his brother's to help hoist him off the beach chair. As he did, he heard shouting coming from the main house.

"Mr. Hank! Mr. Hank! Come quick. It's Peter on the phone!"

The calm of the evening had just been shattered.

CHAPTER FOURTEEN

Saturday, October 19
Tehran, Iran

In those first few moments, they were dumbstruck. A million pairs of eyes fixed in a thousand-yard stare—nerve endings unfeeling, insensitive to what had happened.

Most just stood there. Mouth agape. Barely able to breathe as they comprehended what was happening. Others released a primal, spine-chilling scream before running in all directions in search of safety.

To observe their bodies, arms outstretched, flying away from where they once stood, would make you think your mind was playing tricks on you. Their fingers would begin to melt like a wax figurine in a much too hot enclosed room.

Then the rest of their body seemingly disappeared, evaporated into a cloud of dust, leaving no trace as it mixed with the sands of Persia.

The screaming would continue. Shrieking. Moaning. Agony expressed in any manner of ways.

Hundreds of thousands of victims at once. Maybe millions.

Their fragile corpses, what was left of them anyway, strewn about amid a sea of shattered concrete and glass. A wasteland dotted with the shells of buildings, orphaned walls, and stairways leading to nowhere.

And then as a punctuation mark—a great, big exclamation point —a massive fireball would rise high into the stratosphere, carrying with it the bowels and guts of the once proud city and its inhabitants. A massive act of cremation of the dead corpses and the homes where they lived.

This was Tehran after the Israeli nuclear counterstrike. The Supreme Leader of Iran, the highest political and religious authority of the Islamic Republic, together with his Ayatollah advisers, was ready to administer justice. He needed to punish the Jews. Once that succeeded, he would turn his ire on the Americans. Death to Israel! Death to America! A mantra that was repeated a million times a day in Tehran.

Except he miscalculated.

He chose to believe the words of the scientists who'd recently been killed at Isfahan when they said their first-strike capability against Israel would be successful. He chose to believe his admired generals within the Iranian Revolutionary Guard, who assured him they had the capability to defend Iran from Israel's counterattack. He chose to trust Allah, who told him those who might perish would rise to face the great resurrection followed by guaranteed admittance into Heaven.

He was wrong.

Iran pulled their nuclear trigger. In the first wave of their attack on Israel, they fired four fifty-kiloton warheads via Shabab 3 missiles upon Tel Aviv and two more upon Haifa up the coast. Tel Aviv was located on a flat, open plain with a high population density, making it the Iranians' most likely target. Haifa, because of its population, was the next likely target. Jerusalem, because of its thirty-five percent Muslim population, was spared.

The superior Israeli anti-missile and anti-aircraft defenses performed admirably against the surprise attack but not perfectly.

Both Tel Aviv and Haifa were struck with a nuclear warhead. The cities were devastated, but not destroyed. The aftermath would be another issue.

In Iran, its cities were particularly vulnerable to nuclear attack due to geography, building construction, and population densities. Israel was merciless in their counterattack, sending several one-megaton warheads at Tehran just seconds behind a cluster of Jericho 1 and 2 missiles to draw Iranian defenses. While the Russian-made S-300 missile defense system knocked down most of the Jericho missiles, they were preoccupied when the nuclear-armed cruise missiles arrived.

Tehran, with its thirteen million inhabitants and fifty percent of the republic's manufacturing and education facilities, never stood a chance. The simultaneous detonations obliterated the city.

The limited nuclear war, which was over in hours, had long-lasting effects on the planet, especially in Tehran. The topography, specifically the mountains around Tehran, obstructed the distribution of the blast caused by the nuclear explosion, forcing the debris upward. This, coupled with climatic conditions that included high concentrations of airborne dust, exacerbated the size of the mushroom cloud.

The massive hot bubble of gas rose in the form of a fireball, carrying with it debris and radioactive material. Within days, it would have circumnavigated the planet.

PART III

ONE WEEK IN OCTOBER

Day three, Sunday, October 20

CHAPTER FIFTEEN

Sunday, October 20
White House

Washington was in a frenzy. Staffers working at the White House, the State Department, the DOD, and Homeland Security were all called in on a Sunday as the world reeled from the nuclear war that had broken out between Israel and Iran. Years later, it would be known as the Six-Day War although for all intents and purposes, it was over in six hours.

The delusional Iranians still had a lot of fight in them. Despite Tehran being leveled from the twin nuclear detonations delivered by Israel, the Iranians had planned a ground attack coupled with naval activity in the Persian Gulf. They were seemingly prepared to do battle in the region regardless of the consequences for the Iranian people, who never had a chance.

The Iran Navy, led by Commodore Hossein Mohammed, was a small but formidable force. They'd war-gamed a blockade of the Strait of Hormuz as the cruise missiles began to fly. This action was consistent with their prior threats of stopping the flow of oil out of the Middle East and permanently forcing the U.S. out of the region.

Had the attack occurred a day later, the USS *Georgia* would've been positioned in the middle of the Persian Gulf and ready to join the fight. The *Nimitz* Carrier Strike Group, steaming toward the region, was still a day away. Had it been in position, there would no longer be an Iranian Navy, assuming the president gave the order to join the fray.

The level of stress in the White House was at its highest since the days of the Cuban Missile Crisis. The Kennedy administration had engaged in a thirteen-day political and military standoff with Nikita Khrushchev and the Soviet Union in October of 1962.

The U.S.S.R. had attempted to deliver nukes to Cuba, but not in the same manner of delivery as Iran and Israel exchanged. As Soviet ships steamed toward the tiny island nation just ninety miles from the Florida Keys, the U.S. moved into position to initiate a blockade in their path. The world held its breath as the nations came to the brink of all-out nuclear war. The standoff ended, in that instance, with diplomacy.

It was a different world now. In 1962, only two nations maintained nuclear stockpiles. Today, there were ten countries—the U.S., the UK, Russia, France, China, Pakistan, India, Israel, North Korea, and, with help from its allies, Iran.

In theory, any nation with the technology, intelligence, and facilities could develop nuclear weapons. Nations like Russia, China, and North Korea had been accused of facilitating the development of nuclear programs in Iran and, most recently, in Syria. It had also been rumored that China and Russia had worked with Venezuelan dictators to position nuclear warheads on the South American continent.

A new arms race had begun as the mid-twenty-first century approached. Nonproliferation agreements designed to prevent the spread of nuclear weapons and promote disarmament had been mothballed. The illusion of a world free of nuclear weapons had faded of late. Now the hope of them never being used had been dashed.

President Carter Helton had a concerned look on his face as he was ushered by Secret Service personnel through the bowels of the East Wing of the White House into the Presidential Emergency Operations Center, more widely known by its acronym—PEOC.

In the early years of the Cold War, beginning in the 1950s and continuing through the Reagan administration of the '80s, America's defense warning system evolved from duck-and-cover protocols to advanced computerized responses being initiated to defend the nation's citizens and prepare the military for an attack.

The wholly underground facility, initially constructed during the Roosevelt administration, had undergone substantial changes over many decades so that it was impenetrable to any form of nuclear missile threat.

The president glanced up at the low-hanging ceilings and the elaborate network of pipe that contained hardened wiring designed to protect the facility's electronics from an electromagnetic pulse attack. In the event of a nuclear-delivered electromagnetic pulse, the PEOC's communications and mechanical equipment wouldn't be destroyed by a massive burst of energy known to destroy or disable anything electronic.

The president was escorted through the final stretch of tile-covered hallways into a reception area. Several members of his national defense team had gathered in the small conference room near the entryway. He nodded his head toward them and managed a slight wave, but was abruptly pulled away by Secret Service toward a large room that adjoined the main command and control center of the PEOC.

Harrison Chandler, his chief of staff, and several aides and uniformed members of the military were huddled around the long rectangular table. He was the first to notice President Helton enter the room.

"Mr. President!"

Everyone came to attention and stood to the side so the president could make direct contact with his chief of staff.

"Talk to me, Harrison. What the hell happened?"

Chandler gestured toward a chair at the head of the conference room table, but the president didn't move. He glanced through the large one-way mirror that overlooked the PEOC's nerve center, the equivalent of the Situation Room that was located below the Oval Office in the West Wing, only much larger.

He folded his arms and stared at his chief of staff, which was his nature, a posture that often intimidated those locked in the president's dark eyes.

"Mr. President, we are still awaiting details from our recon satellites. We've analyzed video obtained from the news networks, as well as footage provided to us by Israel. It's apparent that in revenge for the killings at Isfahan, Iran chose to retaliate with several nuclear warheads attached to their Russian-designed ballistic missiles."

"They had no proof Israel was behind that attack! You solve these matters through diplomacy, not firing off nukes." The president was incensed.

Chandler moved on with his explanation. "Israel's defenses worked, although parts of Tel Aviv and Haifa to the north were both struck. We have reports of extensive damage and mass casualties."

"Israel retaliated?" the president asked.

"In a big way, sir. Tehran was mostly leveled."

"I take it they've stopped."

"Yes, sir. At least with respect to the nukes. Iran is still active military. If I may, please let me defer to the Pentagon on this." Chandler motioned to the Pentagon's representative to brief the president on Iran's naval blockade and other troop movements.

After he finished his portion of the briefing, Chandler brought the White House communications team into the conversation.

"Mr. President," the communications director began, "we're under tremendous pressure to comment on our response."

President Helton, who'd stood for the entire briefing with his arms crossed, nodded and spread his hands apart. "Of course. Of course. Naturally, we're saddened by the loss of life, and we strongly condemn the actions of the Iranian regime. There is no place in our civilized world for the use of nuclear weapons."

"Yes, sir. I understand. However, the pressure relates to what actions we plan on taking to defend our closest ally in the Middle East—Israel. The media wants to know whether we are going to declare war on Iran and enter the Persian Gulf to restore order. Also, they want to know if we're willing to state unequivocally that our use of nuclear weapons in response is off the table."

The president shook his head in disbelief. Only hours ago, two nations had devastated one another with nuclear missiles, and the media wanted to know if America was prepared to fire off a few more. This was going to be a long day.

CHAPTER SIXTEEN

Sunday, October 20
Washington Times
Washington, DC

Every young person who dreamed of becoming a journalist enjoyed seeing a vintage, yellowing photograph of the city desk of a newsroom from the mid-twentieth century. Scrambling to put together the afternoon paper, a once-grand tradition in America, had gone the way of manual typewriters and carbon paper. Gone were the tape recorders and spiral notebooks. Editing consisted of retyping whole paragraphs and pasting them on top of the material to be deleted. There were no computers or internet or smartphones to record news in real time.

Newsrooms were filled with furnishings that looked like they'd been picked up at a garage sale. Scarred wooden desks were covered with papers and perhaps a nondescript desk lamp. To the side, perched on a rolling table, was a manual typewriter made by companies like Royal and Smith-Corona. Reporters who were assigned to the field or to travel with a high-ranking government official were assigned a Remington Portable, which was basically a typewriter in a box.

What hadn't changed over the years was the journalists' zest for reporting the news. The desire to use their intuition, or hustle, as necessary to seek out the facts considered newsworthy and to break the story was the same today as it was in 1950.

The newsrooms, therefore, had a similar sense of urgency and excitement as decades past, only the furnishings and tools used by journalists had advanced in the twenty-first century. Telephone desk sets were gone. Typewriter keys clacking coupled with the ding of the return handle being engaged disappeared. Calls for the copy boys were no longer necessary. Everything was digital.

But the feeding frenzy during a breaking news story remained the same. Back in the day, the news came in mostly by telephone, called in by *legmen*, reporters who scoured the town for stories. Their calls were rerouted to one of the city editors, who, depending on the urgency or sexiness of the story, would reassign it to a rewrite man. He was the guy who got the byline, credit for the article, even though it had been scooped by someone else.

All of this had changed with technology.

Peter had scheduled two interviews that morning to discuss what he'd experienced in Abu Dhabi. However, that, as they say, was yesterday's news. In today's twenty-four-hour news cycle, an ordinarily newsworthy event just a few hours ago could easily be forgotten and displaced with a much sexier story in the present. Such was the case as the mutual nuclear attacks between Iran and Israel overtook any other story the reporters at the *Washington Times* were working on.

Every desk in the *Washington Times* newsroom was filled. The energy was at a fever-pitch as reporters called sources and others banged away on their computers, conducting research. These were the hired guns who continued to work tirelessly to produce the second largest newspaper by circulation in Washington. Only the *Washington Post* had a larger subscriber base. The journalists who occupied these desks were irreverent, brash, and above all, competitive, even with one another. It was all about making a name for themselves, a direct result of the success of Bob Woodward and Carl Bernstein's notoriety achieved during their investigation of President Richard Nixon.

All of their cutthroat tactics were designed to become known. Every attempt to break the news was in furtherance of their insatiable desire to pursue a Pulitzer. None of their tactics gave them the notoriety and respect Peter Albright had achieved by being at ground zero of the terrorist attack in Abu Dhabi. However, fame was fleeting, and his fifteen minutes had burned up quickly.

Because the secretary of state was involved in White House discussions all day, Peter was able to touch base with his boss at the *Times*.

"Peter, grab a seat," Doug Beasley said without looking away from his computer monitor. "Glad you're back in one piece."

That's it? Peter had been hoping for a little better pat on the back for his efforts in Abu Dhabi than the one Beasley was offering.

"Thanks," was all Peter could think to say in response.

"Peter, things are developing rapidly after the nukes started flying. There's an angle I want you to run down for me."

"Um, I'll do my best, but the secretary is expected to be at the White House all—"

"It doesn't involve your coverage of her movements. It has to do with her political ideology."

Peter was genuinely puzzled. "Um, sure. But shouldn't I focus on the Middle East picture rather than her future political aspirations?"

Beasley looked away from his monitor for the first time. He peered over his glasses at Peter, who was casually dressed in a long-sleeve, striped polo shirt and khakis. It was his uniform of choice when not in the State Department press room representing the *Times*.

"I'm talking about her political ideology as it pertains to the use of nuclear weapons. She's been known to be a dove in these respects, always pushing the president in a direction that does not involve military conflict."

Since the founding of the American republic, doves were often associated with a political ideology promoting peace and pacifism. Politicians of this ilk were opposite of the hawks, who favored war and a continuation of any existing conflicts as opposed to other, nonmilitary solutions.

"Sir, her opinions are well known and in line with the president's. I can't imagine he'd bring her into his cabinet if it were otherwise."

Beasley continued. "I'm hearing there is an exception."

"An exception as in *they're doves ninety-nine percent of the time except for ...?*" Peter allowed his question to dangle in the air.

"The DPRK," Beasley replied flatly. "There is something in both of their backgrounds that indicates they might take a different approach toward North Korea than Iran, in the present circumstances."

"Why would they have a hard-on for Kim? Are you thinking it's something personal? Since Helton's election, the Hermit Kingdom has been very quiet."

"Too quiet, don't you think?" asked Beasley. "Lying low to the point of being obvious. Like they're scared."

"I suppose, sir," said Peter. He didn't want to argue with his boss. He was getting the impression he was being assigned busywork as some form of punishment. Regardless, he'd do as instructed.

Beasley removed his glasses and leaned forward so his elbows rested on his desk. "Listen, Peter. This is a hunch of mine that doesn't need to be shared with anyone else in the newsroom. I've tasked you with it because you have connections at State, the Pentagon, and the White House.

"Something in my gut is screaming at me regarding the administration's treatment of North Korea. The whole dynamic is off-kilter. Will you look into it and see what you uncover?"

Peter sat a little taller in his chair now that he realized he wasn't being sidelined and relegated to the bench. "I'll jump on it right now."

CHAPTER SEVENTEEN

Sunday, October 20
Driftwood Key

Hank walked onto the beach that morning, as was customary. He was in a pensive mood as he strolled along the water's edge, where the calm, gently lapping waves barely rose up the slight incline. He followed footsteps that had been left in the sand by another early riser. His bare feet were larger than the other beach walker that morning. He picked up the pace to see who it was.

Up ahead, he caught a glimpse of Erin Bergman. She was wearing her swimsuit and her white linen coverup. He hadn't seen her the day before, even assuming, until later told otherwise, that she'd returned to Washington. He was anxious to speak with her about the nuclear exchange.

Hank glanced ahead of her as he approached. He didn't mean to startle her, but she was about to encounter a rarity in the Keys, one that might shock her.

"Erin, wait," he announced with a tone of caution.

She swung around. "Um, hi, Hank. Is everything all right?"

"Yes, just don't move."

Erin stopped in her tracks and tilted her head with a puzzled look on her face. He caught up to her with his hands spread apart, waving them up and down as if he wanted her to remain calm.

"Slowly. Back away from where you're standing," he instructed as he held his hand out to her. She took it and carefully picked up her feet, which had sunk somewhat in the wet sand. Her first instinct was to look around her feet, presuming there was something dangerous nearby. She couldn't see it, but she followed Hank's suggestion nonetheless.

Still holding her hand, he led her up the slope a few feet away from the water's edge. "This is your lucky day," he said with a smile. He hesitated to let go of her hand. It was soft and warm. It felt right. But he did and walked just to where the wave line was created in the wet sand.

"Is it a jellyfish?" she asked.

"No, better. Let me introduce you to a stargazer."

"Where?" Erin asked as she gingerly inched forward and bent over to see what he was referring to.

Hank knelt down and drew a semicircle in the sand when the water receded. Erin looked closer until the water lapped over the space again. He redrew the line in the sand.

"Do you see it?" he asked as he waved for her to come closer.

She placed her hand on his shoulder and bent over at the waist. "Well, I'll be damned. It is a fish."

"A stargazer. It's very unusual, but we happen to get them all the time on this desolate stretch of beach. Look closer. You can see that its eyes, gill slits, nostrils and most of its mouth are on top of its body."

Erin studied the twenty-inch-long fish that was half-submerged. It's dark blackish-brown body blended in perfectly with the wet sand.

"How did you see it from back there?"

"After living here for all my life, you notice slight variations in the sand. Most people might think it's a rock or something under the surface. Until, of course, they step on it. These guys are stout, and they have a special organ just behind their eyes that produces an electric shock for anyone who unknowingly grabs it."

"Or steps on it," added Erin.

Hank nodded, and the two of them stood upright to study the unusual creature. "May I join you? I usually walk along the beach in the mornings, you know, just to get ready to do battle with hostile and ornery hotel guests."

Erin let out a hearty laugh. "You mean like my sisters?"

Hank had no intention of his joking remark to be associated with her three older sisters. "No, not at all. And I was just kidding. Only rarely do we have a guest we simply cannot please. It happens. Not everybody gives out five-star reviews."

"Don't I know it. I'm in politics, remember. You piss off half your constituents. Initially, you please the other half until at some point you piss most of them off as well. By the time your career in public service is over, most everybody is mad at you, making you wonder why you bothered."

"Why did you? Bother, I mean."

They continued to study the interesting stargazer.

"It wasn't my idea," she replied casually. "My ex was politically connected, but he made too much money as a personal injury lawyer to seek public office. He made a living out of suing the wrong people, corporate giants, for example. Therefore, he had a résumé that was easy to shoot at. Instead, at a dinner party one night, he offered me up as a better candidate."

"Were you surprised?"

Erin laughed. "Well, we'd discussed it, but nothing serious. Because of my degree in public administration, I had an aptitude for the operations of government. My minor in transportation and work with Florida's highway commission as a lobbyist made me an ideal candidate for a transportation position."

"Not agriculture?" Hank asked a logical question considering her current position.

"Well, that came later. The governor appointed me to head the Florida Department of Transportation. When the commissioner of agriculture became embroiled in a sex scandal, the governor looked to a familiar face with no skeletons in the closet to fill the post. As a result, with only a year of public service under my belt, I became one of four members of the Florida cabinet behind the lieutenant governor, attorney general, and the state's chief financial officer."

"Wow. You moved fast."

Erin looked down shyly and smiled. "Well, the temporary appointment was easy. Running in the special election is what got me put on the so-called political radar as a proverbial up-and-comer."

Hank shrugged. "I'm sorry, but I don't follow politics, really. I vote for president, and that's about it."

"That's okay. Ordinarily, I would've been one of those down-ballot candidates that folks fill in the circle next to because it was on a certain side of the page. As it happened, my first campaign was in an off-year election cycle where the race was the most prominent in the state. Hell, we had debates. Mudslinging. Outside money pouring in. All the hallmarks of a gubernatorial race except it was for Ag commissioner."

"And you won."

"Decidedly so in an evenly divided state."

"I bet your husband was proud of you."

Erin laughed and ran her fingers through her hair. She glanced up at the cloudless sky and smiled. "One would think, but alas, no. It led to our divorce."

"Why?" asked Hank, hesitating to pry but doing so anyway.

"He became jealous of my success and notoriety. He tried to take credit for my win until one day, during a press conference, a reporter set him straight. He took his anger out on me, and our marriage was over."

"I'm sorry," said Hank.

Erin shrugged and smiled nervously. "You know, it probably should've happened long before. He never supported me or encouraged me to pursue my goals and dreams. He wanted me on his arm at social gatherings or as a smiling face for his television commercials."

Erin was talkative, and Hank enjoyed listening to her, so he decided to take the conversation further. "How long were you in Tallahassee? You must've impressed some important people to reach the top of the totem pole."

"Well, I actually did a lot of things for Florida farmers and orange growers in particular. But more importantly, I built coalitions with both parties to get things done. I won my second election by a landslide. When the president began his campaign a couple of years ago, I pledged my support even though we were in opposite parties."

"I bet that was awkward," said Hank with a smile. "Didn't you piss off your side of the aisle?"

"Like I said, eventually you make everyone mad."

"Obviously, that bold step was appreciated by the president."

"Okay. I'm gonna toot my own horn for a moment. The fact is, I practically delivered Florida for him on election day. My statewide campaign team worked tirelessly to get out the vote for the president. Without Florida, he couldn't have been elected. Anyway, our efforts didn't go unnoticed, so he rewarded me with secretary of agriculture. I'm the only one in the cabinet who isn't in the president's party."

Hank was impressed. She was a politician, yet she wasn't. She was a straight talker, a rarity in Washington, Tallahassee, or the Florida Keys, for that matter. He still sensed she was troubled.

"I didn't see you yesterday, so I thought you'd returned to Washington."

"No. Sadly, or fortunately, depending on how you look at it, they don't need me up there. If I were leading transportation, then certainly. That was the job I really wanted, but the president had to offer it to someone more acceptable to unions."

"You're still a cabinet member," said Hank. "Wouldn't you be involved in the national security meetings?"

She shook her head side to side. "I have the requisite security clearance but would have little to offer from the agriculture side, or at least that's what they probably think."

Hank glanced at her face to make eye contact. "I take it you disagree."

There was a fallen palm tree ahead, and Erin pointed toward it, indicating what she had to say was worthy of sitting down to explain. Hank followed her lead and took her hand to help her up the slope through the soft sand. Once they'd settled in to watch a fishing boat meander out toward a reef, Erin dropped a bomb of her own.

"If we were to be attacked with nuclear warheads, the transportation secretary would have to deal with the threat of an EMP. However, the aftermath of what happened between two nuclear powers, even on the other side of the world, will bring a plague on our planet that could be much worse—nuclear winter."

CHAPTER EIGHTEEN

Sunday, October 20
Driftwood Key

Hank was not completely unaware of the terms—EMP and nuclear winter. He'd heard them mentioned in movies, news documentaries, and books he'd read in the past. However, he'd never bothered to study or research what they meant. Erin was about to enlighten him and open his eyes to the very real threats their nation faced from nuclear war.

"There are many aspects to the use of nuclear weapons most of the public is unaware of. They all can visualize the massive mushroom cloud full of debris and fire because they've seen the videos from testing decades ago or how it is digitally portrayed in movies.

"That part is certainly accurate. The tremendous amount of energy that is released at the impact site annihilates virtually everything within the blast radius, depending on the size of the warhead.

"World powers, namely the U.S.S.R. and the U.S., learned through a series of nuclear tests in the late fifties there was an unexpected side effect to atomic bomb detonations. In 1958, testing at the Pacific Proving Grounds located in the Marshall Islands, known as the Starfish Prime project, revealed the energy generated also had the ability to destroy the tiny vulnerable wiring of electronic devices. This side effect, as they initially called it, is known as an EMP, or electromagnetic pulse.

"The government began to experiment with warhead detonations at different altitudes. The higher above ground the nuclear warhead was detonated, the broader the reach of the energy waves and the highly charged particles released into the atmosphere. Ground detonation, while releasing the same types of particles, had a significantly smaller EMP effect because its particles were not launched into the atmosphere but were thwarted by geographic features like mountains."

Hank was aware of EMPs and what they were capable of, but he did not know the altitude of the detonation made a difference on the area it impacted. He looked for clarity. "Let's use an example. The Russians nuke St. Louis. I don't know why they would, but it's the center of the country. Now, if the nuke hits the city, how far out will the electronics be impacted?"

"Again, keep in mind that the size of the weapon and the altitude are very important variables. Low-yield nukes coupled with a ground-level detonation will have less of an EMP effect. High-yield, high-altitude detonations could potentially place the entirety of the continental U.S. in the dark.

"Now, a caveat. Our power grid is tied together from coast to coast, except for Texas, which I'll explain in a moment. The Eastern and Western Interconnection grids rely upon one another to maintain the continuous flow of power to the highest-demand users. For example, electricity generated by hydroelectric dams in Tennessee might not need to send as much energy to the rural parts of the state, but they transfer it to major cities like Atlanta and Memphis in the region.

"If the nuclear blast produces a large enough EMP to impact an entire region, like the West Coast, then the other power grids will work overtime to supplement the needs of areas outside the impact area. This may result in a cascading failure of the entire Eastern and Western Interconnection power grids."

"But not Texas?" Hank asked.

"Right. They have their own grid separate and distinct from the rest of the country, operated by ERCOT, their power company."

Hank stood to stretch his legs but also to absorb what Erin had relayed to him. "This is a real problem for the rest of us who aren't directly in the line of fire of a nuke that might hit LA or ..." His voice trailed off as he avoided identifying the most obvious East Coast target—Washington.

"Correct. Don't get me wrong. A targeted EMP attack designed to destroy our grid would be devastating and result in the deaths of nearly ninety percent of Americans, according to some reports. However, with a herculean effort and international cooperation, power grids can be rebuilt. That's not the case with problem number two."

Hank sat down again. He'd begun contemplating selling the inn and moving to Texas. "So the power grid crashes. Electronics won't work. Does that mean cars, too?"

"Yes, depending on the nature of the energy release. Trust me, Hank, our scientists have run as many simulations as there are warhead yields, targets, and altitude scenarios. We won't know until it happens."

"God forbid."

"I agree," she said before moving on to the concept of nuclear winter. "During my years in Tallahassee and even in the first hundred days as secretary of agriculture, the concept of nuclear winter has often come up in our policy meetings."

Hank interrupted as he sought clarification as to whether this would impact their tiny part of the world. "Is the potential for nuclear winter serious for those of us who live away from obvious nuclear targets?"

Erin sighed and swallowed hard. "Electromagnetic pulses may

be the last thing we need to worry about in the event of a nuclear attack. Not just on our soil, but anywhere in the world."

"Whadya mean?"

"Nuclear war would spawn a climate catastrophe, including a global nuclear El Niño."

Hank stood and began pacing again. He looked around to see if any other guests were approaching. He'd hoped for the opportunity to be alone with Erin. He enjoyed her company, and he'd visualized them having a conversation filled with laughs and even, perhaps, flirting. Instead, he found his palms getting sweaty from anxiety.

"Well, that doesn't sound like a lot of fun," he said, hoping to find a way to inject humor into a subject that wasn't funny.

"Hank, I'm sorry," she apologized, hanging her head. Then she made eye contact with him. "My sister told me that you'd asked where I was yesterday. I was coming to grips with all of this stuff myself. The fact is the entire world suffers in a nuclear war, even if it's regional in nature in places far away from America.

"Nuclear explosions bring radioactive fallout as well as an unrelenting winter as it kicks off the most intense, longest El Niño the planet has experienced since the last eruption of the Yellowstone supervolcano.

"Last month, I attended an ocean sciences meeting in San Diego suggesting global cooling from a nuclear conflict would disrupt normal upper-level wind circulation, leading to severe changes in the atmosphere above the Pacific Ocean.

"Their studies were conclusive. A limited, regional nuclear war in the Middle East like the other day, or in South Asia between Pakistan and India, would provoke a cascade of changes to the Pacific Ocean, the world's largest ocean basin. Trade winds will reverse direction. The height of the sea surface on either side of the Pacific will adjust, bringing more water to South America's shores than Australia's, for example. With this profound change in the normal sea levels near the equator, the volume of nutrient-rich waters made available to marine life will become depleted. In essence, there's the potential for a total reversal of ocean circulation."

"Geez," said Hank as he suddenly turned to the calm waters of the Gulf.

"The thing is," she began before pausing. "These nuclear detonations represent a pretty big hammer slapping the planet's climate. Depending on the number of nuclear weapons exchanged, the unusual nuclear El Niño could last up to ten years."

"During which time, what happens?" asked Hank.

"A massive die-off of the marine food population, especially in the Pacific. The disruption in the weather patterns coupled with substantially less light due to the fallout circumnavigating the planet results in less food resources for fish."

"What about our coast?"

"Well, there haven't been many peer-reviewed studies of the impact to the Atlantic or the Gulf of Mexico. The Pacific is an ecosystem in and of itself. However, the limited light resulting from nuclear fallout, nuclear winter, if you will, would severely hamper food production around the globe.

"Without natural grown foods for wildlife, animals can't eat. Without adequate sunlight and rainfall, crops can't grow. Without food from animal and plant sources, humans can't eat. If nothing eats, famine is the natural result."

"Are we talking about the end of civilization? I mean, surely the people who press the buttons know this is a really bad idea, right?"

Erin stood to join Hank and dusted off the back of her coverup. She took him by the arm, a touching gesture that prompted Hank to smile for the first time since this whole nuclear-aftermath conversation started.

"Hank, imagine a room where the walls and floors are soaked with gasoline. Inside, you have two bitter enemies facing each other. One has a thousand matches, and the other has only nine hundred. Both enemies want to show their firepower is superior to the other's.

"That's where we are today. We have an enormous stockpile of nukes, as does China to our west and Russia to our east. There is this unsteady understanding that none of us win in an all-out nuclear war.

"Now, consider this. Iran and Israel were on equal par with one another thanks to a recent surge in Iran's stockpiles. They thought it was a fair fight, but it wasn't because Israel had planned for this eventuality many years ago. Its defensive capabilities were far superior."

The results were obvious.

Erin stopped and began to draw in the sand with her toes. Hank stood back to give her plenty of room. She drew a big circle and reached out to take his hand.

"You stand here, Captain America." She smiled and sent him a wink. He eagerly stepped into the circle.

She stood to the side and made a circle representing China. Then she walked around Hank to create another one for Russia.

"China and Russia, okay?" She furrowed her brow as she identified the circles. Hank gave her a thumbs-up.

Then, below China toward the left, near the water's edge, she drew another circle and looked up to Hank.

"This is Pakistan and India. Now, they've been in their own gasoline-soaked room for a while now. They don't have a thousand matches, but they have more than enough to incinerate the room. If they were to light their matches, the billowing smoke and ash would flow upwards into the atmosphere and, within four days, spread around the globe.

"We would experience nuclear winter, albeit on a lesser scale at first. This will gradually become worse as the days go on. Naturally, if the nukes were dropped on top of us, the results would be immediate."

"I see," said Hank. He began to step toward her, and she raised her hand, indicating she wasn't finished.

She walked to the opposite side of the China circle, closer to Hank, and drew an oblong shape from the water's edge to the upper side of China. She stood off to the side and put her hands on her hips to survey her work.

"This represents the Korean peninsula. Now, there's a whole lot of gasoline here, but only one side has matches, and they're held by a ruthless dictator."

Hank chuckled. "I call him *Little Un*."

Erin laughed with him but cautioned, "Short on stature but tall on threat. You see, if the balance of power between you, China, and Russia over there were to stay the same, *Little Un*, as you call him, might do something stupid because these big guns have his back. Likewise, these guys who are facing off in their own gas-filled room might decide to have at it." She walked across China and pointed to India and Pakistan.

"What would trigger all of this?" asked Hank, sweeping his arm across the map in the sand. "Surely that whole mutually assured destruction thing would apply, right?"

"One would hope," she replied. "But if it doesn't, the consequences would be dire for all of us regardless of whether we were at ground zero of the nuclear strike."

Hank shook his head in disbelief. He wondered how politicians could sleep at night knowing that nuclear Armageddon hung over us all like a mighty sword. He stepped out of his circle and motioned for Erin to walk back to the hotel. They shared casual conversation in an effort to get their minds off the prospect of somebody else striking a match in a gasoline-filled room that could result in their extinction.

CHAPTER NINETEEN

Sunday, October 20
Oval Office
The White House

"Clear the room, everyone. Please." President Helton had spent the entire day with advisors and analysts and staffers chirping in his ear for one reason or another. He needed some peace and quiet. Especially the peace half of the equation.

After the Oval Office was empty, he removed his jacket and loosened his tie. He made his way to a small cabinet located to the right of the Resolute Desk. It was perched below a painting of Lady Liberty holding the torch high above her head.

He retrieved a leaded crystal glass and the bottle of Glenfiddich scotch whisky. After pouring his glass half full, he returned to his desk and flopped in the chair. He mindlessly spun back and forth, taking in his surroundings.

He realized how rare it was for him to be left alone in his sanctuary. As president, he was afforded precious little free time. Once in a while, he was left alone to peruse briefing documents for a meeting before the ever-present Chandler would have a need to return to his office.

In addition to the briefings he received from all parts of government, he had figurehead functions to perform, ranging from meeting with world leaders to hosting the Little League World champions. As of this morning, his entire schedule had been cleared for the next several days as the nation's vast intelligence apparatus kept him apprised of events in the Middle East.

It was nice, for a change, to set other matters aside to focus on one thing and make sure he got it right. As a former senator, he hadn't run a government like a governor runs a state. Governors, like presidents, were the chief executive officer of a massive financial operation that dealt directly with the well-being of its citizens. Matters of health, finance, and national defense all had to be taken into account.

The Oval Office had hosted seventeen presidents before him since it was constructed by President Franklin Roosevelt in 1934. The president turned in his chair and stared into the darkness that had engulfed the District as nightfall set in. Lights twinkled off in the distance. He stood from the chair and casually strolled up to the three eleven-foot-tall windows overlooking the South Lawn.

The president was philosophical as he spoke to the empty room. In his mind, he was speaking to the American people. "This office comes with great responsibility. There is no perfect decision on any subject. I can support Israel, but I cannot fight their battles.

"I refuse to go to war over the free flow of oil. Past administrations have done that already. Any decision I make is gonna be met with criticism. That comes with the job."

He stopped speaking, but his thoughts continued. *So let the media pitch a fit. We're gonna sit on the sidelines for now.*

These were similar to the words he'd just spoken to his chief of staff, with instructions to forward them to Pentagon officials. He was certain to receive pushback, but he was firm in his resolve.

Their argument was that their failure to defend their ally Israel, and engage Iran, forcing them to open the Strait of Hormuz, was a sign of weakness. It would embolden their enemies and create doubt in the minds of their allies as to whether the U.S. would back them up in a similar conflict as had been pledged in the past.

Maybe those arguments were valid, but the president didn't believe any nation was going to test his mettle based upon a limited nuclear strike in the Middle East. For now, he'd continue to study his intelligence briefings and allow the military to keep him abreast. If, and when, a threat of this type directly impacted the U.S., then he'd act accordingly.

CHAPTER TWENTY

Peter called Jenna and invited her to a late lunch at their favorite Asian restaurant, Zen Bistro. Located at Pentagon Row, it was a blend of unique retail stores and restaurants on the south side of the Henry Shirley Memorial Highway across from the Pentagon. He also called upon another acquaintance of theirs, Brian Stephens, an assistant to the White House director of political affairs, or DPA.

Peter felt guilty about failing to disclose the real purpose of calling the three friends together. He actually missed Jenna and could tell in her voice during the phone call that she was under considerable stress. Brian dealt with foreign policy matters on behalf of the DPA and might have some insight into the president's opinion of North Korea.

Zen was referred to in the restaurant business as Asian fusion, a mix of several different Asian dishes and ingredients. Chefs served up sushi, Korean cuisine, Thai foods, and Chinese delicacies. The trio, who'd been frequenting Zen for years during happy hour, opted for sushi. After their tea was served and each of them snatched a piece of the red dragon roll, their favorite, the conversation turned to the president's response to the nuclear attack.

"We're all off the record, pinky sworn to secrecy and all of that, right?" asked Brian.

"Of course, man," replied Peter. He might pinky swear, but he certainly would second-source whatever was about to be shared if he planned on revealing it to Beasley. "What are you thinkin'?"

"There's a real concern in the White House that this thing could expand to a much larger, extra-regional conflict."

"I can echo that," added Jenna as she munched on a piece from her crunchy shrimp roll. "The Pentagon believes the president needs to act decisively to show the world America won't stand down to despot rulers."

Peter turned to Brian. "Whadya mean by extra-regional? Are you saying beyond the Middle East? Like Europe?"

Brian shook his head vigorously from side to side as he swallowed the hot tea. "No. South Asia. There's chatter."

Peter's eyes darted from Jenna to Brian. He then fixed his gaze on his friend with benefits, although they hadn't been *friendly* in a few weeks due to Peter's travel schedule. "Do you know about this?"

She shrugged and looked guilty. "Vaguely. Echoes of conversations in the halls. You know how that goes. The Pentagon is a big place with a lot of conversations, if you know what I mean."

Peter shook his head in disbelief. "Why would Pakistan and India go at it now? In the midst of what just happened? Didn't they see the visuals out of Tehran and Tel Aviv. Nuclear war sucks."

When he woke up that morning, he'd hungrily, yet with trepidation, scoured the internet for video clips and photographs of the devastation. Human beings, if not obliterated altogether, were left maimed and twisted. Buildings were incinerated. The entire landscape was covered with gray soot and ash. The sun was blocked out by the debris floating overhead. It was as if the world had turned whitish gray except for the raging fires all around.

"It's complicated," replied Brian.

Peter pressed them. "Pakistan and India seemed to have a working, albeit tenuous peace, for decades. Sure, their nuclear programs have advanced greatly during that time, but they're next-door neighbors, for God's sake. They're not gonna shoot at each other, right?"

Jenna replied, "I never thought the Iranians would have the balls to fire on Israel."

Peter chuckled. He liked when Jenna used locker-room talk. His mom had been the same way.

He shook his head and used his chopsticks to pluck a piece of sushi. "Well, it was stupid. Look how it turned out for those fools. I just can't imagine Pakistan and India going after each other."

Brian felt the need to defend the information he'd shared. "Actually, Peter, it isn't that surprising. Listen, there's a war going on in the White House between the Helton faction, who is adamantly opposed to war, and the longtime advisors to administrations, who see it as a necessary evil. The president sees America's defense of its ally Israel as initiating an act of war on Iran. Others see it as a promise kept, one that has endured for decades."

Peter looked over his drink to Jenna. "Is the Pentagon thinking this way as well?"

She nodded. "From what I'm hearing, the defense secretary firmly believes that bad actors like Pakistan will see the president's inaction as a sign of weakness. They're willing to take their chances on a head-to-head war with India if they believe Washington will stand down."

Here was Peter's opening. "Well, hell. If the administration's opinion is to stand down in a nuclear conflict between two equally matched adversaries, what'll they do if Kim fires off nukes at Seoul and Tokyo, two nations with no nukes of their own?"

Brian leaned back and sighed. "Personal opinion?" he said inquisitively.

"Sure," replied Peter.

"That's a different scenario. He'd defend South Korea and Japan."

"With nukes?"

Jenna and Brian replied simultaneously, "Yes."

Peter continued with his questions. "And this is because of the balance of nuclear power differential?"

"I think so," replied Jenna. "At least from the Pentagon's perspective."

Peter looked to Brian. "Same from the White House?" He intently studied his friend's facial expression, searching for clues.

Brian squinted his eyes and furrowed his brow. He looked around at the mostly empty restaurant. Most people were home tuned into the cable news stations. The nuclear showdown in the Middle East was high drama for most Americans. He leaned in to reply.

"Okay. This is totally water cooler talk, understand? This has never come out of the mouth of my boss and is strictly passed around the Eisenhower and EOB cafeterias." There were two cafeterias open to White House staff. One was located in the Eisenhower Executive Office Building, and the other was in the New Executive Office Building, both of which were part of the White House complex.

Brian continued after both Jenna and Peter nodded in agreement. "There is something personal between the president and Kim. Nobody knows what it is and where it originated. Did you notice during the campaign the subject of North Korea rarely came up?"

"Yeah, you're right," replied Jenna.

"Are you saying he and Kim are best pals or something?" asked Peter.

"I don't know," Brian quickly answered. "There is some kind of unwritten understanding between the two that none of us can put our finger on. It isn't discussed much because, frankly, Kim has toned down his rhetoric since the election, and the president hasn't found a need to address this particular foreign policy matter."

"Well, I'm gonna throw this out there," began Jenna. "Regardless of what the North Koreans are up to, I can say that Pakistanis are certainly on a war footing. That didn't come from me."

CHAPTER TWENTY-ONE

Sunday, October 20
McDowell Residence
Hayward, California

Lacey, Owen, and their son, Tucker, were not unlike millions of other American families gathered around the dinner table that night as they discussed the nuclear attack. They'd grimaced when, despite the warnings of the media that the following images were graphic in nature, they couldn't look away from the devastation wrought by the nuclear bombs.

Lacey cried when she saw orphaned children, maimed and burned, crying for their parents while they clutched a doll or toy. Owen set his jaw in anger as the pundits explained why Iran thought they had a right to attack Israel. Tucker scowled in disbelief when some reporters warned a nuclear war could be brought to American soil.

The solemn news overshadowed what should've been a celebration for the family when Owen broke the news that he got the promotion together with a substantial raise. He was even rewarded with a few days off at the end of the upcoming week.

"Okay. Enough of this," began Lacey as she turned off the television that had been playing in the background as they ate. "We've heard it all, and now they're just regurgitating and speculating, their favorite pastime." She and Peter had vastly different opinions of the role of the media in America. Lacey's was more closely aligned with her father—why can't they just tell the truth from all sides. Peter's perspective was different since it was his passion and job.

"I agree, Mom. I've been thinking about a way to spend Dad's extra days off besides him doing chores around the house."

"How do you know that's what I had in mind?" asked Owen.

"'Cause that's what you do lately, Dad. The three of us haven't been hiking and camping since last spring."

"You and your mom have gone," said Owen with a tinge of guilt in his voice. He knew his son was right. He'd been far too focused on his career at Yahoo, promotion and raise notwithstanding. He needed to live in the present with his family.

"As luck would have it," interjected Lacey, "there are no honey-dos on the hubby's to-do list. We can all just chillax or—"

"You can pull me out of school for a few days, and we can head to the mountains," said Tucker, finishing his mom's sentence in a manner she hadn't planned. "I've got it all planned out."

Owen chuckled and leaned back in his chair. He and Lacey exchanged subtle smiles and encouraged their son to continue.

"Have you guys checked out the weather forecast for the Sierra Nevadas?"

Lacey started to laugh and shrugged. "Um, can't say that I have. How about you, Owen?"

"Nope. What did I miss?"

"Snow, you guys. *No cap*. The forecast is calling for snow at the end of next week."

Owen and Lacey burst out laughing. They tried not to show their age when talking with their fifteen-year-old son, especially since they were in their late thirties and hardly ancient. Phrases like *no cap*, the new-and-improved version of *for real* or *no lie* used often in their younger years, required evening internet research sessions to decipher.

Once Tucker had entered high school, new words were introduced into his vocabulary. While playing football one afternoon, Lacey heard Tucker and his buddies shout *yeet* from time to time. She learned *yeet* was an expression used by teens instead of *bam* or *boom*, with the presumed accompanying explanation point, of course.

Lacey recalled laughing so hard she was in tears that evening as she relayed her observations to Owen. Without a word, he'd hustled off to the kitchen, returning with a stockpot and a wooden spoon. Then he retrieved a white dinner jacket out of his closet and a pair of tighty-whitey underwear. He pulled the drawers on top of his head and adjusted them just so in the mirror. Then he put on the white jacket and turned to Lacey with pot and spoon in hand.

"Who am I?" he asked nonchalantly, starting the guessing game they played often, along with *would you rather?*

"More clues, please," asked Lacey as she laughed, already amused by his antics.

Owen smacked the pot with the wooden spoon, held it high over his head, and yelled, "Yeet!"

Lacey immediately picked up on the reference to Chef Emeril Lagasse, who was known to throw out the word *bam* during his food presentations. She laughed and cried so hard she couldn't manage to get out the words.

This did not deter Owen from beginning round two of the *who am I?* game. He dropped all of his props and rustled through the closet. He located an orange and black soft-shelled jacket bearing the San Francisco Giants logo on the back. Then he retrieved a wooden baseball bat out of the closet that had been autographed by Barry Bonds at a Yahoo corporate event he'd attended.

He rushed into the bathroom, found some hair gel, and worked with his sandy blond locks to get the raggedy surfer-dude look. Then he emerged, donning the orange and black jacket, with bat in hand.

"Who am I?" he asked with a straight face. He pulled the bat up and rested it on his right shoulder and struck a pose with his chest puffed out.

Lacey struggled to reply. Her sleeves were already covered with mucus mixed with tears that continued to stream down her cheeks. She waved her arms and tried to reply but couldn't. Owen was glad to help her out.

"More clues?"

She nodded.

Owen proceeded to hop around the bedroom, slamming the bat toward the floor, yelling, "Yeet! Yeet!"

"Bam! Bam!" she joined in the shouting and nearly peed herself as she lost any semblance of composure.

Tucker's voice invaded her subconscious. "Whadya think, Mom?"

"Um, about what?"

"The plan. Are you in?"

Lacey glanced at Owen, who nodded. She shrugged. "Yeah, let's do it. But, um, can we go over it again?" She started to laugh to herself. It felt good.

"Go ahead, Tuck," said Owen. "I'm gonna pour us a glass of wine."

"Make it three," said his son. "Sooo lit." Cool, in teen-speak.

"Not a chance, pal."

Tucker frowned and then explained what was happening with the cold front that had swept through the mountains and the other one that was approaching.

"They had a record snowfall in Lake Tahoe overnight. It kinda got lost in the news with all that's happening over there, but some of my friends who are farmers are pretty stoked."

Lacey was surprised. "Snow in October? I can't even remember the last time that happened."

"More than just snow, Mom. I'm talking GOAT levels." GOAT was an acronym used for greatest of all time. It was often overused, but in the case of the unusual winter precipitation that was ongoing, it was the truth. The snowmelt to follow was much needed by Northern California farmers.

The horrific drought conditions had made it difficult for farmers to make ends meet. Pressured by banks to pay their notes despite the lack of crop production, many of them took to growing grapes to supply local wineries. Others in the higher elevations converted their lands to grow hemp and marijuana like so many others in California.

The drought had another significant impact. Wildfires had devastated hundreds of thousands of acres across the state. The drought conditions and high winds at that time of year created a worst-case scenario in the event a negligent camper or a careless smoker started what might ordinarily be a harmless flame. The fires had been burning since September but were largely contained.

"So you're thinking South Lake Tahoe for snowboarding?"

"You name it, Mom. Wouldn't it be great to get away? Heck, we can even unplug the television in the room so we don't have to listen to that crap anymore." He pointed over his shoulder with his thumb.

Lacey glanced into the living room. She was tempted to turn it back on and see if there were any new developments. It was like watching a train wreck that you couldn't take your eyes off of. Only it was much larger.

PART IV

ONE WEEK IN OCTOBER

Day four, Monday, October 21

CHAPTER TWENTY-TWO

Monday, October 21
Near Key Largo, Florida

Mike had raced up A1A after receiving the phone call from Jessica. She'd been called out to assist two snorkelers when they'd made a discovery. Fortunately, Mike was in Islamorada, only seventeen miles down the highway. To expedite matters, Jessica met Mike at the Calusa Campground Marina located on the Gulf side of the Overseas Highway.

When he arrived, Jessica stood on the dock, waving to get his attention. She had several MCSD deputies with her and a young couple sitting cross-legged on the dock with colorful beach towels wrapped around their shoulders. The young woman was still crying, and her boyfriend appeared to be shaken as well.

Jessica walked toward Mike to meet him halfway.

"Hey, whatcha got?" he asked. Ordinarily, the two would exchange a kiss on the cheek, but not while on duty.

"Another body. May or may not be related."

"Out there?" Mike nodded toward Tarpon Basin, a circular body of water surrounded on all sides by land except for a couple of openings to the Gulf.

"Out at Bush Point," replied Jessica, pointing toward the north and the mainland. "They'd taken their kayaks up Dusenbury Creek to do some snorkeling around the point. They didn't tie their kayaks off properly, and they'd both floated away, too far for the couple to swim to. Fortunately, the young guy had brought his cell phone secured in a waterproof pouch, so he could call for help."

"Okaaay," Mike began, stretching out the word. "How does a dead body fit into all of this?"

Jessica led him by the arm toward the college kids. "I'll let them explain."

When they arrived at the end of the dock, the deputies stepped away, and Mike knelt down in front of them. "Hi. I'm Detective Mike Albright. I know you've told these other guys about what you found, but would you mind telling me, too?"

The young girl sniffled and nodded her head in agreement. Her boyfriend took the lead.

"Well, we lost our kayaks, so I called for help while we were treading water. She was gettin' tired, so I looked around the point to find some solid ground or at least a few mangrove branches to hold onto.

"Anyways, we snorkeled around the point, and that's when this large cluster of lobsters grabbed my attention. It was early this morning, and I've been around long enough to know that lobsters are more active at night, so I thought it was weird.

"We floated there for a minute, watching them gnaw away at something until I noticed something metallic flash up ahead. I kicked my fins a little and moved toward it. It looked like a broken piece of dead coral stuck out of another cluster of lobsters. Only, the reflection of the light striking something shiny made me wanna take a closer look.

"I reached down to grab the coral branch off the bottom. When I pulled it up, the hand came with it. Then an arm floated by me with a watch around it. I started to panic. I broke the surface and gasped for air, and that's when she started screaming. The hand floated toward her, and she twisted her body in the water, kicking her fins really fast to get away. I guess the turbulence stirred up the bottom enough until more body parts were dislodged.

"Another arm. A foot. An ear. We freaked out and swam away as fast as we could until she rescued us." He pointed at Jessica.

The girl began to cry again, and the young man welled up in tears. Mike decided to give them a break, so he stood to speak with Jessica.

"Did you call it in, too?"

"Yeah. They're sending forensics. Also, we have another one of our units out at the scene to preserve it and, um, gather up evidence."

"Great. I wanna go out there. First, did you happen to bag what these two found."

"I did," she replied with a smile. "Just like the boss taught me."

Mike chuckled as he followed Jessica to her boat. She jumped over the side and opened up a large ice cooler underneath the rear seat. On one side were several water bottles. On the other were several body parts secured in Ziploc baggies, identified by location and time. A bluish-white stretch of arm, or at least what remained after the crustaceans had fed off it, was lying on top of the ice. It had been drained of blood.

He joined her side and studied the hand, foot and ear. "There is some decomposition here. If this is related to our serial killer, it happened sooner. Forensics will tell us that. Also, look at the arm. How it was severed. Do you see here? On the side just above the elbow? It's not a clean cut. This arm was brutally hacked off."

"With what?"

"An axe maybe? Hell, there is a whole field of science on the various cutting tools to dismember a body. All I know is the wounds are different from the two victims we've already examined."

Jessica asked, "If this person was murdered before the other two, as the decomposition suggests, it could be unrelated."

"Or the killer is getting better at what he does," said Mike, his voice trailing off. Mike stood and shielded his eyes from the sun to look out across Tarpon Basin.

"You wanna take a look?" she asked.

"Yeah. Wait. The kid said something about a watch."

Jessica turned around and pointed toward an open compartment in the boat's center console. "I didn't put it in the cooler. Nice watch, see?" She handed him another Ziploc.

Mike held it up. "Well, we can either rule out robbery, or the killer didn't know what he had."

"Whadya mean?" she asked.

"This Omega is expensive as dive watches go. It's not a Rolex Submariner, but a Seamaster like this one sells new for about four grand."

"Can you use this to ID the victim?"

"Maybe," Mike muttered before retrieving his cell phone. He placed a call into the conference room where the other detectives were following up on leads related to the two existing homicides. "Hey, on this new Key Largo case. I need someone to run down our list of missing persons. Contact the families and see if any of the missing persons own an Omega Seamaster Diver 300 wristwatch. Also, check Miami-Dade missing persons."

Mike might have just taken on another case, but he might have caught a break as well.

CHAPTER TWENTY-THREE

Monday, October 21
Driftwood Key

It was another beautiful day in the Florida Keys. As the operator of a resort hotel, Monday wasn't especially different from any other day. Guests came and went seven days a week. Meals were prepared. Drinks were served. Entertainment was offered. Daily maintenance functions were undertaken.

Fantasy Fest was underway in Key West, and thousands of people were jamming A1A as they descended upon the southernmost point of the Continental U.S. The Driftwood Key Inn was full, as always, with another couple of bungalows turning over that morning.

Two elderly couples had arrived early, and while their room was being prepared, Hank took them on a short tour of the beach amenities. He offered to walk them down the dock, and then he'd return to the main house to meet with Sonny and Phoebe to place their wholesale orders and discuss their work projects for the week.

"I believe this is your first visit to Driftwood Key," said Hank casually as the group strolled along the dock toward where Hank's fishing boat would normally be tied off. Jimmy had taken a family fishing early that morning for half a day. "Is it your first time in the Keys?"

One couple came regularly, and the other had never been to Florida. They were residents of Colorado. As if on cue, just as they arrived at the thatched covering, Bob Marley's music began to softly play through the speakers that dotted the beachfront. It set the tone for the group to observe the turquoise waters swarming with fish that day.

"Would you mind telling us about the Conch Republic?" asked the man from Colorado politely, pointing at the flag gently flapping in the breeze.

Hank smiled and nodded. This question was often asked while he interacted with guests. He reached into his back pocket and retrieved his Conch Republic passport. The novelty item, issued by the official Conch Republic office in Key West, was bent and cracked from decades of spending time in Hank's pockets. He studied its crest, a combination of the Conch Republic flag, a dolphin jumping out of the water, and a sailing ship on the ocean. He ran his fingers across the official motto and read it aloud to his guests.

"We seceded where others failed."

He handed the passport to the man from Colorado, who opened it and began to flip through its pages. It looked as official as any passport from any nation he'd visited.

As they admired it, Hank explained. "Here's what happened. Many folks down this way believed the United States declared war on the Florida Keys. In April of '82, as part of its anti-drug programs, the U.S. Border Patrol set up a roadblock and customs checkpoint just before A1A crossed over to the Florida mainland, which, as you probably know, is the only way in or out of the Florida Keys.

"It was the first time the U.S. government had set up an armed checkpoint that was within the territory of the U.S. itself and not actually at any internationally recognized border. Customs agents began checking IDs and systematically searching every vehicle leaving the Keys, looking for drugs. Within hours, the stopped cars had produced a traffic jam nineteen miles long, forcing travelers to wait for hours before being allowed to continue on.

"Over the next few days, as word spread across the country about the massive delays, tourists began cancelling their Key West vacations. Delivery trucks from the mainland stopped going to the Keys. The businesses, like ours, that were so dependent on outside tourists and supplies, were completely paralyzed.

"It so happened that Skeeter Davis, the owner of the Last Chance Saloon right in front of where the border patrol had set up the roadblock, was a friend of Key West mayor Dennis Wardlow. After a day, he was on the phone to the mayor, asking if he could do anything about the situation. The Key West City Council met and decided to have their lawyers seek a federal court injunction to force the border patrol to lift the roadblock.

"To avoid the traffic, Mayor Wardlow and a few other officials flew to Miami to make their case. On April 22, the court ruled against them and refused to issue an injunction. As they were leaving the courthouse, reporters asked him what the city would do next, and Mayor Wardlow announced to the reporters, 'We're gonna go home and secede. Tomorrow at noon, the Florida Keys will secede from the Union!'"

The group laughed as Hank relayed the mayor's words with an excited voice as if he'd uttered them himself. He'd told the story hundreds of times before, so he continued with the unwritten script that he'd recited from memory and practice.

"Well, the story flew around the country, and when the Key West city government gathered at Clinton Square, in front of the old customs building, at noon on April 23 to formally announce their secession, they were surrounded by reporters from across the US. They were also surrounded by federal agents wearing earphones and blue suits, who stood out amongst the locals, who were wearing tee shirts and flip-flops.

"The mayor stood on the back of a flatbed truck and announced that since the U.S. government had decided to treat the Keys as a foreign country and had already established the border to be at the Last Chance Saloon, Key West might as well be a foreign country.

"He declared himself to be the *prime minister* before presenting the Conch flag just like the one above us. He even had a pledge of allegiance."

"Do you know it?" asked one of the guests.

Hank smiled and placed his right hand over his heart. "Of course, I'm a Conch." The group chuckled as he turned reverently to face the flag and recited the pledge.

"I pledge allegiance to the flag of my tiny island nation, And to the Republic for which it stands. One nation, under the sun, indivisible, where the liberty is true and the justice is divine. Long live the Conch Republic!"

Hank thrust his fist into the air as the group of four guests cheered him on. Everyone exchanged high fives, and Hank imagined they'd be racing down the highway shortly to join the movement.

Hank left out the part of how the newly anointed prime minister then formally declared war on the United States of America, and for one full minute, the citizens of the new Conch Republic attacked the US Navy and Coast Guard officials who were present by pelting them with stale Cuban bread. It was all in good fun, of course, but would generate a far different reaction if it had occurred today.

While the guests got a good laugh, Hank felt his phone vibrate in his pocket. It was a text message notification from Peter.

Peter: Call me. 911.

CHAPTER TWENTY-FOUR

Monday, October 21
Washington, DC

The U.S. Department of State was headquartered in the Harry S. Truman Building in an area of Washington, DC, known as Foggy Bottom. It was one of the oldest neighborhoods in the District located just west of the White House. In the nineteenth century, Foggy Bottom received its name because it was in a low-lying marshy area near the Potomac River. Fog, and later industrial smog, would settle there, lending the appearance of a perpetually cloud-covered part of the city.

The State Department had been labeled with the metonym Foggy Bottom when the Truman Building was constructed in the late 1940s. Peter's friends would often ask him, "How are things over at Foggy Bottom?" Today, the answer was *not so swell.*

He paced the grassy lawn across C Street from the Truman Building. The National Academy of Sciences was closed for refurbishment, so pedestrian traffic was light. It was the only place he could think of without prying ears.

"Come on, Dad," he muttered as he checked his phone's display for the fifth or sixth time. Finally, the phone rang, and Peter picked up the call before the first ring finished.

"Son, are you okay?"

"Yeah. Yeah, Dad. I'm fine. Listen, I need to tell you something. Nobody outside Foggy, um, the State Department is aware of this yet. Definitely not the media, okay?"

"Sure. I understand. What's up?"

"My friend at Defense tells me Pakistan is on a war footing with India. Here's the thing. The Kashmir region—the disputed borderlands between India, China, and Pakistan—has always been a flashpoint for a war. Overnight, there were tit-for-tat airstrikes across the cease-fire line established by the UN last year. These two have been fighting over the Himalayas for nearly forty years."

"Son, that sucks, but how does that affect the U.S., or me for that matter?"

"An hour ago, India sent military jets into Pakistan and bombed its nuclear facility at Chashma. Dad, this is two hundred miles into the center of Pakistan from the Indian border. Islamabad is freakin' pissed!"

"What does that mean, exactly?" asked Hank.

"NSA recon birds indicate Pakistan is repositioning their nuclear-capable, road-mobile ballistic missiles. It could be a bluff, or they could be preparing to retaliate."

There was silence on the other end of the line. Finally, Hank said, "Bottom line it for me, son."

"Dad, the president is already on the hot seat for not coming to Israel's aid after Iran shot first. If Pakistan does the same, and he chooses to stay out of it, this will make us look weak to Russia, China, and the North Koreans. We'll be vulnerable to attack."

Hank still appeared uncertain of how that impacted the U.S. or Florida. "Are you suggesting we need to be searching for a bunker?"

"No. Well, maybe. I am saying you need to know where one is. At the worst case, if war breaks out over there and we're not drawn into it, supply lines and commerce will be disrupted worldwide. It will have a huge impact on everything, including food and gas prices, as well as availability."

"Okay, son. Listen, I trust you. This is actually the second conversation I've had about this in as many days. Let me relay what you've said to Mike, and do you have a moment to call your sister?"

"I'm on it, Dad. Listen, you know I don't like to interrupt you with phone calls. I'll text if I have solid news, okay?"

"Love ya, Pete," said Hank.

"I love you, too, Dad."

The two men disconnected the call. Peter wandered around the lawn and thought of how he might approach his sister. She was not an alarmist and probably had a more level head than he did. He'd just lay out what he knew. It would be up to her and Owen to decide what was best for them and Tucker.

He dialed Lacey's number and got voicemail. His chin dropped to his chest. He fired off the same text he'd sent his dad, hoping for a quick reply. After several minutes, she hadn't, and he'd just received a text to report to the Office of Press Operations at the State Department. With a worried look on his face, he ran across C Street, dodging taxis and travelers going about their day, oblivious to the events in South Asia.

CHAPTER TWENTY-FIVE

Hank hailed Sonny on the island's two-way radio system. He told him to find Jimmy, who'd returned from the fishing trip and was on a lunch break. He wanted them to meet at the main house before he sat down alone with Phoebe to place their food and liquor orders.

While he waited for his top employees to arrive, he sat in his office and took a moment to log in to his portal on the First State Bank website. They'd been the Albright family's bank since 1955 when they first opened an office in Key West. He navigated between the primary business checking account and his personal account.

Hank was a saver, and he'd managed the business well. Although Mike had no part of running the inn, he was an owner by virtue of inheritance. Hank made sure Mike was kept abreast of the inn's financial affairs. Hank received a fair salary, and Mike received an annual stipend. The two brothers used to joke that Mike's share was *protection money* because of his law enforcement career.

He logged out of his accounts and checked his watch. It was almost three. He could hit the branch in Islamorada before it closed at four, or for sure make his way to the drive-thru by five that afternoon. What he planned on doing couldn't be handled by an ATM machine after hours.

Hank glanced out his office windows in the direction of the beach. He wished Erin hadn't left with her sisters for Key West like so many others that day. They were interested in seeing what Fantasy Fest had to offer without getting caught up in the madness brought by the larger crowds as the weekend approached. Without giving away Peter's inside information, he felt the need to talk with her about what he'd learned.

A light tapping at the door interrupted his thoughts. "Mr. Hank, can we come in?"

The door was ajar and then opened slightly. The three faces of the Free family poked through the opening from shortest, Phoebe, to tallest, Jimmy. Hank managed a smile despite his serious mood. He loved them all as if they had Albright blood running through their veins.

"Come in, guys."

Phoebe led the way with her oversized ledger pulled tight against her chest. She'd used the same Wilson Jones ring ledger system for years. Every January, she'd set it up for the year and filed the previous year on a shelf in the outdoor storage building where cleaning supplies and other housekeeping related items were kept. Nobody entered that storage building without Phoebe unlocking it. She ran a very tight ship.

She took a seat in an armchair in front of Hank's desk while Sonny and Jimmy sat on the rattan sofa across the spacious room. All three of them had a look of concern on their faces, as it was unusual for Hank to have a meeting such as this.

"Mr. Hank," began Phoebe tentatively, "I hope there's no bad news."

"No, Phoebe. Not yet, anyway. That said, we need to do a few things. Unusual for our normal routine, but nothing that will go to waste. Let me get Sonny and Jimmy started first because they have some errands to run."

"Okay, Mr. Hank," said Sonny, who sat up on the edge of the sofa.

Hank spun around and pulled out two small notepads bearing the Driftwood Key Inn logo on them. They were complimentary in each guest room. He tossed them to Sonny and Jimmy along with a logo'd pen.

"This is gonna seem out of the ordinary because, well, it is. At the same time, I'll feel better when we're done."

"Yes, sir," said Jimmy.

Hank stood and paced the floor, mindlessly glancing out the windows of the corner office space as he gave instructions. He tried to process everything logically, thinking of the operations of the inn during any given day and week.

"Jimmy, you first. I need you to take every vehicle on the island. I mean trucks, personal cars, and even the golf carts. Top them all off with fuel. While you're at it, find every available gas can and fill them up as well. Diesel, too. I want you to use a different station with each fill-up. Also, while you're there, buy more gas and diesel cans. Fill them up, too."

"Mr. Hank, is a hurricane coming that we didn't know about?" asked Jimmy as he exchanged glances with his parents.

"No, not exactly. However, we're gonna get prepared in the same way and then some."

"Okay, how many gas cans do you want me to buy?"

"All of them," replied Hank without emotion. Noticing the questioning looks on their faces, he added, "Just go with me on this. We need to stock up. The worst case is we'll use it over time and this afternoon was unnecessary."

Jimmy shrugged. "Anything else?"

"No. You're good to go," he replied as he looked from Jimmy to Sonny. "I've increased the spending limit on your debit card, so you shouldn't have a problem."

Jimmy rose and started out the door. "I'll see ya later."

Hank raised his voice slightly. "Oh, Jimmy, also buy several cases of bottled water at each stop. Again, no discussion or explanation is owed to anyone. That's why I want you to use different stations throughout Marathon, okay?"

"Yes, Mr. Hank."

He turned to Sonny. "I need you to contact the propane company and our gas suppliers. Fill up all the storage tanks we have on the property. Then take the boat to the marina and fill it up, too. When you get back, come find me. I'll have a list for the Home Depot in Marathon."

Sonny left with his marching orders, leaving Hank alone with Phoebe. Hank knew he wouldn't be able to brush off her questions as easily as he had the others'.

She calmly set the food and supply ledger on his desk, followed by her glasses. She leaned back in her chair and folded her arms. Then she gave him the look. It was the look all women learned from their mothers and grandmothers. The one that shouted *no bullshit, mister*, without saying a single word. Hank had experienced it his entire life.

He stood and closed the door, which Sonny had left open. "Okay, it's just you and me," said Hank as he eased back into his chair, locking eyes with Phoebe.

She forced a smile and nodded. "That it is."

Her tone was threatening, in a motherly sort of way. In seconds, she had Hank spilling the tea without asking a single question. He held back the direst of warnings garnered from his conversations with Peter and Erin from the day before. He revealed enough to Phoebe to provide her a sense of urgency and to not question his intentions. After he was done, she summed up the preparations succinctly.

"It's like preparing for a hurricane, except on steroids."

"That's a pretty good way of putting it," he said.

"I can place the order on Sysco's website. Some of the things, like cleaning supplies and personal hygiene, I'll order from Southeast Wholesale." Phoebe thought for a moment as she made notes in her ledger. She looked up over her glasses and asked, "For how long?"

Hank gulped as he thought to himself, *I don't know. How long do you wanna live?* However, he resisted the urge to share his inner drama.

"A few months for nonperishables. A year, odd as that sounds, for basic supplies."

"Like?" she asked.

"Think of your everyday activities. Not just as Phoebe the chef but as Phoebe who just rolled out of bed. Consider what you do first, second, third, etcetera. Same is true for every waking moment until you go to sleep. Whatever products you use, stockpile a lot of it. Make sure you buy for both men and women, if you know what I mean."

"I understand. We're gonna need more storage space."

Hank closed his eyes and nodded. "If you order this afternoon, when will the trucks deliver to us?"

"Tomorrow, first thing. As long as it's in by seven this evening, it'll be dropped off early in the morning."

"Good. We'll find the space to store it."

She continued to ask for direction. "What about perishables? Produce, dairy, stuff like that."

"Order as much as your walk-in coolers can handle. We can keep them running with our generators until the food is gone."

"Why would we need generators?"

"For when the power goes out."

Phoebe sat back in her chair and removed her glasses. She stared at Hank for a long, uncomfortable moment. She finally spoke. "When? Or if?"

Hank exhaled. "We need to prepare for the worst, Phoebe. If nothing happens, then we have a lot of extra food and supplies to use up before we buy any more. Here's the way I look at what we're doing today. It's kinda like buying insurance. I invest in peace of mind with every payment to Chubb. I hope nothing happens, but if it does, I have a plan. Same is true with what we're doing right now. We are ensuring our ability to deal with the worst-case scenario."

Phoebe glanced at her watch. "All right, Mr. Hank. I'd better get started so I can place the orders before I prepare dinner for our new arrivals. Will you be joining them tonight?"

Hank grimaced. He was far too preoccupied to socialize; plus he wanted to corner Erin when she returned from Key West.

"Will you pass along my apologies and tell them I'll make it up to them this week?"

Phoebe nodded, and then a scowl came over her face. "Mr. Hank, our families have been through a lot. I don't doubt the Albrights and Frees could face any challenge. But we've got eighteen bungalows filled with strangers from all over. What about them?"

Hank's face turned ashen. He hadn't thought about all the people on Driftwood Key that he bore responsibility for. Not to mention those who might be en route to fill their places on checkout. He grimaced as he realized he'd have to get rid of them and cancel incoming reservations. *But when? And what if he was wrong?*

"I don't know. Let me think on it. Now, I've got to go to the bank and make a couple of other stops."

Phoebe waved her hand and left his office. Hank gathered his wallet, car keys and a notepad. He made his way into the master bedroom suite that had been occupied by his parents and their parents before them. He walked to a solid wood door, the only one that wasn't louvered in the main house. The key to the lock was kept in his bottom dresser drawer. Hank bent over to retrieve it and then tentatively unlocked it.

As the door swung open, he muttered, "I never thought I'd need to get in here."

Inside the walk-in closet stood a gray Liberty gun safe with Lady Liberty emblazoned across the front. The safe had been there for many years, still requiring the user to turn a numbered dial to get inside. In the closet, on both sides of the safe, were shelves of ammunition stacked neatly by brand and caliber.

Most of the ammunition was seven years old. Mike, who was an expert marksman and personally managed the Albrights' cache of weapons, made sure the oldest ammunition was used first when he and Jessica went to the range. Hank had never taken an interest in guns, and other than training with Mike years ago, he never practiced. He didn't think it would be necessary. He was wrong.

He started making notes. Tonight, he would consult with Mike, who was really wrapped up in his murder investigation, especially since they'd discovered the third body. Hank would have to make multiple trips to Bass Pro Shops as well as local bait and tackle shops to stock up.

He began his list until he noticed the time. It was 4:30. He needed to get to the bank before it closed. He planned on making a cash withdrawal that would probably make the local branch manager wonder if he was making a drug deal.

CHAPTER TWENTY-SIX

Monday, October 21
McDowell Residence
Hayward, California

Lacey had been at her store, Jefferson Outfitters, working with one of her best customers when Peter called. She didn't see the text message until after lunch, when she frantically began calling him to see what was wrong. After they had a conversation along the same lines as he'd had earlier with their father, Lacey told her employees to close up for her. She decided to pick Tucker up from school so he'd be with her. *Just in case.*

Her son was very level-headed and mature for his age. Fortunately, his interests were similar to his parents'. Enjoying the outdoors. He wasn't into music or the party scene teenagers found themselves exposed to in the Bay Area. Tucker would rather go hiking, camping or snowboarding than attend a concert or hang out with other kids his age.

"Mom, you know Uncle Peter and I are tight. He never goes *highkey*, you know what I mean?"

No, not really, but she caught his drift. Lacey's thought caused her to smile. *Highkey* was Tucker's era. *Catching his drift* was hers.

"Dramatic?" she asked.

"Yeah. I mean, he's a reporter, and I know it's his job to hype things up. He's never done that with us."

Lacey nodded. Her younger brother wouldn't ring these alarm bells with their family if he wasn't genuinely concerned, and certain, that something was coming that could possibly affect them.

"The question is, what do we do about it?" she asked.

"Have you called Dad?"

"I spoke to him briefly. He said he wanted to look into something, you know, on a hunch."

Tucker laughed. "Dad's big on his hunches."

The phone rang. It was Owen. "His ears must've been burning." Lacey connected the call through the SUV's sound system. "Hey, honey."

"Hi, Dad."

"Tucker? Aren't you supposed—?"

Lacey cut him off to explain. "I decided to pick him up. I thought it would be a good idea for us to sort this out together."

"Well, I'm glad you did," said Owen. "Listen to this. I reached out to our department that analyzes internet searches around the world. A lot of people don't realize this, but search engines like Yahoo! have a literal pulse on the mindset of a country or locale based upon their trending searches. It's mind-boggling what information we have access to that can be cross-referenced through search activity.

"Anyway, when you relayed Peter's concerns, I thought I'd check with our people and have them look into Yahoo metrics for Pakistan and India. While they did, I called my buddy at Google. Face it. Google dominates outside the U.S., with like ninety-eight percent of the market share.

"Well, anyway, I heard back from both resources just now. Search terms related to the term *nuclear* are off the charts in both countries. And get this, on Google, one of the top five trending searches today is *nuclear fallout shelter near me.*"

"Wow!" said Tucker excitedly. "Uncle Peter's right. We need to get ready."

Lacey furrowed her brow as she turned into their neighborhood. "What do you think, Owen?"

"Well, most of the time these search results are based on media-driven hype. The airstrikes by India in Pakistan are the top news story in most countries on that side of the world. Here, there's hardly a mention."

Lacey pulled the truck into the driveway and opened the garage door. As she waited for it to open completely, she suddenly put the car in park. Tucker looked over at her with a puzzled look on his face. She held up one finger, indicating he needed to wait a moment.

She took a deep breath and studied herself in the mirror. Her eyes moved from side to side as if to surveil her surroundings, but in actuality, she was making sure everything around her was real and not a dream.

"Honey, are you still there?" Owen asked.

"Yes. I hate to ask this question because I've never wanted you to feel pressure to leave the office. Um, but what time will you be home tonight?"

Owen replied in all seriousness, "As soon as I can shut down my computer and walk out the door, I'll be on my way."

She glanced at the time. It normally took Owen an hour or a little longer to travel from Sunnyvale out to their house in the hills overlooking Hayward.

"Tucker and I are gonna run to Safeway. We should be back about the same time you get here."

"Are you gonna pick up dinner?" asked Owen.

Lacey reached up to close the garage door again. "Something like that. Love you!" She disconnected the call and backed out of the driveway.

"Mom, what's the plan?"

Lacey set her jaw. "We've got some shopping to do, son."

CHAPTER TWENTY-SEVEN

Monday, October 21
Oval Office
The White House

It had been a long day, and President Helton was exhausted. He'd just been briefed on the airstrikes at the Pakistani nuclear facility. He was beginning to be concerned the American military presence in the region was being stretched too thin. They simply didn't have sufficient assets deployed to fight a conflict in the Middle East and defend their Indian allies in South Asia. Tensions needed to be tamped down, and he tasked his most loyal cabinet member, the secretary of state, to handle it.

He had a scheduled meeting with the Iranian ambassador in thirty minutes. It was a rare face-to-face opportunity for the man who was capable of spewing more lies than any propagandist the president had ever met. However, because Iran stubbornly continued to block the Strait of Hormuz with no apparent achievable goal, President Helton wanted to deliver a personal ultimatum. Get out of the way, or we're going to sink every ship in your fleet.

The Pentagon was prepared to back up the threat, and military assets were being positioned to carry out his orders. But then the government in New Delhi gummed up the works. Their preemptive attack on Pakistan wasn't a bad idea; it was the timing that caused problems for American interests. Now, with the intelligence confirmed that Pakistan was maneuvering its nuclear warheads into position via mobile launchpads, the region was a powder keg with a short fuse.

He'd asked his advisors how bad it could get. They equivocated in their response. China was the wild card in the region. The Kashmir region, the source of the ongoing military hostilities in addition to the cultural ones, was in the Himalayas at China's border. A ground invasion would almost certainly draw their attention and likely lead to a declaration of war by Beijing. The land was beautiful, and it had certain religious ties to the Pakistanis, but President Helton couldn't fathom why it was worth fighting a war over. Especially a nuclear war.

To their credit, both India and China had maintained a *no first use* doctrine in which India promised to use its nuclear weapons only in response to Pakistan's first strike. Pakistan had refused to issue any clear doctrine to that effect.

For years, U.S. presidents have grappled with the possibility a false-flag terrorist attack might generate a nuclear response. Through some mishap or error, the nuclear missiles could fly. An escalation in Kashmir could be another cause. Certainly, the air strikes were a very bold provocation, one that angered most world leaders.

President Helton planned on taking the lead in deescalating the conflict. He was going to ask for restraint and demand both countries come to the negotiating table to work toward a long-term fix. He would impress upon them that the last thing either government, or the world for that matter, needed was more mushroom clouds.

With this on his mind, he turned his attention to the Iranian ambassador, who was about to get a promise of his own. Get out of the Strait of Hormuz or prepare to deal with the full brunt of America's military might.

Tomorrow, he'd deal with Pakistan and India.

PART V

ONE WEEK IN OCTOBER

Day five, Tuesday, October 22

CHAPTER TWENTY-EIGHT

Tuesday, October 22
South Asia

Pakistan convened its National Command Authority in an undisclosed location many miles from any population centers. It quietly relocated its highest government officials and their immediate families into the wilderness near Tajikistan, as far away from India as possible. Its citizens were given a siren warning the moment after the launch sequence was triggered.

In Islamabad, the nation's capital, residents had less than twenty minutes to rush into a fallout shelter that could hold less than eight percent of the population. Those with wealth were able to buy their way into a bunker. Others had to look for basements of buildings built on a rocky landscape.

On both sides of the Pakistan-India border, across the entire subcontinent of South Asia, home to nearly two billion people, nuclear war had broken out. Virtually all the residents of these two nations were on their own as the nuclear warheads flew.

India, with a population of one-point-four billion, had more to lose in terms of human life. Fifty of its cities had populations in excess of one million. Five had over five million. Across the country, because nuclear power formed an important part of India's energy mix, Pakistani targets included nuclear reactors and atomic power plants in addition to missile launch sites.

Both nations relied upon a combination of medium- and long-range missile systems deployed close to their mutual border and in hardened silos within striking distance. Some of the targets included the silos, but the moving targets, the rail/road mobile launchers, were constantly relocated. History proved these strategic weapons to have been the deadliest. They were virtually unstoppable, especially at such close range.

Like Iran, and unlike Israel, both nations placed an emphasis on nuclear deterrence through an ever-growing arsenal. Following the twentieth-century model of mutually assured destruction, both governments presumed the other would show restraint. Recently, a reporter from the *Washington Times* had reached out to the Indian Home Affairs Minister and asked how his government was planning to protect its people from a nuclear strike. He laughed at the question, replied *utter nonsense*, and hung up the phone.

There was nothing nonsensical about the regional nuclear war between India and Pakistan. It made the Six-Hour War in the Middle East look like a short quarrel between lovers. The nuclear arsenals possessed by the South Asian nations might have been inferior to the nuclear stockpiles of Russia, China, and the U.S., but the sheer volume of weapons launched during the daylong war was astonishing.

Pakistan and India hosted some of the most densely populated cities on the planet. Calcutta, Karachi and Mumbai contained more than sixty-five thousand people per square mile. By comparison, New York City's population density was less than half that.

Each of the two nations' forty-kiloton nuclear warheads created a firestorm that covered fifty square miles. The immediate effects of the detonations—the fireball, the overpressure wave, and resulting radiation burns—killed hundreds of millions in the region. The larger, one-hundred-kiloton warheads had a greater blast radius, and the overpressure waves reduced hardened structures to rubble while increasing the death toll fourfold.

And that was just the beginning. Like Tehran and Tel Aviv, major cities in South Asia would suffer slow, lingering deaths due to radiation exposure. Their healthcare and other critical infrastructure had collapsed. The nuclear blasts triggered deadly firestorms far worse than the deadly napalm bombings had done during World War II in Tokyo.

As the rest of the world watched in horror, billions said prayers for the dead and begged for peace. Many in America were thankful the nuclear war hadn't taken place in their country. They hugged their families and comforted one another in the thought that the nuclear exchange wouldn't affect them.

Sadly, they were wrong.

CHAPTER TWENTY-NINE

Tuesday, October 22
Driftwood Key

"Let's do this!" exclaimed Hank as he pressed the throttles down on his forty-five-foot Hatteras Sportfish yacht. He and Erin exchanged high fives at the state-of-the-art upper helm surrounded by next-generation electronics and comfortable seating. It was truly another beautiful day in paradise on the smooth coastal waters off Driftwood Key.

Earlier that morning, Hank, like always, made his way to the beach to find solace after a restless night. His mind raced to all of the possibilities raised by Peter's phone call. With the help of a warm brandy and after reading several chapters from a new novel about a massive earthquake along the Mississippi River, he finally drifted off to sleep. He awoke refreshed and anxious to search out Erin, as he hadn't seen her since Sunday.

The smile that broke across his face when he approached the water's edge could've shattered glass. She stood alone, facing the main house, with a breakfast smoothie in each hand. He picked up the pace and was practically jogging toward her after he noticed her standing there.

"I have a special delivery from Phoebe!" she'd said loudly as he arrived. "She told me to give you a lecture on not taking care of yourself and chastise you for skipping your smoothie."

"I'm not drinking both, mom," Hank added jokingly.

"One's for me," she said as she tipped the cup to her mouth, leaving a creamy mustache above her lip.

Hank burst out laughing, and like his new friend, he pushed the straw aside and recreated the act. Only, his mustache was a little too runny, and he looked more like Cujo, the crazed dog in the Stephen King story.

They shyly admitted they'd missed one another yesterday, and without getting into serious subjects, Hank offered to take Erin fishing. Thirty minutes later, with Jimmy's assistance in preparing the Hatteras to sail, the two *kids* were off for a day of sun and fun.

The Albright boat was in excellent condition because Hank, like his father, was meticulous about maintenance. The Hatteras was used by the resort to take its guests fishing, usually captained by Hank or Jimmy, plus a new captain who was used sporadically. Both of them treated it with care, and therefore one never knew it had plenty of hours on it.

"Where are we headed?" she asked as she sat on the raised seat next to him at the helm.

"It's still warm, so reef fishing will probably be a little slow. I love grouper and snapper, but I don't wanna sit around if the waters aren't cool enough. This is a pretty good time to fish offshore for wahoo and blackfin tuna. If you're up for a ride, I say we head out about a hundred fathoms and see how we do." To landlubbers, one hundred fathoms was equal to about six hundred feet of water.

"Whatever you say, Captain!" she replied enthusiastically.

Hank, caught up in the moment, turned on the audio system to fire up his favorite playlist of beach and island songs. Bob Marley, Jimmy Buffett, Kenny Chesney and other artists randomly blared through the speakers. Caught up in the moment, they pumped up the volume and began to sing along.

Once they reached one of Hank's favorite spots to fish, he set up the fighting chair on the aft deck and prepared the rods in their strategically placed holders. As he did, he explained to Erin his thought processes, and she eagerly soaked in the tutorial. Throughout, the two flirted, laughed, and became more physical with one another. Subtle touches of the arm and back. Occasional tender moments of moving Erin's hair out of her face or allowing Hank to wrap his arms around her as she reeled in a fish. They had a mutual attraction to one another that seemed to move to another level each day.

Hank had just pulled out a picnic basket of food and wine packed by Phoebe, when he glanced toward the back of the boat. He startled Erin with his outburst, but then she joined in the excitement.

"Big fish on! Here we go!" He abruptly set down the basket and sprang across the fiberglass deck to the back of the boat. Erin was hot on his heels and set herself in the fighting chair. As Hank had taught her, she strapped in tight because, as he'd said, you never know what's gonna take the bait.

A blackfin tuna could stretch to three feet and forty pounds. The wahoo was a more formidable adversary. Some of them have measured nearly eight feet and a hundred seventy pounds. Then there was the grand prize of them all, the blue marlin, although it was very late in the season for them.

Hank turned to Erin and asked, "Ready?"

She nodded eagerly with a bit of trepidation. She'd learned enough from their morning session that the line told the fisherman a lot about what was on the other end. The five-and-a-half-foot carbon-fiber rod bowed like a tall palm tree in a Cat 5 hurricane.

Hank studied Erin. Believing she was up to the task, he gripped the pole and heaved it from the rod holder. He placed it in the fighting chair's solid stainless steel rod gimbal. Erin held on tight, her muscles protesting as the fish zipped out the line.

Hank hustled to reel in the other trolling lines as a large crested dorsal fin splashed out of the Gulf in the middle of the boat's frothy wake.

Erin was glad she was all buckled up because the powerful fish would've certainly pulled her hundred-thirty-pound body overboard. "Hank! Is it what I think it is?"

"It's a bluey, baby! Hang on. Keep the rod steady. Make sure the butt of the pole stays firm in the holder. It's gonna be a helluva fight!"

"Maybe you should—?"

"Nope. You got this!" Hank dashed up to the flybridge to grab his binoculars. He cranked up the Jimmy Buffett song "Fins to the Left" to offer Erin encouragement. The song was ostensibly about shark fins, but the blue marlin's zigzagged path from one side of the boat's wake to the other called for some lively music. Erin was in for a real fight.

He arrived by her side and studied the marlin. He dropped the binoculars and then looked again. She noticed his movements.

"Is it big?" she said, readjusting her grip as her hands began to cramp.

"Two hundred. At least," he said just loud enough to be heard over the music. "Let's give it another hundred yards. Let it swim a little."

Erin adjusted her grip and let out the line as Hank had taught her. The marlin was now tugging on four hundred feet of line in a primal war of man versus king of the sea. Blue marlin was one of the world's most sought-after game fish. Hank could take a dozen trips during a season and not even see one. Yet here they were, at the most unlikely of times, with a relatively inexperienced angler in the chair battling a real beauty.

"Hank, my arms are on fire!"

"Okay, let me help while you relax."

Hank wrapped his arms around Erin and gripped the rod. Frankly, he hadn't expected to reel in a blue marlin in late October. He was not muscular by any means. Tanned and toned in an island sort of way would've better described his physique. Had he known what was on the other end of the line, he might've taken the lead on this. Reeling in a blue marlin was no easy task, even for a fit and experienced angler.

Hank began reeling the beast in. He fought the tension, reeling and pulling with everything he had. Erin relieved him with a vigor and sense of purpose that astonished Hank. Maybe it was the effort he made in assisting her? Maybe it was the fact the two worked as a team to bring in the mighty fish? Either way, she put the muscle to the task and set her jaw, with determination in her eyes.

"There is no answer on their cell phones either," said Sonny as he nervously stood among the three men who'd suddenly appeared on the front porch of the main house. They were all dressed in dark suits, starched shirts, and blue ties. There was little doubt to the streetwise Sonny that they were from the government. Regardless, he insisted upon seeing their identification. They were with the Secret Service.

"The secretary knows better than being out of communication with her staff," one of the men said. "Where are they?" he asked as he looked out into the Gulf. There wasn't a boat in sight.

"I don't know," replied Sonny. "Hank has a number of spots that he prefers. He may have gone flats fishing up around Duck Key. If he wanted to take a nice ride, they might've gone offshore."

"Good god," the agent said with a huff. He tapped one of his agents on the arm. "Call the Coast Guard. Deploy a couple of choppers to sweep the inshore areas. The boat is a forty-five-foot Hatteras flybridge. Two passengers. Once identified, have them intercept with one of their Defender-class boats. There's no time to waste."

He turned to Sonny, who asked a question. "Can you tell me what this is about?"

The agent sighed and thought for a brief moment. "I guess you'll see it on the news soon enough. Pakistan and India are at war."

"What does that have to do with us?" Sonny asked, genuinely confused.

"Nuclear war."

Sonny stood a little taller, and his eyes got wide. Prior to that statement, he'd been helpful but not the model of cooperativeness.

"Come with me, sir. Let's take a look at the map. I can narrow down your search area."

"Prepare to be boarded!"

The voice blared over a loudspeaker that practically muted Kenny Chesney's singing and Hank's encouragement of Erin's efforts.

He spun around to find the source of the demand. Two Coast Guard vessels were easing up to the Hatteras on both sides of his bow. The twenty-five-foot boats abruptly slowed to a stop but brought their wake with them, causing the Hatteras to sway violently from side to side.

Erin turned her head to see what was happening. Her relaxed grip on the rod and loss of concentration ended the fight. The fish sensed a change in dynamic and cut toward the boat. It broke the plane of the water and launched itself into the air. The massive blue fish whipped its head back and forth in a flash, propelling the hook out of its mouth just before it splashed back down in the water.

The line went slack. Erin cursed loudly and then collapsed back into her chair, dejected. *This'd better be good*, she thought to herself as she immediately cast blame on the intrusion.

Hank helped one of the Coast Guard vessels pull alongside. He worked with the guardsman to place the fenders between the two boats before tying them together. The young man quickly boarded Hank's boat and immediately approached Erin without so much as a glance in Hank's direction.

"Ma'am," he began with a tip of his cap, "we've been sent by the Secret Service. You've been requested to return to Washington."

"Wait? Secret Service. Why?"

The young guardsman glanced at Hank. "I can only speculate, ma'am. There have been some developments between India and Pakistan. Um, similar to the Middle East, only worse, ma'am."

"Shit," Erin muttered. She closed her eyes and shook her head in disbelief. She walked past the guardsman and hugged Hank.

"It'll be okay," he whispered in her ear, not sure what else to say. His mind was also racing, as the information given to him by Peter was deadly accurate.

"Hank, I'm so sorry to leave you. All of this. You're an incredible man."

"I feel the same way, Erin. Please keep in touch."

"I will," she said as she kissed him on the cheek. Then she leaned in to whisper in his ear, "Be ready. Protect yourself and your family. You never know, okay?"

She pulled away, and Hank saw the tears begin to flow out of her eyes. She tried to wipe them away and shield her emotions from the guardsman who stood dutifully nearby. Without another word, she crossed over into the Coast Guard Defender. As they uncoupled and raced off, she never stopped looking at Hank, nor did he stop looking at her as the boat disappeared from sight.

CHAPTER THIRTY

For the second time in a week, the president had been ushered through the corridors beneath the East Wing of the White House into the PEOC. Unlike the moments following the Iran-Israel nuclear exchange, during which the attendees were relatively calm, the military and intelligence personnel didn't bother acknowledging President Helton as he entered. The nuclear war between Pakistan and India was far more serious and was still ongoing.

"Mr. President, thus far, all indications lead us to believe this conflict is regional in nature," began the president's chief of staff. "State has spoken with their counterparts in Moscow and Beijing, who both agree all three nuclear powers should remain neutral."

"That's easy for them to say," shot back the president. "They're responsible for arming Iran and Pakistan in the first place. Everyone might note who the aggressors are in all of this. It's not our allies."

Harrison Chandler, who as the president's chief of staff was anything but a yes-man, provided some context. "Sir, I'm not defending their actions. That said, both Israeli and Indian provocations caused tensions to escalate. Do I believe the Pakistanis and Iranians are blameless? Absolutely not. Now we have to be prepared for the aftermath."

The president turned to the secretary of defense, who was present in the PEOC's large conference room. He was on the phone, but President Helton interrupted him.

"You've raised the defense readiness condition?"

In the event of a national emergency, a series of seven different alert conditions, known as LERTCONs, can be issued. The seven alerts include two emergency conditions, or EMERGCONs, that are national-level reactions in response to an attack on the U.S. mainland from foreign intercontinental ballistic missiles. In the event of a major attack on American or allied forces overseas, the defense emergency levels are elevated under EMERGCON. Likewise, if an air defense emergency exists, such as hostile aircraft or inbound conventional missiles were considered imminent, then the EMERGCON levels were raised.

The other five alert levels fall under national defense readiness conditions, or DEFCONs, a term more widely known among the general public. These levels start at DEFCON 5, which is normal peacetime conditions, up to DEFCON 1, the maximum force readiness that coincides with EMERGCON alerts.

In the history of the United States, DEFCON 1 had never been initiated. During the Cuban missile crisis, the U.S. Strategic Air Command was placed on DEFCON 2 for the first time, without President Kennedy's authority. The action almost triggered a nuclear war that October.

With each passing day during that crisis, the U.S. military inched toward war as it prepared to strike targets within the former Soviet Union. The world held its collective breath during those days in October 1962.

"Mr. President, at the moment, we have no indication of a direct threat to the U.S. or our military installations abroad. Therefore, we have remained at DEFCON 3, as you instructed following the Iranian attack on Israel and their counterattack."

The president turned toward the undersecretary of state. "Are you able to contact either government? I assume both capitals were targeted."

"Yes, sir," the undersecretary responded. "Devastatingly so. We've reached out to our counterparts in China and Russia, as you know, seeking a means of gathering information about the Pakistani government. The Russians are close to the New Delhi government, as are the French. Nobody has received confirmation as to the status of either heads of state or their parliaments."

"I might add, Mr. President," began the defense secretary, "someone must be in charge because there are continuing targeted strikes on both sides of the border. It appears, incredibly, that they intend to empty their respective nuclear vaults."

The president remained standing throughout. He dropped his chin to his chest as he contemplated the deaths of millions of innocent people, none of whom asked to be embroiled in all-out nuclear war. He finally looked up to his advisors.

"Have they all gone batshit crazy?"

His question was crassly worded but clearly understood.

"Mr. President, tensions have been festering—" began the undersecretary of state before the president cut him off.

"No, I get that. I'm talking about all of these rogue nations who have their fingers on the nuclear triggers. Who's next? Is it like a damned lunacy epidemic? Is Kim Jong Un the next maniacal despot to fire off nukes?"

The undersecretary of state really didn't want to answer the question, but the president's stare had him locked in his sights. "Well, sir, the only rogue nation by U.S. diplomatic definition is North Korea. If you are looking for some kind of pattern from these two events, there's no indication either South Korea or our allies in Tokyo would dare initiate military hostilities with the DPRK, especially under these circumstances."

The president, who was generally forthcoming about his

weaknesses, especially as it related to foreign policy, repeated the criticisms by the war hawks of his response to the Iranian-Israeli conflict.

"Let's say my friends across the aisle were right, and my failure to stand by Israel was seen as a sign of weakness across the globe. Might this have emboldened India to launch the airstrikes and Pakistan to counter with nukes? Maybe. Both sides have seen us as all talk and no action, standing down when our allies were in need. Therefore, they took advantage of the chaos in the Middle East to make their move."

The undersecretary of state squirmed in his chair, but to his credit, he continued in an honest assessment of the president's stance, how it was perceived, and how it might relate to North Korea.

"Sir, I'm going to respond this way with a caveat. I don't speak for the secretary of state. However, I believe our assessment of the North Korea situation is closely aligned."

"Understood," said the president, who took his seat at the head of the table for the first time.

The undersecretary explained, "When North Korea reneged on its promise to forgo nuclear weapons in the early 1990s, the Clinton administration put together an accord deemed the Agreed Framework that paved Pyongyang's path to nuclearization. Kim Jong-il withdrew from this Nuclear Nonproliferation Treaty in 2003, confirming that he intended to build a nuclear weapon.

"President George W. Bush pushed for the China-led six-party talks with North Korea that yielded no agreement. When North Korea tested its second nuclear weapon in 2009, President Obama opted for a *strategic patience* approach. This policy led to an expansion of the North Korean nuclear program, and three subsequent tests showed just how misguided these approaches have been."

The undersecretary paused and caught his breath. He gulped before he stated his opinion. "Mr. President, it's time to acknowledge that North Korea has never been interested in negotiating away its nuclear deterrent. Their goals have always been to bide time, get sanctions removed, or even secure humanitarian aid from the West.

"Of course, we should continue to leave the door open for serious discussions if the situation changes. However, sir, in my opinion, our government does our citizens and the world a disservice if we continually discount the central threat of the DPRK's nuclear weapons to the stability of the Korean Peninsula, Japan, and our western shores."

President Helton studied the undersecretary, a young man compared to the elderly military personnel in the room. He was anxious to learn more from him, but an aide had rushed into the room.

"We've made contact with the prime minister of India."

CHAPTER THIRTY-ONE

Tuesday, October 22
U.S. State Department
Washington, DC

Peter had been rushing up and down the halls of the State Department since the news broke about ballistic missiles sailing across the South Asia subcontinent. He raced out of his condo and made it to Foggy Bottom in record time, faster than other journalists assigned to State could ride their subway trains.

The story, and the administration's response, was certainly foremost on his mind. However, he'd begun to get a nagging feeling that the president, and even the secretary of state, were focused on another nuclear-equipped bad actor, North Korea.

Amidst the chaos in the corridors of the Harry S. Truman Building, Peter hoped to catch a State Department official with his guard down. With the right set of loose lips, they might provide some insight into the Helton administration's North Korea policy. His ploy worked.

He'd cornered a harried aide to the undersecretary for Arms Control and International Security. The two retreated to her office, where she began to reveal everything she knew. As the conversation began, Peter learned the president had set up a secret task force designed to bypass the intelligence watchdogs and the media. Their purpose was to study the means and justification for attacking North Korea with a *first strike*.

A preemptive nuclear first strike meant a lot more than being equated with the first ballistic missile to be launched, as had been the case in Iran and Pakistan. Both of those nuclear attacks were ostensibly in response to prior provocations, although most would argue a nuclear response was quite an overreaction.

A first strike was designed to apply overwhelming force against a nuclear-capable enemy with the goal of defeating them by destroying their nuclear arsenal. By doing so, the enemy would be unable to continue with nuclear threats of their own. Targets would focus on missile silos, submarine bases, and other military installations like command-and-control sites. The counterforce strategy had never been employed using nuclear warfare.

No nation had undertaken a first strike although some argue the U.S. attack on Hiroshima fell under the definition. Contrarians argued the bombs on Hiroshima and Nagasaki were designed to end a war, not to avoid or start one. President Kennedy had been urged to initiate a first strike at the Soviet Union during the Cuban Missile Crisis, but cooler heads prevailed.

Peter's conversation with the analyst provided him tremendous insight. He probed further with his questioning after his initial success. "Where do they meet?"

"The building where I used to work before coming on board at State. The one with five sides." She was referring to the Pentagon.

"And the president used an executive order to set it up?"

"Yes. It's kept hidden from public view on national security grounds. That's not unusual. What is unusual is the task force's lack of normal procedures and accountability. They don't even have to report to Congress."

"Wow," muttered Peter. He thought for a moment, and then he asked, "Have they issued any suggestions?"

"Oh yeah," she replied. "That's why all of this business in South Asia and the Middle East has me concerned. Even before today's attack, they'd made up their minds, and they've advised the president on their recommended course of action."

"Which is?"

"A nuclear first strike on the DPRK."

Peter sat back in his chair. The rumors were true. There was something between the president and North Korea, an issue that might never be made public. Regardless, he'd established a task force to give him political cover.

He asked a pointed question. "Are they creating intelligence to justify nuking Kim?" It was the kind of conspiratorial question that would get him thrown out of a press briefing. He doubted the aide would answer.

"Yes."

So much for that. He leaned forward.

"Even though the Chicoms might fire back?"

She nodded in response. "The task force believes it can strategically pinpoint targets to take out Kim's capabilities while minimizing loss of life to the North Korean people. The task force, and the president, I'm told, firmly believes the surgical first strike will be palatable to Beijing, who has been fed up with Kim's independence of late."

"What will be the justification?" asked Peter.

"They will manufacture intelligence, with the assistance of our Far East allies, proving Kim's intentions to fire upon Seoul and Tokyo."

Peter sighed. He shook his head in disbelief as he imagined the political machinations that took place in the dark recesses of DC.

While Peter paused, she added another thought. "There's more. The task force believes the North Korean people would be better off."

"Of course," said Peter. "With the Kim dynasty taken out, South and North can unify."

"That's not what I mean. China wants the territory. Supposedly, just rumor, a back channel has been established between Beijing and the task force, indicating they might be on board with such an operation. It solves a problem for both sides."

"Can they be trusted? Think about it for a moment. We're revealing our plans to nuke North Korea to their biggest ally and one of our deadliest enemies."

She shrugged.

Peter continued with his questioning. "How far along are these discussions? I mean, is something imminent in light of what's happening in South Asia?"

"Maybe. Maybe not. The president is reportedly warming to the concept of a first strike. He wants to believe the Chinese are on board."

Peter sat in amazement as to the aide's blunt honesty. He also contemplated what all of this meant. He had one more question. "What if the task force is wrong?"

"About …?" she asked, her voice trailing off, as she was unsure what part of the conversation he was referring to."

"The Chinese. What if they aren't on board and retaliate?"

Her response was blunt, and her calm demeanor was chilling. "Now, that would suck for us, wouldn't it?"

CHAPTER THIRTY-TWO

Tuesday, October 22
Hayward, California

"So do you guys have the Disaster Alert app installed on your phones?" asked Tucker as they gathered in the kitchen. Each member of the McDowell family had a different way to kick-start their day. Owen needed his coffee, black with a couple of sugars. Lacey wasn't a coffee drinker, opting instead for a healthy, fruit-filled smoothie. Tucker ate whatever leftovers existed in the refrigerator, or an energy bar. "Everybody at school got a text blast from the school, encouraging us to download it. It covers all kinds of stuff like bad weather, active-shooter situations, and nuclear attacks. I think that's the real reason."

"It came pre-installed on my phone," replied his dad. He glanced over at Lacey, who was preoccupied with the imagery displayed on the television. The ongoing nuclear attacks between Pakistan and India seemed to affect her more than the exchange in the Middle East. "What about you, sweetheart?"

"What?" Owen's question grabbed her attention away from the news reports.

"The disaster app, Mom. The government is urging everyone to download it. The school messaged me about it."

"Oh," she mumbled. She walked over to her phone and mindlessly studied it. After a moment, she handed it to her son. "Will you do it for me, Tucker?"

As Tucker went to the App Store and located the download, Lacey wandered out of the kitchen into the family room. She located the remote and turned up the volume.

Owen talked to his son in a lowered voice. "Your mom said she planned on keeping you out of school today. All of this seems to have hit her hard, and I get her concern. However, I don't like unexcused absences."

Tucker completed the download and placed her phone back on the counter where it had been previously. "Dad, I'm way ahead this semester. It's the middle of the week, so there aren't any quizzes or anything. I can get one of the guys to fill me in on what I might've missed."

"Will you keep a close eye on her today? You know, stay with her."

"Sure, okay. But, Dad, she's not going crazy. Uncle Peter seems to think this is the start of something bigger. Don't you agree?"

"Your uncle Peter knows a lot more than I do about these things, but I try to apply common sense. The last thing our country needs is a nuclear war. I can't imagine any president getting us involved in one."

"Did anyone imagine they'd drop those bombs on Japan during World War Two?" asked Tucker.

Owen grimaced. His son had made a good point. "No, but times are different. We know the devastating effects of these things. Listen, I'm not saying your mom is overreacting. Just, you know, text me if you feel she needs my support. Okay?"

Tucker smiled. "Sure, Dad."

"What does she have planned for the day?" asked Owen.

Tucker responded with a question of his own. He wondered if

the family's plans had changed in light of what was going on. "We're still going to Tahoe Thursday, right?"

"You betcha," said Owen, reaching up to scruff the long, sandy blond locks of his son. He styled it like a surf bum who'd just rolled out of a hammock for the day. "We'll get loaded up tomorrow afternoon. I'm gonna bug out of the office as early as I can."

"That's lit, Dad. Mom has us running errands all day. She has to stop by the store, and then we're going to Costco."

"More stocking up?" asked Owen.

"I guess so. Hey, I'm along for the ride. We're gonna have In-N-Out burgers for lunch. Works for me, you know?"

Owen rubbed his son's hair again and then made his way into the family room. "Hey, babe. I gotta roll. You guys have fun today."

Lacey had switched stations to the Weather Channel. They were discussing past record-breaking winters in the Sierra Nevada Mountains and how this early-October snowfall had followed a similar timeline as the others.

"Are we still good to go?" asked Owen, startling Lacey, who was deep in thought. She flinched, and he immediately felt bad. "Honey, I'm sorry. I didn't mean to—"

Lacey turned around and spontaneously kissed her husband. It was a meaningful kiss. The kind longtime married couples share less and less often over the years.

"I love you, Owen," she said in a serious tone.

He hugged her. He tried to use humor to break her out of her melancholy mood. "What's not to love? Smart. Handsome. I still have all my hair and teeth. See?" He provided her a Cheshire cat grin.

"Now I hate you," she said with a laugh. She playfully slugged him on the chest.

He laughed with her. "Good, that's better. Now, is makeup sex an option?"

She pounded him in earnest this time. "Get out of my house!"

They embraced again, and she sighed. After a moment, she pulled away and wiped a solitary tear that escaped her eye.

"Part of me is upset about Peter's call. Then the other side, the wife and mother side, wants to do everything I can to prepare for my family. I don't know if any of this crap is gonna come our way, but I feel the need to do something."

She pointed over her shoulder toward the television, which was still showing scenes of snow in Nevada. Owen knew she was referring to the nuclear devastation that had occurred between the two warring nations.

"Listen, I admire you for taking care of us. I know you're not gonna go shopping for Humvees and shipping containers to bury in the ground like those people in Idaho."

"Too much rock."

"Rock?" asked a confused Owen.

"Because we sit up on this ridge, our backyard has too much rock for a shipping container."

Owen furrowed his brow as he studied her face. "Seriously? You've thought about this."

"Yes. After you fell asleep watching the news, I did a bunch of research. The shipping container won't work for us, so we need to find out where the nuclear fallout shelters are."

Owen glanced past Lacey and saw that she had her iPad sitting on the table next to several stacks of paper. Each one had a yellow Post-it note stuck on the front, identifying the purpose of the stack.

"Is this part of your research?" he asked, pointing at the table.

"Yes."

"Geez, Lacey. Did you sleep at all?"

"A couple of hours," she replied. "Here's the thing, Owen. There is no man-made scenario worse than a nuclear war. Sure, large asteroid strikes and supervolcanos are extinction-level events, but man doesn't control those things. Nuclear weapons can kill a lot of people all at once. Exhibit A ..." Her voice trailed off as she grabbed the remote and switched back to the cable news network. The video footage was beginning to emerge out of the war-torn region in South Asia. It was Tehran all over again, times fifty.

Owen tried to tamp down her concerns. "I really don't think that'll happen here, but if you wanna do some things, I'm all for it."

"I'm not going crazy, Owen. Nor will I empty the bank accounts on this stuff. I'd just feel better knowing we had some semblance of a plan. You know?"

He embraced his wife. "Now it's my turn. I love you, Lacey McDowell." Then he gave her a meaningful kiss.

CHAPTER THIRTY-THREE

Hank had spent the day with Sonny, walking every square foot of Driftwood Key's twenty-eight acres. His mind was too cluttered to work from memory as to what aspects of the resort's operations needed to be analyzed for backup mechanical parts or maintenance supplies. They had an extensive produce-growing operation on the key, which included greenhouses and hydroponics. Sonny was, in addition to virtually everything else, the man with the green thumb. Hank prided himself on his fishing skills, and Sonny carried the burden of growing fruits and vegetables. The division of responsibilities had served them well over the years.

With a new list in hand and half a dozen stops, Sonny set out for the day to purchase backup supplies and fertilizers for the gardening aspect of Driftwood Key. He also bought backup parts, fluids, and more shells for the marine shotguns he owned.

Hank took a few hours that morning to drive to Sea Tek Marine in Marathon, a local supplier of solar energy equipment. He bought additional panels to be mounted with their existing array that provided power to the bungalows. He also purchased their entire supply of charge controllers, batteries and power inverters that were compatible with their existing setup.

Then he stopped by the True Value in Marathon and purchased several medium-sized galvanized trash cans. He had been up late the night before studying the effects of an EMP on electronics. Erin had cautioned him that electronics would be unable to function if America was attacked with an electromagnetic pulse weapon, so Hank had decided to do a little research on the concept.

The complex subject gave him a wicked headache, so he took the last of his Advil to overcome it. That simple task, one that he did several times a week when his muscles were sore, reminded him that over-the-counter medicines and first aid were of vital importance. He searched for a checklist of commonly used medical supplies and provided it to Jimmy, who headed over to Walgreens to fill the order.

His research into EMPs revealed a method of protecting small electronics from the highly charged particles generated by a massive burst of energy. By placing these electronics, whether it be related to his solar array or communications devices, into the galvanized cans, he could protect them from the effects of an EMP.

The instructions were remarkably simple. Line the inside of the galvanized trash can with cardboard and Styrofoam, if available. Then wrap the electronics in heavy-duty aluminum foil. Secure the lid and wrap the rim with aluminum tape used by HVAC contractors. The result was an impenetrable place to store electronics known as a Faraday cage.

All of his research led him down a rabbit hole of preparedness websites that seemed to contradict one another at times. He applied his own logic and common sense and formulated a plan for the day.

After Phoebe served breakfast, Hank met with her in the kitchen. Their food suppliers had delivered early that morning, and cases of supplies were stacked in every available square foot of the kitchen and all along the back porch of the main house. They discussed a storage plan, and then Phoebe brought up the issue of their guests.

"Mr. Hank, you know I'm not one to question your decisions," she began before Hank started laughing.

"Since when?"

"Okay, only once in a while," she said with a tinge of guilt. "The thing is, I don't know anything about politics or wars and don't want to know about nuclear missiles. If you think something is gonna happen, you know, because your lady friend said so or Peter, then we need to make a decision about our guests."

"They need to go, Phoebe."

"Yes, Mr. Hank. If you believe this in your heart, you owe it to them to send them home. Some of these folks are from Colorado. That would be a long walk, if you know what I mean."

His mind immediately shifted to Lacey. California was even longer. He had to convince her to come here. And soon.

"I agree. I'm thinking about telling them the water main between here and the mainland broke. They'll have to evacuate because we don't have any fresh water. I can have Laura cancel the incoming reservations."

"If that's what you think is necessary," she added. "I just don't know, Mr. Hank. It's kinda like the chicken screamin' the sky is falling."

Hank sighed and shifted his feet as he rubbed his heels along the perpetually sand-covered wood floors. "Financially, we could close for more than a month and everything would be fine. It's just, um, if I wait too long, we'll be in a mess. I'm in a situation where we can't support these people. But I feel obligated to take care of them. Every meal we serve them is a meal we won't have for ourselves."

Phoebe nodded in agreement. "You sound like you've thought it through."

Hank laughed nervously. "I did last night. A lot, in fact, until I got a headache. To be honest, the nuclear attack this morning just sealed the decision. I'm gonna need to tell everyone in the morning that we can't refill the water tower because of the water main break, and they have to check out. I'll start Laura on cancelling the new reservations for the rest of the month right now."

"Um, Mr. Hank. Are you gonna bring Lacey and Peter home? Family should stick together in troubling times."

"That's the next order of business. I'm calling Mike, Peter, and Lacey next. I just hope they'll listen to me."

Hank touched base with Peter first to get the latest news. Peter relayed most of the conversation he'd had with the State Department aide as well as a few additional tidbits. Earlier in the day, as the missiles were still flying in South Asia, North Korean president-for-life Kim Jong Un spoke to the DPRK's 13th Party Congress, the Hermit Kingdom's highest legislative event. In addition to his usual chest-puffing, he was intent on sending a message to his citizens and the rest of the world as to how dangerous he was capable of being.

Kim spent most of the speech reciting a list of advances in their missile and nuclear programs. He also outlined his plans for expanding them even more regardless of international sanctions. Then he immediately targeted South Korea and Japan with his threatening rhetoric.

His outlaw-like behavior was so convincing that both of the neighboring nations immediately raised their threat-assessment levels and placed their military defenses on a war footing. He then proceeded to attack President Helton. He pointed out the United States, and the new administration in particular, was full of empty threats and hollow promises. Specifically, he echoed what American political pundits and many within in the Department of Defense were saying. President Helton's failure to act in defense of Israel, especially, was a sign of geopolitical impotence.

Peter cautioned his father that he was more concerned now than in their prior conversation. Hank, in turn, insisted Peter should come home. That was where the two men disagreed. Peter saw this as the biggest news story of his lifetime, at least thus far. He wanted to stick it out in the DC area so he could use his sources to bring the behind-the-scenes dealings into the public eye.

He made a hollow promise to heed the warnings and be prepared to leave the Washington area as soon as possible. From Newport News to the south, all the way up the East Coast, nuclear targets were abundant. He'd already mapped out a bug-out strategy that took him away from the city and the potential fallout resulting from a direct hit. And he honestly promised to act on it when he got a chance.

With this new information in hand, Hank touched base with Mike and Jessica. He convinced them to come to the inn for a late dinner and drinks. Mike had a break in his case and looked forward to discussing it with his brother.

Finally, the toughest nut to crack, because she had her mother's somewhat stubborn, independent streak, was Lacey. Hank spoke to her for thirty minutes and hung up pleasantly surprised. He was relieved that Lacey was taking the threat seriously. He applauded her two-day-long effort to be ready for a possible nuclear attack.

He was disappointed by her lack of commitment to hop on a plane with her family and head for Miami, where he promised to greet them. Owen had one more day in the office, and then they'd promised Tucker a four-day vacation in the mountains. She promised to think about it and, like Peter, claimed to have a plan in case they were warned of an impending attack.

The sun was beginning to drop over the horizon when Mike and Jessica arrived. The three of them pulled cigars out of the humidor and stopped by the bar for their favorite adult beverages. This, of course, reminded Hank that cigars needed to be stocked as well. Simple pleasures during the apocalypse might help him keep his sanity. He made a note on his iPhone.

"Let's talk about your case first," began Hank after the trio was settled in their chairs, with their toes buried in the sand.

"Yeah, it's a break in the case although it raises a number of questions," began Mike. "On the most recently discovered victim, the kids retrieved a fairly new model of Omega's dive watch line. In addition to our detectives looking through missing persons reports and trying to cross-reference the watch, we were able to make out the serial number. It was laser-etched in very small type on the back of the lug closest to the eleven o'clock position. It's a titanium model, so cleaning off the effects of sitting under water for over a week was a little easier.

"Anyway, the serial number was connected to a New York man who'd flown into Miami on business. He and a lady companion were seen leaving a bar in Coconut Grove early that evening. His rental car was found abandoned nearby."

"How did he get to the Keys?" asked Hank.

"We believe the woman—who was described as tall, as women go, nearly six feet—helped the guy out of the bar. The man was apparently inebriated although the bartender claimed he only had a couple of scotches. Anyway, drugs might be involved, and I'm still waiting on the toxicology report."

"That's something," said Hank.

"We caught a second break. After getting the vic's photo from family, our people began canvassing hotels, restaurants and bars in the Upper Keys. We got a hit at WaterLOO, the gay bar in Key Largo."

"Maybe they didn't know—" Hank said as his voice trailed off.

"He didn't, but she, or shall I say, the other he, did."

"Wait. What? The dead guy was picked up by a—?"

Mike interrupted his question. "Quite possibly. Yes. We might be onto something here. We have a working theory, anyway. The only issue is motive."

"The watch is high end," observed Hank. "Robbery doesn't make sense. Are you thinking a crime of passion? Or just an accident gone bad?"

Mike winced as he finished a sip of his drink. "Not an accident. The next two victims, if connected, rule that out. Crime of passion is a possibility. But again, how does that connect the three killings?"

"I have a theory," interjected Jessica.

"Whadya think?" asked Hank.

"Okay, this sounds very Netflix or Hulu-worthy, but what if our suspect is a frustrated male who is trying to find himself in an LGBTQ world. Especially the Q part. I saw a documentary once about a guy who killed gay men in Toronto a while back. He thought he was gay but tried to deny it. He apparently grew angry with himself and took it out on other gay men."

Hank turned to Mike. "Viable?"

"Absolutely. Listen, serial killers come in all shapes, sizes, and sexual orientations. To kill like this, they must have a serious screw loose. Anyway, I have our people taking the Key Largo vic's photo around to all known LGBT hangouts in the Keys."

"You might have to go beyond that," added Jessica. "If he is dressing as a woman, he may be trolling all the bars. Especially the late-night ones."

Mike finished his Jack on the rocks and hoisted himself out of his chair. "We don't have enough people for this. I'm gonna have to ask Tallahassee for more help."

He walked away to the bar, allowing Hank and Jessica to talk.

Hank finished his drink but kept his seat. "He's taking this hard, isn't he?"

"Yeah. Mike loves his job, and he's driven to solve these murders. The break in the case helps, but it also concerns him. He didn't mention this, but the witness who works at the Coconut Grove bar vaguely remembered the couple. The woman was described as very attractive, and the grainy image pulled from security footage bears that out. Hank, he's looking for a person who's capable of morphing from man to woman easily. It's a helluva challenge."

Hank glanced toward the bar and saw that Mike was chatting with the bartender. "Well, I have another challenge. However, this one is for you. I need you and Mike to agree to move back to Driftwood Key for a while. And I'm talking about tomorrow, if not tonight."

CHAPTER THIRTY-FOUR

Tuesday, October 22
Oval Office
The White House

The White House was bustling with activity as panicked staffers raced around carrying sealed banker's boxes with files destined for an undisclosed location. Outside the West Wing, white unmarked box trucks were lined up to accept the cargo. The vast majority of the staffers would be furloughed until further notice as the president prepared to be removed to a safer location, one whose floors, walls and ceilings were impenetrable to a nuclear blast.

While the National Security Agency was not prepared to affirmatively state the U.S. was under an immediate nuclear threat, the combination of the events of the last three days and the saber rattling by the North Koreans was enough to evacuate the Helton administration to a more secure facility.

Since President Truman had been in office, U.S. presidents have had access to fortified bunkers to ride out a nuclear war. If the missiles were in the air, the president would be hustled back into the PEOC. However, it was designed to house only a few people for a very limited time. Another option was Greenbrier in the Blue Ridge Mountains of West Virginia. Formerly a nuclear bunker for Congress, it's now a tourist attraction but can immediately be repurposed in a state of emergency.

To the north of Washington was Raven Rock in the hills of Southern Pennsylvania. It is mostly dedicated for the military. Peters Mountain, also known as Spy Mountain, was a fortified bunker north of Charlottesville, Virginia, dedicated to America's intelligence agencies.

The Cheyenne Mountain Complex in Colorado was the most well-known of them all. Built deep within a mountain, it housed NORAD, the North American Aerospace Defense Command, charged with the responsibility of defending America from a nuclear attack.

Today, the president was going to be evacuated as part of the U.S. continuity of government readiness condition known as COGCON 1. In the event of a credible threat of nuclear attack, the Administration and the U.S. government would be relocated to a secure, fully staffed bunker.

His destination was Mount Weather, a mountain peak near Bluemont, Virginia, just fifty miles outside Washington. Run by FEMA, Doomsday City, as it was known, had been activated and kept in a constant state of readiness since the terrorist attacks of 9/11. Mount Weather was built during the throes of the Cold War and was capable of taking a direct hit. It housed the president, his aides, and hundreds of others necessary to operate the government during a time of war.

All of these facilities were designed to ensure continuity of government during an anticipated foreign invasion, nuclear war, electromagnetic pulse attack, or a natural catastrophe of enormous magnitude.

The evacuation was not the president's idea. He had to defer to the defense department. However, the decision aligned with one that he'd made. He was tired of America living under the thumb of her enemies. Namely, North Korea. If Israel and India could take the bold step of beating back their archenemies, so could he. However, there was more to his decision-making process.

President Helton's family had experienced the horrors of the Kim regime. In fact, he was surprised nosy reporters or opposition researchers for his political opponents had never picked up on it.

His uncle, the brother of his deceased mother, had joined a humanitarian contingent to visit a disease-stricken village in the western regions of North Korea. Part of Doctors Without Borders, the beloved uncle of the president had been like a father to him growing up. He'd paired with another medical provider, an epidemiologist who happened to be the mother of Secretary of State Carolyn Sanders.

While examining and treating patients in a remote village away from their assigned areas, the two encountered a North Korean security patrol. They were brutally beaten simply because they were Americans. Their mauled corpses were returned to the Doctors Without Borders camp. It was explained to the director of the contingent that criminals had attacked the two and were immediately killed by brave North Korean soldiers.

Nobody ever believed the story. Days later, the group was expelled from the country, and any chance of learning the truth was lost.

President Helton had discovered the commonality with Secretary Sanders many years ago at a political fundraising dinner. They compared notes, comforted one another, and became longtime friends. They also shared a solemn promise. To avenge their loved ones.

When he was elected, the president never imagined he'd have the opportunity to exact his revenge on the murderous regime. He'd laid the groundwork to gain the opportunity by bringing Sanders into his cabinet. Once in office, he learned how the U.S. government worked. In secret. He established a commission of loyalists to find an opportunity, as well as a justification, for wiping Kim Jong Un off the face of the planet.

That opportunity was now.

After clearing the Oval Office, the president retrieved a celebratory cigar he'd planned on smoking following his inauguration. He'd gotten caught up in the moment, and the opportunity, or just the right occasion, never presented itself.

He rolled the glass tube containing the Gurkha Churchill in his fingers. The top was sealed with green wax reminiscent of a Maker's Mark whisky bottle. The cigar, known as His Majesty's Reserve, sold for $750 each. A hefty price for a smoke but preferred by elites inside the Beltway and considered one of the most expensive cigars ever made.

He peeled off the seal and retrieved his butane lighter. Earliest man had a fascination with fire. It represented life as well as destruction, the president thought to himself as the hot flame hissed out of the lighter. He became mesmerized by its various hues of red, orange, and blue where it was the hottest.

He lit the end, rotating the cigar in his fingers to provide an even burn. With each puff of the cigar, the fire created by his lighter rose several inches. His mind deceived him as the fire morphed to a tower of flame stretching thousands of feet skyward until it formed a billowing, ever-expanding mushroom.

As he puffed on the cigar, the flame continued to dance up and down as it was fed and deprived of oxygen. His mind continued to play tricks on him. He saw a fireball spread across the nation he was elected to protect, incinerating large cities and rural towns, scorching the heartland while reducing to ash the bodies of millions of Americans. All of it floated into the clouds and beyond, swept up by the jet stream and carried for thousands of miles, leaving the remains of America around the globe.

With one final draw, the burning cherry glowed bright red, and he exhaled, sending smoke spiraling upward. And, within the smoke, there was a set of eyes looking back at him. Evil. Lifeless. Unblinking. Narrowing with scorn. Piercing his psyche. Leaving the words to float through his mind.

First strike.

In that moment, President Helton, a sly smile on his face,

confirmed his decision. Once he was settled into the bunker at Mount Weather, he was going to make the case for a preemptive first strike against North Korea.

Do unto others before they do unto you, or something like that, he thought to himself, drawing a slight laugh from deep within him. His mind continued. *Screw me? No, screw you!* He could go on, but he'd settled on his decision.

Yes, he would exact his revenge while eliminating a despot at the same time. The world would be a better place for his efforts. He was convinced of it.

CHAPTER THIRTY-FIVE

Tuesday, October 22
Hayward, California

It was late that evening, and Owen was tied up at the office. By the time he broke away, a torrential rain swept down San Francisco Bay toward Palo Alto. Owen was on the Dumbarton Bridge, crossing the lower end of the bay, when a multi-car accident half a mile ahead of him occurred, effectively locking him down on the bridge in the midst of a multilane, thousand-car parking lot. He sat there, frustrated, waiting for emergency vehicles to clear the wreckage. And growing increasingly apprehensive as he listened to news stations on his satellite radio.

After thirty-six hours, the nuclear war between Pakistan and India had finally come to an end. It was being called the worst humanitarian and environmental disaster in history. Countless millions had perished in a blink of an eye as one nuclear warhead was detonated after another. Wildfires raged out of control across both countries, consuming millions of acres of farmland, destroying buildings, and sending noxious materials into the stratosphere.

It was during one roundtable discussion on NPR that Owen

learned about the concept of nuclear winter. When these nuclear warheads struck the earth, not only did they propel millions of cubic yards of debris and radioactive material into the sky, but they spawned widespread firestorms across the landscape of both nations.

The fires were not quite as prevalent in the brief Iranian-Israeli exchange due to the geography surrounding the primary targets, Tel Aviv and Tehran. South Asia was a different matter.

The multitude of targets in both nations were located in fertile valleys used for growing food for the enormous populations in the region, especially India. The blasts created a mushroom cloud, but they also spread incredible heat and fire outward from the detonation site. The soot from the burning cities and plant material following the nuclear blasts entered the atmosphere and immediately began to spread around the globe.

Scientists interviewed by NPR claimed the soot, radioactive debris, and other materials could circumnavigate the globe within four to five days. As they did, sunlight would be blocked from reaching the Earth's surface, resulting in a significant drop in global temperatures. In addition, rainfall would decrease substantially, thus increasing ultraviolet radiation levels due to the badly damaged atmosphere.

That was how nuclear winter began, a term of art dating back to the early eighties when Carl Sagan and a team of scientists brought the concept to the attention of the world. Their studies, as refined by present-day scientists, talked of unfathomable loss in agriculture productions and massive global starvation.

Owen's pulse raced as those interviewed made their case. He changed the station to CNN. More of the same. FoxNews? Ditto.

The consensus was that the direct death and destruction was the obvious result of a nuclear war between nations. The widespread firestorms following the bombings would burn out of control for months in some locations, or longer. The millions of tons of soot and ash would absorb sunlight for a minimum of five years as the ability to grow the world's four main cereal crops—corn, wheat, soybeans, and rice—would plummet for nearly ten years. It would be the single largest famine in documented human history.

Owen switched his radio to ESPN, hoping for a respite from the doomsday discussions. He would soon be disappointed.

It had been a long but productive day for Lacey and Tucker. She monitored the news but didn't obsess over it. There were too many things on her to-do list for hand-wringing. She and her family were resolved to get ready for the worst-case scenario. Tucker had spent time on the internet and revealed a horrifying fact. The San Francisco Bay Area was a high-value target for the three nuclear-powered enemies of the U.S.—Russia, China, and North Korea.

Silicon Valley, the area where Owen worked, was the high-tech capital of the world. It was home to over two thousand companies, including Apple, Microsoft, Google, Yahoo!, and the social media giants. As the military pundits pointed out earlier in the day, a strike against the Bay Area would devastate the American economy and its high-tech dominance for a decade.

After Lacey heard that report, she stepped up her preparations. Tucker's innocent proposal to get out of town for a family vacay suddenly took on a new meaning. That morning, she replayed Peter's warning in her mind and felt the urge to run away from home as fast as she could. However, first, there was work to be done.

Lacey knew they'd have a twenty-to-thirty-minute warning in the event a nuclear missile was launched toward the West Coast. That would require fast action on the family's part. Living on the east side of Hayward on the ridge was a plus. They wouldn't have to battle traffic like the millions who lived in the Bay Area. In minutes, they could be on I-580 heading east, and thirty minutes later, they'd be past Stockton, roughly sixty miles away from San Francisco.

The first order of business was to prepare to leave on a moment's notice. Staying was not an option in the event of a nuclear attack. After consulting with Owen, they agreed to use their Ford Expedition to tow their vintage Ford Bronco, nicknamed Black & Blue. The 1967 classic had been a purchase made by the family after Lacey's first hugely successful year with her new business, Jefferson Outfitters. The family vowed to spend more time exploring the outdoors in Northern California and Nevada. They enjoyed watching the Paramount television series *Yellowstone*, starring Kevin Costner. One of the beloved characters drove a classic Bronco. That was how the choice had been made.

She focused on all of the things the government harped on—water, batteries, candles, etcetera. Lacey spent the better part of the morning focusing on food that was easily transportable. She purchased all of the high-calorie MRE bars at Bass Pro Shops to supplement her own store's inventory. MRE was an acronym for meals-ready-to-eat. Her store sold a wide variety of easily transportable, long-lasting food products designed for campers and hikers. As of noon that day, she was completely out of stock. Every case of anything edible was sitting in her living room.

She doubled the quantity of her camping and hiking gear. The same was true of their clothing. If the time came, they'd be heading into the Sierra Nevadas as an early snowstorm arrived. If Peter's warnings were correct, they might not be able to return home, a reality that hadn't quite set in yet.

By nightfall, when the deluge of rain had invaded the coastal areas, Lacey and Tucker had filled the living room with gear, supplies, food, and water. Their focus on the basic necessities was a success. However, it was Tucker who was the first to point out a potential shortfall.

"Hey, Mom, why don't we have a gun?"

Lacey, who was exhausted as she sat on the only seat on the sofa not covered with piles of clothing, responded, "Well, frankly, we never found the use for one. We're not against guns like a lot of people around here. It's just that we aren't hunters, and because we live in a safe gated community, we're not afraid of break-ins."

Tucker just stood there for a moment, and then he, too, surveyed all of the items they'd amassed over the last twenty-four hours. He glanced back toward the hallway leading to the garage where the Expedition awaited.

"Mom, this is a lot of stuff. Is it all gonna fit?"

Lacey pushed herself off the couch and stood in the middle of the room, slowly rotating in a complete circle to take it all in. They'd need to go back to U-Haul to rent a box truck, she thought to herself half-jokingly.

Owen was listening to the ESPN hosts discuss the ongoing World Series when the inside of the car exploded in a cacophony of warning signs and computer-generated voices.

The ESPN programming was interrupted to issue an ominous alert. The screen on his SiriusXM radio changed to read:

EMERGENCY ALERT
BALLISTIC MISSILE THREAT INBOUND TO CALIFORNIA.
SEEK IMMEDIATE SHELTER. THIS IS NOT A DRILL.

Owen received a text message from the California State Warning Center, known as Cal OES, which issued a push alert to all cell phones and handheld tablet computers located within the state's IP address locations.

Cal OES: The U.S. Pacific Command has detected a missile threat to California. A missile may impact on land or sea within minutes.

THIS IS NOT A DRILL.

. . .

If you are indoors, stay indoors. If you are outdoors, seek immediate shelter in a building. Remain indoors well away from windows. If you are driving, pull safely to the side of the road and seek shelter in a building or lie on the floor. We will announce when the threat has ended.

THIS IS NOT A DRILL. Take immediate action measures.

The disaster app began to wail. Outside the car, through the driving rain, California's siren warning system, which had been tested just weeks before as part of a missile preparedness exercise, had been activated, emitting a high-pitched wail.

Owen, like many other motorists, froze for a moment, unsure what to do. Then, as if prompted by an invisible cattle prod, they reacted.

Some jumped out of their cars, leaving their doors open and engines running. They raced away toward the east, logically trying to get away from the coastline. Others calculated the shorter distance to land was back toward the west. Large groups of people collided with one another, resulting in a massive human scrum on the bridge.

Owen pushed his way in between the three lanes of stalled vehicles toward home. Behind him, horns were blaring and tires were screeching as motorists tried to force their back way off the bridge. Several panicked motorists tried to jump over the concrete barrier separating the east- and westbound lanes of the causeway. They were plowed down by speeding traffic as drivers raced to perceived safety somewhere in East Palo Alto.

It was mayhem, and San Franciscans weren't handling the threat very well. As Owen ran, he tried to call Lacey and Tucker. Cell towers were overwhelmed with millions of others doing the same. His mind raced as he thought of the buildings and facilities on the east side of the Dumbarton Bridge. He'd passed by there twice a day, five days a week, for years, yet his mind drew a blank.

Was there a nuclear fallout shelter over there? Was there even a building with a basement considering its close proximity to the bay? How much time did he have before the bombs hit?

Owen wanted to throw up, but he kept moving. He focused on his love for Lacey and Tucker. He prayed they'd taken off to the east like they'd discussed. He wanted them to live, even if he couldn't. He refused to let despair overtake him. So he pressed forward. He abandoned all sense of decorum or politeness. Like so many others were doing, he knocked anyone down who prevented him from reaching safety.

Lacey had been marshalling their assets. Picking and choosing what was a priority based upon the survival rule of threes. A person can only live three hours in extreme weather without adequate shelter. Without hydration, the human body begins to deteriorate rapidly without water after three days. Without food and adequate nutrition, the body begins to cannibalize itself after three weeks.

With that being her focus, she started giving things to Tucker to pack into the back of the Expedition. After the Bronco was affixed to the tow dolly and the hitch of the Expedition, they'd fill it with their most essential gear.

"Mom!" yelled Tucker from the garage. His disaster app had issued an incoming ballistic missile alert.

Lacey heard it as well, and the television screen was filled with the warning. She ran down the hallway toward him as he raced back inside. They nearly collided but spontaneously hugged one another instead. She gripped her son by the shoulders and looked up to the taller young man.

"No panicking. Okay."

Tucker nodded. "What about Dad?"

"Let's see where he is. Try calling him on both your cell and our landline in case you can't get through. Let me check the app."

The McDowells' cell plan enabled them to link their locations together. At any given time, they could check on each other. Lacey thought that was an essential feature with a teenage boy in the house. She opened the map and searched for Owen. It showed him on the Dumbarton Bridge, moving slowly in the direction of the Nimitz Freeway.

"Anything?" she hollered at Tucker in the kitchen.

"Circuits are busy!" he yelled his response. "I'll try to text!"

Lacey ran into the living room and located her laptop. In all her preparations, with the assumption they'd immediately be leaving town when the warnings were issued, she hadn't bothered to locate the nearest fallout shelter.

She searched *nuclear fallout shelters near me* and viewed the results.

Besides Ready.gov, which was essentially worthless because the advice it gave was to hide under your bed, the other results were survivalist websites trying to sell products or backyard buried shelters.

She drilled down in her search, using *fallout shelters near San Francisco*. Her mouth fell open as she viewed the results. The words *abandoned, thing of the past,* and *no plan* were common. She shook her head in disgust as she ran her fingers through her hair.

Tucker joined her in the living room. "Mom, what are we gonna do? We have to wait for Dad."

Lacey closed her eyes. She couldn't believe the words that came out of her mouth. "It'll be too late."

CHAPTER THIRTY-SIX

Tuesday, October 22
Driftwood Key

Although Hank was exhausted by the end of the day, he was having difficulty finding sleep. He'd started before dawn at just after five that morning, resulting in a fast-paced, seventeen-hour day. He tossed and turned as a myriad of scenarios ran through his head. He questioned himself several times as he tried to determine whether he was overreacting. However, Peter had been so convincing, and when the nuclear skirmish in the Middle East transitioned into an all-out war between India and Pakistan, Hank began to believe the potential threat to the U.S. was real.

But which threat should he prepare for? Would America be subjected to a nuclear detonation on her soil? Or would it simply be subjected to the aftermath of these other conflicts—nuclear winter?

The best-case scenario, of course, was that nothing happened. Certainly, the concept of nuclear winter was largely theoretical, based upon the works of Carl Sagan many decades ago. Comparing the global environmental implications to the eruption of the Yellowstone supervolcano, he thought, might be a little too much. Then again, would it have to be that bad to throw the world into a period of rapid cooling and famine as plant material died off?

If nothing happened, then he'd sent his guests home for no reason and he'd cancelled reservations that would have to be rebooked. It would cost the inn revenue, but he had sufficient savings to cover the losses.

In his restless state, his mind chased several scenarios. When would it be safe to say *all clear*? Or *the threat has passed. The modern-day equivalent of the Cuban Missile Crisis is over.*

Hank's planning had relied on Peter's inside information and judgment. He would not take the advice of the talking heads on the news networks. They'd lost his trust and confidence years ago.

He worried about Peter, who was a headstrong risk-taker. Peter was not one to shy away from a fight or danger, as his career had proven. His son was prepared to stay in Washington, an obvious nuclear target, until the end so he could cover the story. While Hank admired his dedication, he'd feel a whole lot better if Peter were settled in one of the guest bedrooms upstairs.

Then there was Lacey. His adorable baby girl who'd grown up, left the nest for college, and was hustled off to Northern California to start a family. He didn't begrudge her choices in life. In fact, Hank truly admired Owen and enjoyed his company on the rare occasions they traveled back to the Keys. And Tucker was a heckuva young man. Polite. Smart. Head screwed on right. A model teen, if that was possible nowadays.

It was impossible to ask a parent who their favorite child was. Their intense feeling of guilt in choosing one or the other would result in a response full of equivocation and caveats. The same was true for Hank although there was a special bond he'd had with Lacey.

From the beginning, he could look into his baby girl's eyes and see his wife, Megan. Megan created a mini-me as she raised Lacey, something that thrilled Hank. He loved his wife, and the thought of Lacey growing up in her image comforted him. When Megan died,

Lacey had been there for Hank more than anyone else that summer in between her junior and senior years.

When she was a child, the two had a classic hero dad–princess daughter relationship. Hank included her in all of his activities, and Lacey found a love for the outdoors just like Hank. To be sure, she was the darling little princess although she was more Ariel, the Little Mermaid, than she was Cinderella.

Hank was there for her, teaching her to be self-reliant and a problem-solver. Megan believed Hank's time spent with Lacey as a young child boosted her self-confidence and encouraged her to overcome her inhibitions. She was fearless, much like her brother, Peter.

Lacey's teen years were different. Well, they actually started at twelve. The eye roll became a commonly used response to Hank's attempts to employ the same parenting tactics he'd used when she was younger.

Hank hung in there and persevered. The phase passed, and Lacey's relationship with her dad grew, especially after the death of Megan. They helped one another through it, and now the bond between the two of them was as strong as ever.

It was for that reason that Hank bolted upright in his bed that evening as he struggled for sleep. Something sent chills up his spine, and his forehead broke out in a cold sweat. He fumbled to turn the light on, and he retrieved his cell phone from its charger. In the moment, Hank was incredibly lucid, and worried.

He tried to dial Lacey's number first and got no answer. He moved on to the home phone and received a fast-busy signal. When he tried again, the fast-busy signal was replaced in the earpiece by dead, staticky silence. He checked his watch. It was barely seven o'clock on the west coast. He navigated through his address book to call Owen's and Tucker's cell phones.

No answer.

Hank cursed himself as his mind went there. The worst-case scenario. A nuclear strike on American soil, with the West Coast being the first of many targets. He jerked open the nightstand drawer to find the television remote that was rarely used. The entire drawer and its contents spilled out onto the floor. Hank rolled out of bed and searched for the remote, which had found its way under the bed.

The expletives were being hurled at this point. He took a deep breath to regain his composure. He powered on the monitor and struggled to switch from the Weather Channel to any of the cable news networks.

He finally found CNN. His eyes grew wide as the words *BREAKING NEWS* were splattered across the screen together with a graphic depicting California, Oregon, and Washington, with several red dots flashing on the screen. Along the chyron, the words *Ballistic Missile Alert* issued.

Tears poured out of Hank's eyes as he turned up the volume.

CHAPTER THIRTY-SEVEN

Tuesday, October 22
Falls Church, Virginia

Peter had flopped on the sofa with a beer. He'd spent the bulk of the afternoon at the State Department, attempting to confirm the information he'd received from his sources. He didn't have sufficient corroboration to satisfy his editor, so a story for the print edition of the *Times* didn't have a chance. Their journalistic standards also applied to the digital edition online. Peter planned on settling in with his MacBook to review statements made by the president during past electoral campaigns to determine if he'd tipped his hand unknowingly. As was his practice, he watched his television with the volume muted and the closed captioning turned on so he could monitor events around the world.

Fox News was airing a commercial, so he perused his social media accounts before getting started. He moved from the new platforms, MeWe and Gab, to the dinosaurs, Facebook and then Twitter. By the time he scrolled through his Twitter feed, the digital media world had exploded.

"Holy shit!" he exclaimed as he jumped off the sofa, spilling his beer in the process. He grabbed the bottle off the floor and set it on the coffee table as the foamy head spilled out. He quickly turned his laptop sideways so the droplets of beer slid off the screen.

Peter grabbed the remote and turned up the volume on the television. *Breaking News* was emblazoned across the screen. He turned up the volume to listen as he studied the tweets. The news opinion host stuttered at first. She was normally level-headed, but the magnitude of the event had clearly rattled her.

Laura Ingram read from a printed page instead of a teleprompter. "We have received reports from KTTV, the Fox affiliate in Los Angeles, that the California State Warning Center, Office of Emergency Services in Sacramento has issued a digital warning to all residents of California that an incoming ballistic missile has been detected. This is unconfirmed as of yet."

Ingram paused as someone spoke to her off camera. Then she continued. "I've also been told that as is their protocol, Oregon and Washington state have issued similar warnings. According to this, the alerts took place in the last seven minutes. From my recollection, America's west coast is thirty to thirty-five minutes away from a nuclear strike from our nearest adversaries, North Korea and China."

She took a deep breath and looked into the camera. "Everyone needs to seek shelter immediately. Don't hesitate. Go now. Your life depends on it."

Peter's first instinct was to call Lacey. He tried twice on her cell phone and got no answer. He scowled as he paced the floor. He called Jess. She'd been at the Pentagon late that evening and had bailed on a previously scheduled dinner with him.

Her phone rang and rang.

"Come on, Jess, pick up."

Peter paced the floor, glancing twice at the beer as he resisted the urge to drink it. He needed to keep his head clear.

He returned to his phone and tried Lacey again. No answer. He was mad at himself for not having Owen's number, or Tucker's, for that matter.

The Fox coverage switched to live shots of panicked partiers in West Hollywood and motorists who were rushing away from the city. A traffic helicopter hovered over Interstate 210 through Pasadena as cars traveling east away from the city had taken over one of the westbound lanes.

He called Jess again. It rang twice, and she picked up.

"Peter! We've got nothing inbound."

"What? Say that again."

"Initially, they went into a full-blown panic over here. There are no missiles inbound. They've called USCENTCOM and confirmed with Pacific Command. There are no ballistic missiles in the air. I know for a fact they reached out to the governor of California and his OES people to shut the damn warning alerts off."

Peter said nothing for a long moment. Fox was still reporting on the mayhem and had done nothing to retract their initial reporting.

"Jess, I'm watching reaction on the news. They've got to tell people. There are reports of people jumping from high-rise balconies to commit suicide. Cars are crashing head-on into one another along the freeways coming out of LA."

Jess was on edge and agitated. "The Pentagon is on it. We're preparing a press release and a nationwide text alert now. It should go out any second."

The federal government had established a program to notify every cell phone user in the nation of emergency alerts sent by state and local public officials regarding severe weather, missing or abducted children, and silver alerts related to senior citizens who might suffer from deteriorating mental faculties. Through the Emergency Alert System, or EAS, the president can address the American people within ten minutes of a national emergency.

"What about POTUS?" he asked.

"They hustled him off to Mount Weather already in light of the South Asian conflict," Jess responded.

"He, or someone, needs to issue a retraction. Every second that goes by could mean hundreds of people dying unnecessarily."

"They know, Peter. Listen, I gotta go."

"Okay, call me when you can," he insisted, but she'd already disconnected the call.

Peter's hands were shaking when he reached down for his beer. It had become warm, but he didn't care. He drained the bottle in three hard gulps.

He tried to open SFGate.com, a well-known Bay Area website for local news, sports, and weather. The servers had crashed. His palms were sweaty as he dialed Lacey's number again. He prayed they were home at this hour.

The phone rang, and finally, Lacey picked up the phone. He could hear the blaring of car horns in the background. Lacey dropped the phone.

"Watch out, Mom!" Tucker shouted in the background. Lacey slammed on her own horn in response to whatever Tucker had warned about. She finally came to the phone.

"Owen? Are you okay?"

"Lacey!" Peter shouted so she could hear him. "Listen to me. It's a false alarm. Do you hear me? It's a false alarm!"

"What? Peter? They've been sending out these—"

"Lacey, I know. I talked to the Pentagon. It's a mistake. Somebody made a mistake."

"Are you freakin' kidding me?" Lacey shouted at the phone, her incredulity obvious in her tone of voice.

"I confirmed it. The president will be issuing an emergency alert notification withdrawing what California started. Get home. Get to safety. There is no missile threat."

"I'm gonna hand you off to Tucker."

"Uncle Peter?"

"Yeah, big guy. Listen, I'm gonna hang up. Help your mom. There is no missile, okay?"

"Stupid idiots," Tucker groaned.

"Yeah, for sure. Listen, I take it Owen isn't with you?"

"Right. We think he's on the Dumbarton crossing the bay. I'd better try to call him again."

"Do that. Be careful and call me later."

Tucker hung up, and Peter collapsed onto his sofa. Seconds later, the president's text message was disseminated through the emergency alert system, cancelling the alert.

The nation breathed a collective sigh of relief.

CHAPTER THIRTY-EIGHT

Tuesday, October 22
California State Warning Center
Office of Emergency Services (Cal OES)
Sacramento, California

Alix Adams was a loyal soldier. She'd been hand-selected to join the Cal OES about six months ago. Prior to that, she'd worked on the president's election campaign in the state. Her experience procuring signatures to initiate ballot referendums had landed her a lucrative position in Sacramento within the California State Warning Center.

At first, she didn't understand why she was offered the full-time position at just over fifty thousand a year but also given a consultant contract by the president's campaign team that doubled that annual salary.

The prior evening near the end of her shift, she'd received a text message to meet a campaign coworker at the Thai Bistro restaurant nearby for drinks. Adams hadn't heard from the man she'd casually dated during the campaign since the inauguration. She liked him and was willing to let him buy her a few drinks.

Upon arrival, he got right down to business. He slid her an

envelope with five thousand dollars in cash enclosed. His request was a simple one. Accidentally hit the wrong button. Nothing more. Nothing less. Afterwards, apologize profusely. Cry, if she felt compelled to do so. "Don't worry about your job or your side gig," he'd said to her. "Just push the wrong button when the time comes."

They shared one drink and made small talk about the new administration. He abruptly left, and she went home. The next night, as her shift was in its last hour, her supervisor advised her that during the shift change, he wanted to run an unscheduled drill to make sure everyone was *on their toes*, as he put it. He advised Adams that he was going to contact the emergency management team, pretending to be with U.S. Pacific Command. He just wanted to give Adams a heads-up so she would do the right thing when she was instructed by the team to act.

Adams was thoroughly confused. Was her supervisor part of the subterfuge? When he said do the right thing, was he actually referring to pushing the wrong button, as she'd been instructed?

Minutes later, as the emergency workers began filing out of their offices and cubicles, Adams remained at her post. About the time the room was cleared, she received a call.

"This is not a drill. Activate incoming ballistic missile alert received via USPACOM. Exercise. Exercise. Exercise."

Adams froze. The first sentence indicated the instructions were valid and to be followed. The last three words were agency code to indicate a test rather than an actual emergency. She'd been paid to push the wrong button and given a heads-up about the drill by her supervisor. But which command should she follow?

She did her duty. *Push the wrong button.*

Adams sent out an actual notification that triggered the state's ballistic missile preparations computer program. She even clicked through on a second screen, per safeguard protocols, to confirm the directive. Instantaneously, the alert message interrupted radio, television, and satellite broadcasts in California and, moments later, in Oregon and Washington, too.

Once the false alarm was rescinded and the panic subsided,

Adams told the head of Cal OES that the directive from her superiors had been confusing, and out of an abundance of caution, she'd issued the alert. She never revealed the payment she'd received or the brief conversation with her supervisor. She claimed to be one hundred percent certain issuing the alert was the right thing to do, and if anyone was to blame, it was the government for their system and process failures.

It took the Cal OES twenty-three minutes to override the alert and notify its citizens of the false alarm. Fear and panic spread across the West Coast like wildfire as residents were gripped with confusion. With no warning and little in the way of instructions, most people were unsure of what to do.

The next day, the death toll was in the hundreds from accidents, suicides, and heart attacks. Criticism was directed toward the governor of California and Cal OES. The governor immediately called on the legislature to form a commission to study the cause of the incident and the aftermath when it came back into session next week. Congress vowed to start hearings to assess the nation's emergency alert protocols to coincide with California's investigation.

The state and national politicians were unified in their statements condemning the mistake. They also agreed that hearings beginning on Monday would focus on the fact it was time to prepare the nation for the types of nuclear strikes endured by the people of the four countries on the other side of the world.

Next week, the politicians promised, they would tackle this very important issue.

CHAPTER THIRTY-NINE

Tuesday, October 22
Dumbarton Bridge
San Francisco Bay

Owen ran like the wind after he'd reached the end of Dumbarton Bridge and hit terra firma. Word had spread amongst the pedestrians fleeing to the east that Patterson Elementary School near the Nimitz Freeway had a fallout shelter. Thousands of people from the surrounding neighborhood coupled with stranded motorists attempted to cram into the closed school. They broke through windows and doors only to run helter-skelter in search of the basement facility that didn't exist. About the time Owen gave up on the quest for safety and exited the school into the driving rain, the notification came through the alert system advising Californians of the false alarm.

Relief turned to anger. People whipped each other into an angry mob that vowed to march on Sacramento the next day to voice their displeasure. *Things have to change*, they yelled. *Recall the governor* was shouted by some.

Owen ignored the rancor and focused on how he was going to

get his car off the bridge. Hundreds of motorists had fled their vehicles, looking for safety. Some had perished as they'd crossed the concrete dividers into oncoming westbound traffic. The bridge was littered with mauled and mangled bodies that had been run over repeatedly. Owen suspected many of those who'd died drove cars abandoned ahead of his.

He was at least twenty miles from the house. In the rain, and wearing Johnston & Murphy dress shoes, he'd be lucky to make it there in seven to eight hours unless Lacey could meet him somewhere in between.

Then there was the matter of Lacey's car, which he'd driven so she could pack the Expedition. The four-door Nissan sedan would probably be towed to an impound lot somewhere. It would be aggravating trying to find out, and he suspected a fee might be charged. But the prospect of waiting for hours that might even stretch into daytime tomorrow to fix the mess didn't appeal to Owen.

He tried to call Lacey and Tucker. The call wouldn't go through, as everyone else in the state at the time was doing the same thing. Owen thought of what was left in the car. He didn't bring his work home at night, so there was no briefcase or laptop. There were no valuables in the glove box. He felt his pockets for the keys and realized, in his panic, he'd left them in the ignition. If it was stolen, he had insurance.

He loosened his tie, set his jaw, and started the trek home, doing his best to avoid the angry motorists who couldn't decide if the traffic jams or the overall predicament should be the target of their ire. The streets were clogged with debris, vehicles, and pedestrian refugees. A continuous downpour from the sky added to the aggravation.

In that moment, barely a mile into his walk home, he decided the family should start their vacation a day early.

CHAPTER FORTY

"Where are they all going, Mom?" asked Tucker, not expecting his mother to have a definitive answer. "I thought they always said to shelter in place. Maybe they think there are actual shelters somewhere when there aren't." Tucker shook his head in dismay when seconds later the alert cancelling the prior notification was transmitted to their cell phones and through the Expedition's satellite radio.

"Finally, right?" asked Lacey facetiously. She'd questioned leaving the house during those frantic few minutes when she'd unsuccessfully tried to reach Owen by phone. She'd made the decision to load up Tucker and some supplies into the truck so they could flee toward the east. It was what she would've instructed Owen to do.

"Yeah," muttered Tucker as he tried to call his dad again. They were both amazed at how overloaded the cell phone network was. "Look on the bright side, Mom."

Lacey chuckled. The windshield wipers were whipping back and forth as the heavens were bringing a lot of rainfall to the Bay Area but not inland where the farmers needed it. It was an odd weather anomaly caused by Pacific Ocean currents and the Santa Ana winds.

"There's a bright side?" she asked.

"Yeah. We got to do a practice run."

"And failed miserably," she added.

"Maybe so, but at least we'll be ready if it does happen someday. You know, I've got a friend in school whose dad is into ham radios. I wonder if they'd work instead of cell phones right now."

Lacey shrugged and then nodded her head. "You know, I've got the Garmin two-ways that we use when we go hiking, but they have a limited range."

Tucker laughed. "For sure. The box says fifty miles, but that's if nothing is in the way. Heck, pine trees block the signal sometimes. I think ham radios, even those portable ones, might work better."

"We had marine band radios at Driftwood Key," Lacey recalled. "Granddaddy taught me how to use them. He said they were like two-ways except stronger."

"I've seen them at Walmart. We should get a few. You know, just in case."

Lacey turned the truck down the winding road that led back to their neighborhood. Traffic began to dissipate. They'd arrived at the wrought-iron security gates and entered the subdivision. Their neighbors were standing on their covered porches, commiserating with each other. A couple waved to her in an effort to have her join the conversation, but she continued home. Lacey had a single focus, and that was to make sure her husband was safe.

As soon as she parked the truck and began to open the garage door, Tucker jumped out and raced underneath the half-open door. She followed him shortly thereafter, and by the time he entered the hallway through the garage, he was shouting to her.

"Dad left a voicemail. He's okay. He's walking home. He got stuck on the bridge and just left the car. He thinks it might take him seven hours or so."

"What time did he call?"

"Twenty minutes ago," replied Tucker as his mom joined him in the kitchen.

She walked over to the *junk drawer*, as they called it. It was in the far end of their expansive kitchen counter. The junk drawer was the least useful for purposes of cooking but was ideal for filling up with notepads, pens, rubber bands, and just about anything else that didn't have a regular, family-approved storage location. She pulled out a pen and paper.

"I'm gonna write him a note to let him know we're safe. We'll head down the ridge toward the Dumbarton to find him. I'm hoping we can connect by phone in the meantime, but just in case, he'll know to stay here."

Tucker grabbed a Red Bull for himself and a Cherry Coke Zero for his mom while she wrote out the note. Lacey was full of emotion as she wrote the final words—we love you. She wiped the tears off her face and nervously laughed at herself.

Tucker was leaning against the counter. He took a swig of Red Bull and stifled a belch.

"You're such a girl, Mom."

"Brilliant observation, son," she said with a chuckle. "I'm just glad your dad is okay. Now, let's go find him."

Tucker handed his mom the can of soda. "Should we bring him some clothes?"

Lacey beamed. Tucker had more common sense and empathy than she'd had when she was a teen. Hank had taught her to be a boy, but her mom had raised her as a young woman. Tucker was all boy, yet he had flashes of maturity she hadn't had growing up. She gave him a smile and darted up to their master bedroom to retrieve a gym bag, which she filled with jeans, a sweatshirt, socks and sneakers.

"Hey, Mom! Text messaging between phones is working again. It's Dad. He's at the Safeway on Decoto Road."

"Tell him we're on our way!"

Lacey raced down the stairs, two at a time, just like a boy.

CHAPTER FORTY-ONE

Tuesday, October 22
Mount Weather Emergency Operations Center
Northern Virginia

The Mount Weather Emergency Operations Center was hidden away in the small community of Bluefield, Virginia, near the state's border with West Virginia. It was one of America's best-kept secrets as an unacknowledged continuity-of-government facility operated under the auspices of FEMA.

The two-hundred-thousand-square-foot facility, with multiple structures both above and below ground, encompassed a four-hundred-thirty-four-acre mountain site. Two hundred forty employees kept the lines of communication open between the high-level government officials buried deep underground and their counterparts around the world.

Based on a favorable evaluation of the hardness and integrity of the mountain's rock by the Bureau of Mines in the 1930s, construction began on the facility's tunnels in 1954, which was completed by the Army Corps of Engineers under the code name *Operation High Point.*

The billion-dollar facility included a system of tunnels with roofs shored up by iron bolts driven eight to ten feet into the overhead rock. The entrance was protected by a guillotine-style gate and a ten-foot-tall by twenty-foot-wide thirty-four-ton blast door that was five feet thick. It took almost fifteen minutes to open or close.

The underground bunker included a hospital, crematorium, dining and recreation areas, sleeping quarters, reservoirs of drinking and cooling water, an emergency power plant, and a radio and television studio, which was part of the Emergency Broadcasting System. A series of side tunnels connected with a total of twenty belowground office complexes, some of which were three stories tall. The East Tunnel included a computer complex for directing emergency simulations and wartime operations.

An on-site sewage treatment plant capable of processing ninety thousand gallons a day was coupled with two quarter-million-gallon aboveground storage tanks designed to support a population of two hundred for more than a month.

Although the facility was designed to accommodate several thousand people with sleeping cots, only the president, members of the cabinet, high-ranking military commanders, and Supreme Court justices were provided private sleeping quarters.

The president was told this might be an intermediary holdover until after the threat had passed. Based upon confirmed, active intelligence, he'd either return to the White House or be sent to Cheyenne Mountain, where he could better interact with his military commanders.

The planning of the president and the staffers who made up the White House operations team was timely, although complicated by the ballistic missile alert issued on the West Coast. The human side of the administration was safely tucked inside the bombproof bunker. However, the computers and files necessary to operate the government hadn't arrived before the blast doors were forced to shut. The delivery trucks had been redirected to secure locations, and it wouldn't be until the next day before their contents were delivered.

For the first time late that evening as midnight approached, the former Pennsylvanian who grew up in a coal-mining family got settled into the former Bureau of Mines property. He wasn't sure if the false alarm was intentional or truly human error, as the young woman had professed to investigators. He tried to think through the events, especially the timing, to determine if there was a connection to the activities of his secret task force.

He couldn't discern what the purpose might be. Why instigate a panic now when the possibility of actual nuclear retaliation by North Korea or China could come very soon? He shrugged off his own questions. He'd been assured by those he'd hand-selected for this job that their experience immersed in the inner workings of the DC bureaucracy would yield the result he sought.

The president insisted upon plausible deniability. When the time came to cross the Rubicon and pull the nuclear trigger, he needed to be shocked and disturbed that he, as president of the most powerful nation on earth, was forced to take such a dangerous, hostile action.

The term *crossing the Rubicon* was based upon an ancient event. In 49 BC, Julius Caesar prepared to cross the Rubicon River in present-day northeastern Italy during his quest to conquer Rome. To cross the Rubicon was a metaphor that meant to take an irrevocable step toward a risky or even revolutionary course of action. Many equate it with the more modern phrase *passing the point of no return.*

President Helton understood the risks and ramifications of his plan. It was calculated, to be sure, but also predicated on the counsel of the men and women who'd worked in Washington most of their adult lives. He felt certain their advice was sound, and because it comported with one of his unstated goals to accomplish as president, he likely downplayed the risks to suit his purpose.

The hour was fast approaching. He, like Julius Caesar, stood on the precipice of greatness or an abyss that would resemble Hell on Earth.

PART VI

ONE WEEK IN OCTOBER

Day six, Wednesday, October 23

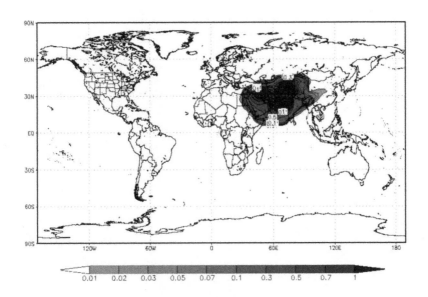

CHAPTER FORTY-TWO

Wednesday, October 23
Driftwood Key

Hank Albright wasn't a very good liar. In fact, he was terrible at it. That, coupled with the look of genuine guilt on his face, made many of the guests he was evicting from the hotel question his reasoning. They most likely understood his motives.

All of them had spent much of their vacation time monitoring the news in one way or another. In society, it was not unusual to observe any given public setting and see eyes focused on smartphones, perusing news or entertainment websites. Walking down the sidewalk of a busy city street, heads were bowed to read the screens. Sitting in the stadium of sporting events, fans alternated their attention between the actual game and the replays shown on streaming television via an app. A couple sitting at dinner in a restaurant or at home shoveled food in their mouth with one hand while scrolling through their media source of choice with the other. Rarely would they speak to one another except to point out a perceived newsworthy item.

Those outside habits and influences had found their way into the Driftwood Key Inn. So that morning, when guests woke up to no water in their bathrooms and a gentle knocking at the door with a letter containing the bad news about the water main break, many were not surprised. Some actually welcomed it. The directive to leave the inn made the decision for those who were on the fence of whether they should stay or go home.

By noon, all the guests had hurriedly left. The reservations for the rest of the month had been rescheduled. The housekeeping staff and bartenders had been instructed to button up their various areas of responsibilities as if a hurricane were coming.

Once the final guest had departed, Hank and Sonny closed the iron gates leading across the private bridge connecting the two keys. Only Mike and Jessica had keys to unlock the dual padlocks holding the thick steel chain wrapped through the doors.

Hank stood there for a moment. His hands were thrust into his pockets as he stared off into the mature groupings of mangroves that lined the bridge on the other side. Their exposed roots clung to the fine sandy soil surrounded by brackish water. He wondered how many mangrove snappers were feeding just below the surface. The thought reminded him of a gift he'd purchased himself, as well as one for Jimmy—a gutting and cleaning knife with a spoon attached to the handle, made by Morakniv.

He turned to Sonny. "What do you have Jimmy doin' this morning?"

"Same as the others, really. Hurricane preparations. You know, putting away anything that's not tied down. I don't know what's gonna happen, Mr. Hank, but your idea to treat it like a hurricane made perfect sense."

"Did he fish this morning?" asked Hank.

Sonny gave him a puzzled look and then made a joke. "Ain't nobody got time for fishin' in the apocalypse."

Hank laughed. At least that particular morning, anyway. Once the key was secured, they'd have to continue their daily routine, and fishing was a big part of it. The catch of the day, whether reeled in by Hank or Jimmy, fed the guests and those who resided on Driftwood Key. They'd need to continue that practice to avoid eating the foods stored by Phoebe. Besides, for Hank, it was therapeutic.

As they walked back to the main house, Jimmy emerged from a trail leading through a variety of palms to the corrugated storage building where all the beach chairs, umbrellas, and kayaks were stored.

"I put everything away, Mr. Hank. What's next?"

Before Hank could answer, his phone rang. It was Mike.

"Hey, I thought you guys were gonna bring over your stuff this morning," Hank answered without so much as a hello.

Mike spoke loudly over the sounds of running car engines and the occasional horn blaring. "Yeah, that was the plan. Jessica's truck is loaded with our gear. Just as we were about to come over, we both got called in. The overseas highway is one helluva hot mess."

"People leaving?"

"By the thousands," Mike replied. "Central tried to treat it like a hurricane evac, but that was an epic fail. Sure, there are a lot of people spooked by all this nuke shit. They checked out early, trying to get a head start home. Either they all had the same idea at the same time, or this is just the beginning."

"Why don't you guys send all lanes northbound?"

"Because there are still people who don't care about the news. They'd rather waste away in Margaritaville than see the doom and gloom on the television."

"Geez. You've got 'em comin' and goin'."

"That's right, Mr. Innkeeper. Not all of these hotels down here are as conscientious as you are. All of these people should stay home."

"Well, they don't know what we know either. Maybe the people in Washington should get a clue? Just put it all out there, and let adults decide for themselves."

Horns started screaming in a variety of pitches. Mike screamed in the phone. "Hey! Back off, asshole!" He returned to the call. "Hank, I gotta run. We'll get there as soon as possible."

"Good luck."

"Oh, Hank? One more thing. Jess is gonna bring the rescue boat this afternoon. She's not comfortable leaving it at our place if we're not gonna be staying there."

Hank looked over at Jimmy and then glanced down the dock at his Hatteras. "I'll have Jimmy make room."

The SAFE Boat, its trademark name, had been purchased with grant funds from the Department of Homeland Security. Built for speed and endurance and designed to handle both Atlantic and Gulf waters in all conditions, the thirty-one-foot boat, used in numerous patrols and emergencies, had been credited with saving the lives of many people in distress over the years.

The inboard diesel jet boat had a weatherproof cabin with an eighteen-person capacity. Its top speed was about fifty-five mph. It was built to withstand harsh conditions, designed to be unsinkable, and was equipped with advanced technology, including radar and digital performance data. Jessica, a PADI-certified rescue diver, kept her tanks and gear on board at all times.

The two brothers disconnected the call just as the men reached the main house. Once inside, they found Phoebe sitting at a table in the bar, going over her ledgers and watching the news. The split screen revealed a scientist on one hand and a raging wildfire in India shown from the perspective aboard the International Space Station.

The screen switched to a graphic showing the spread of soot and debris from the nuclear war between India and Pakistan. Deep purple on the graphic indicated extensive soot coverage. The lighter tones of red were found on the outskirts of the cloud that spread across the planet. It stretched from Japan in the Far East across the whole of Europe.

The scientist then explained what his modeling projected. The billions of tons of soot in the air from the nuclear explosions and resulting wildfires would almost completely circumnavigate the Earth in just a matter of days. When pressed by the news host as to when it would dissipate, he simply shook his head and replied, "Years, hopefully."

CHAPTER FORTY-THREE

Wednesday, October 23
Islamorada
Florida Keys

"It's gonna take years to clear this damn traffic out of here!" Mike shouted to one of his fellow detectives relegated to traffic duty in response to the mass exodus out of the Florida Keys. Both men would rather be finding the serial killer in their midst rather than waving their arms and chiding motorists for driving along the shoulder to get ahead of the rest of those hustling home.

Panic had spread amongst the visitors as the second nuclear exchange not only provided Americans a glimpse into the aftermath of an attack but speculation began to ramp up as to what might happen next.

On the one hand, many had been pressuring President Helton to take a stance and join in the defense of America's allies Israel and India. Political pundits had gone so far as to lay blame on the president for the Pakistani strikes because he'd failed to stand by Israel.

On the other hand, there were those who argued battles abroad, whether nuclear or conventional, were none of Washington's concern unless they directly affected American interests.

Regardless of which political position the experts took, all agreed that the world had become increasingly unstable, and the threat of North Korea, China, and Russia joining the fray had increased exponentially.

The night before, Mike, Jessica and Hank had had their own roundtable discussion on the beach with cocktails and cigars. None of them expected the Florida Keys to be the target of a nuclear strike. They presumed the highest-value targets for America's enemies were political, populated, and nuclear related.

The discussion of EMP weapons came up. This concerned them as much as the nuclear strikes. While they wouldn't be directly in the line of fire from the nuclear detonation, the electromagnetic pulse generated from the ground strikes could cause the nation's power grid to collapse. The three agreed it would take years to repair, and they'd have to be prepared for this eventuality.

Today, all three of them were supposed to scour the Middle and Lower Keys for supplies that would keep them alive in the event something like that happened. Instead, Mike and Jessica were forced into traffic control.

Mike and his fellow detective were attempting to have this conversation at an intersection packed with motorists. They'd stopped both lanes to allow vehicles to exit the Publix shopping center and the residential areas behind it. Frustrated drivers slammed their steering wheels and dashboards over the one-minute delay.

At one point, Mike chuckled to himself, although his thought was not meant to be humorous. *How are these people supposed to handle nukes landing on America if they can't keep from losing their minds over a traffic delay?*

"Is it true the people from Tallahassee are pulling out?" the detective asked, shouting his question to Mike.

"Yeah!" he replied in an equally loud voice. "They've got the jitters up there about what might happen. They watch the news like the rest of these folks."

"Are we changing our schedules?"

"Not as far as I'm concerned. The killer doesn't plan on changing his."

"Good work on identifying the vics!" the detective yelled.

"The problem is there is no connection between the three whatsoever," said Mike as traffic was cleared to move again. He lowered his voice as the two men joined each other on the side of the road. "Listen, here's the thing. We need more evidence. A clue of some kind. Sadly, that means another body or even a foiled attempt by the killer."

The detective waved his hand up and down the highway. "Maybe all of this will disrupt his habits? You know, take away his opportunities or at least make them more difficult."

"Even better, wouldn't it be nice if he was in one of these cars headed north?"

Seconds later, a black Lexus sedan drove by the two detectives. The darkened windows designed to block out the sun also served to deter prying eyes from seeing inside. Its tan interior had been scrubbed several times with bleaching agents, and every fiber of the sedan's carpets had been vacuumed to perfection.

The driver, the branch manager of the Island State Bank, kept his face forward, but his eyes moved to study the two men directing traffic. He recognized Mike Albright. Mr. Big Shot homicide detective. The man who didn't have a clue as to who just drove past him.

It was lunchtime, and he was ravenous. Not just for the local fare from Bad Boy Burritos, aptly named for a man with a gruesome secret fetish. The fish tacos would provide him sustenance. However, they'd do nothing for his hunger.

Tonight, he'd hunt. Again.

The heavy traffic headed toward Key West didn't aggravate him like the other drivers around him. They represented new opportunities. Fresh meat. Happy vacationers ready to release their inhibitions.

To take a walk on the wild side.

With Patricia.

CHAPTER FORTY-FOUR

Wednesday, October 23
Hayward, California

Lacey and her family slept in after the harrowing events of the day before. They'd stayed up until near dawn rehashing the events and discussing their plans. The consensus was to wrap up all loose ends and prepare to travel into the mountains. None of them believed a nuclear strike was going to happen. They were not a family of alarmists. Nonetheless, their planned getaway seemed to fit nicely with leaving one of the top nuclear targets in America.

Lacey was the first to rise and immediately noticed the rain had stopped. It wouldn't start again. For a long, long while.

Everyone was tasked with a variety of activities to prepare for their afternoon departure. After retrieving Lacey's car, Owen spent an hour or so in the offices of Yahoo, ensuring his projects were able to move forward in his absence. He'd advised the team working on the transition he'd implemented to contact him through their North Lake Tahoe hotel, as they planned on camping most of the time and wouldn't have cell phone service.

Lacey and Tucker went shopping for additional supplies that had come to mind following the disaster app's false alarm. As saddened as they were about the loss of life, the family agreed the trial run was an eye-opener.

In the event of a real emergency, there would be no order. They couldn't necessarily expect help from their fellow man, much less first responders, who'd be overwhelmed with calls. As Owen put it, it was incumbent upon them as responsible adults to be ready. To take care of themselves rather than be a burden on emergency services.

As late afternoon arrived, the sun was lowering on the horizon. Owen and Tucker had finished attaching the tow dolly to the Expedition. The Bronco was firmly secured, and both vehicles were packed with gear and supplies.

Lacey had chosen not to follow her father's request to buy plane tickets for the three of them and flee to Driftwood Key. There was no guarantee that the media speculation would result in the U.S. becoming embroiled in a nuclear war. Even Peter had equivocated when his best advice was to prepare and know where to seek cover. He'd never advocated abandoning their home and racing to the Keys.

Not that Lacey could have anyway. Flights leaving the West Coast were completely full for days. Standby passengers slept on the floors of airports, hoping to get a seat. Families split up, using separate flights and destinations, all in an attempt to get to a safer location in the event war broke out.

Interstate highways leaving the major West Coast cities were jam-packed. Impatience resulted in accidents. Accidents resulted in more accidents.

It was five o'clock when they pulled out of the driveway. The normally orange sun was setting as always. Only, on this evening, it cast a different hue. Tucker called it a halo. Owen recalled a visit to Saudi Arabia when he'd observed the sun rise in the throes of a sandstorm. Lacey described it the most accurately. It was if the sun were in fact setting in the Pacific Ocean, and its heat was sending vapor clouds into the sky all around it.

The soot, black carbon remnants of the fires and debris from India and Pakistan, had begun to cross the Pacific Ocean. The sun fell over the horizon, as always, but it was obscured by the smoky film that began to cover the Earth.

As the family zigzagged through back roads toward Sacramento and North Lake Tahoe beyond the state's capital, night set in, and their view to the west was darkened. Had they been at home the next morning, they would've been awakened by the smell of charred wood, and their eyes would've watered from the soot.

And there would've been a noticeable chill in the air.

Their drive would've normally taken three and a half hours on Interstate 80. They liked to travel at night to avoid the rush-hour madness in San Francisco and Sacramento. Based on traffic reports indicating a mass exodus from the Bay Area, they chose small highways and county roads to make their trip, adding an extra hour or so to the drive.

Because they all slept until late morning, they were rested and in good spirits. None of them wanted to discuss the threat of nuclear Armageddon. They recalled past trips camping in the Tahoe National Forest or snowboarding at the ski resorts around Lake Tahoe. Even though they checked into a relatively inexpensive, $99 hotel room at the Biltmore Lodge & Casino, they rarely stayed in the room. It was merely a base of operations, as Owen called it, in the event of bad weather or, heaven forbid, an injury. Hotel rooms filled up quickly around Lake Tahoe, so Owen always made sure they had a place to stay besides their tents.

The drive soon grew tiresome for Owen. The amount of traffic headed eastbound away from the coastal region astonished them all. Tucker checked his disaster app from time to time, wondering if something had happened they were unaware of. Eventually, they turned on their satellite radio and even scrolled through some of the local news-talk radio stations.

People were afraid. They were looking for a safe harbor from the coming storm. A haven where they could seek sanctuary in the event of the unthinkable—nuclear missiles flying toward them.

As midnight approached, it had taken them several hours longer than on any normal day to get to Sacramento. News reports equated Interstate 80 with a parking lot. Owen, with Tucker's navigational assistance, made their way around the south side of the city, hoping to pick up the interstate on the mountainous east side of the city near Auburn. From there, they could pick up the Eisenhower Highway toward Colfax, through Donner Pass, and into Nevada.

Well, you know what they say about the best-laid plans.

They often go awry.

CHAPTER FORTY-FIVE

Wednesday, October 23
The Pentagon

Peter roamed the Pentagon in search of anyone who'd speak to him about the North Korean threat. He was now intrigued about the special, albeit hidden relationship between the secretary of state and the president. He'd spent an hour at Foggy Bottom, scouring the State Department for leads, but nearly everyone of consequence had been instructed to shelter-in-place at home and work remotely on their laptops. He was finding the same type of skeleton crew working the Pentagon that afternoon.

He'd checked his watch continuously as he awaited Jenna's exit from a meeting. She'd reported to him the night before that the vast majority of Pentagon top brass had been relocated to either Cheyenne Mountain in Colorado or to Raven Rock in Pennsylvania. Only a few members of the Joint Chiefs were traveling with the president to Mount Weather.

The meeting she was attending would be her last in the Pentagon until the crisis was over. She was being taken to the Raven Rock Mountain Complex, commonly known as Site R, although members of the media preferred calling it the Underground Pentagon.

Regardless of its moniker, the massive subterranean bunker was designed to be an alternate seat of government but later became dedicated to Pentagon operations. The multilevel, self-sufficient bunker had two underground water reservoirs, its own power plant, food reserves, and tunnels connecting the equivalent of several three-story freestanding buildings.

"Hey, Peter," she greeted him from behind. He'd been deep in thought and was startled somewhat by her sudden appearance. He jumped slightly and then turned to meet her.

"Hey. How'd it go?"

Her response was simple. "Raven Rock."

In that moment, Peter realized why he was in a melancholy mood. He and Jenna had never taken their relationship to the next level, and now he was faced with the reality they might never have that chance. The two young and attractive people were dedicated to rising the ladder of success within the Beltway rather than looking for their soul mates. The dour moods they emitted was an indicator they both felt the same way.

"When?" he asked, hoping for one more night with his best friend with benefits.

"Sixteen hundred." Jenna looked down at the polished tile floor nervously. She looked around the hallway to see if anyone was eavesdropping on their conversation. "Um, Peter, there's something else."

He stepped closer with a concerned look on his face. "What is it?" Peter studied her eyes.

She moved closer and gripped him by the arm. "You need to find a safe place. Away from DC. Far away."

"It's happening, isn't it?"

She grimaced and looked away. "Let's put it this way. We're as close as we were during that October of '62. Only, Khrushchev was sane and predictable compared to Kim Jong Un."

"Do you think he'll fire on us?"

"Not necessarily. The war planners feel he could take a shot at Seoul. If he does, we'll have to defend South Korea. That will necessarily result in an escalation that might bring in ..." Her voice trailed off, so Peter completed her sentence.

"China," he said just above a whisper. "Jenna, this is crazy out of control. Can't they find a way to tamp all of this down?"

"Maybe. The president is conferring with the secretary of state this afternoon. The United Nations is one option. Moscow is another, if you can believe that."

"What? Seriously? Why would they step in?"

"One, they have a lot of nukes pointed at us. While they tend to lean toward China from a geopolitical standpoint, they recognize the damage that would be caused by Washington and Beijing duking it out. There's a belief in this building that Russia could convince cooler heads to prevail."

Peter shrugged and shook his head. "That's a long shot."

"It is. The other pressure is from the UN, but they've had little influence over North Korea in the past."

"Bribery," quipped Peter. North Korea was notorious for demanding a king's ransom from world powers for the mere promise of behaving like a civilized nation. It had always worked. For a while.

"Yes." Jenna glanced at her watch. "I'm sorry. I don't have much time. I need to meet with the rest of the communications team as we divide up our responsibilities. Others are being dispatched to Cheyenne Mountain and Mount Weather."

Peter looked glum. "I know. You gotta go."

Jenna spontaneously hugged and kissed him. They'd always made a point to avoid public displays of affection since they were technically on opposite sides of the podium.

Peter hugged her back, and they held their embrace for nearly a minute. Then, with a final kiss, a goodbye, and a promise to be safe, the two parted ways. One left for the safety of a hardened nuclear bunker. The other for his condo, his mind full of conflict as to what he should do.

PART VII

ONE WEEK IN OCTOBER

Day seven, Thursday, October 24

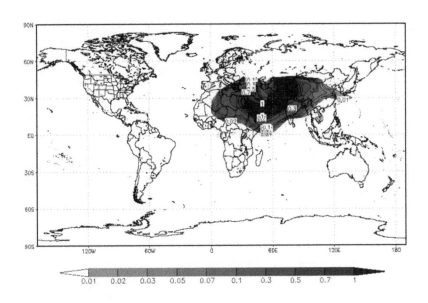

CHAPTER FORTY-SIX

The 2008 Democratic primary campaign advertisement had been deemed one of the best in modern history. The scene, ominous, if not creepy, began in the middle of the night. It was 3:00 a.m. Sleeping children. A ringing telephone. The undertone of a matter of grave importance in the narrator's voice. It was a who-do-you-want-in-charge, Cold War-esque display asking voters whom they trusted to lead the country during a world crisis when that phone rang in the middle of the night.

Every president had their three-in-the-morning phone call moment. This was President Carter Helton's. Ironically, just after 3:00 a.m.

He was awakened by his chief of staff, and he hurriedly dressed in a pair of Penn State University sweats. There was no time for decorum, as nuclear weapons had been launched once again.

North Korea had been relatively quiet throughout the exchange of ballistic missiles in South Asia. In the past twenty-four hours, that had changed. During the DPRK's 13th Party Congress, Kim did a lot of chest-puffing. Apparently, he was prepared to follow through on his threats.

Most analysts believed if a second Korean war broke out with the use of nuclear weapons, it would be deadly, producing millions of deaths just in the South Korean capital of Seoul. However, if North Korea deployed their nuclear arsenal toward Japan as well, countless more millions would die.

Following the war handbook developed by Russia, the North Koreans had amassed troops and accompanying military assets on the border with South Korea in a show of force. Many thought they were feigning an invasion in an attempt to gain concessions at the UN bargaining table.

Then, mere minutes ago, they fired two nuclear-tipped ICBMs into South Korea. The first was successfully destroyed by the U.S. Aegis ballistic missile defense system located in Japan. The second warhead struck the heart of Seoul, vaporizing a million South Koreans instantly.

Seconds after the Aegis missiles were fired from Japanese soil, Kim turned his sights on Tokyo. He immediately declared war on Japan and initiated the launch sequence. Within minutes, three ICBMs were launched from missile silos on the east coast of North Korea toward Japan.

Tokyo's population of nine million plus lived in one of the highest density cities in the world. Two of the three ICBMs found their marks, devastating the city, including the famed Imperial Palace. Once again, the Aegis defense system worked, but with only marginal success.

Kim wasn't through yet. He saw the use of the U.S. built and maintained Aegis system being deployed against his nuclear arsenal as being tantamount to Washington declaring war on Pyongyang. He chose to ignore the defensive nature of the Aegis deployment.

He fired four ICBMs across the Pacific toward the West Coast of the United States and one toward Hawaii in rapid succession. Their estimated time of arrival was half past the hour of three in the morning. They were followed by a second wave of three more ICBMs that followed a different path over the Arctic Circle toward East Coast targets.

The U.S. missile defense system was a global network with twenty-four-hour surveillance by land, sea, and space-based sensors, all of which were constantly looking for signs of anything amiss in North Korea. Regional missile interceptors were deployed in Japan, South Korea, Guam and on U.S. Navy ships, while military bases in Alaska and California were equipped to intercept missiles headed toward the United States.

When North Korea launched their missiles, U.S. satellites detected them almost instantaneously through infrared signals. In less than a minute, the satellites raised the alarm, and the command-and-control center at Schriever Air Force Base near Colorado Springs, Colorado, sprang into action.

Minutes later, President Helton entered the operations center at Mount Weather. Thus far all decisions made in the defense of South Korea and Japan had been made by pre-established protocols and programmed responses. The same was true of the U.S. intercepts of the incoming ICBMs.

The command center at Cheyenne Mountain in Colorado immediately got involved. They directed the radars in the region to track the multiple missiles as they climbed toward outer space. During that five-to-seven-minute period of time, the radar systems gathered data, like trajectory, velocity and altitude, to send back to the command center. Complex computer analysis was applied so the military could identify what type of missile was launched and whether it could reach the U.S.

During this *boost phase* was the ideal time to intercept a missile, but the current defense system wasn't equipped to do so yet.

Normally, the officers at the command center would consult with U.S. Northern Command, Northcom, based at Peterson Air Force Base in Colorado Springs, where a round-the-clock watch officer would be responsible for approving an interceptor launch. If there was time, they might notify the secretary of defense in Washington, too.

However, under the circumstances, all hands were on deck, and the president himself was included in the discussions. It was agreed. Launch orders were approved and sent to Fort Greely and Vandenberg Air Force Base, both of which were best positioned to intercept.

It had been ten minutes since the North Korean missile launches were first detected. America's ground-based interceptors, or GBIs, were the only weapons capable of destroying an ICBM. Until that early morning on the seventh day of the global nuclear war, they'd only been tested against such a missile once—with success.

The U.S. only had thirty-six GBIs—four in California and thirty-two in Alaska. The secretary of defense recommended they launch two-to-three GBIs per incoming missile to improve the odds of success during an attack. That stockpile reduced the American defenses, and those advising the president cautioned U.S. defenses could theoretically be overpowered if North Korea were to fire multiple missiles after these first two barrages.

The president immediately ordered a counterstrike. While they acted to defend American soil, he surmised, they should shut down Kim's ability to hit them twice. The launch sequence was initiated, and seven powerful ICBMs were launched from their missile silos in the Northern Rockies toward North Korea.

At this point, the North Korean warheads were three-quarters of the way through their thirty-minute journey to the U.S. The military's success in defending against the multiple ICBMs was equated with hitting a bullet with another bullet. It had been done in simulations.

Against a single incoming ICBM.

In their simulations, never had the nation's nuclear defenses fought off multiple incoming missile threats at once.

"Ten minutes to first strike," a computer-generated voice announced through the operation center speakers mounted overhead.

There was nothing else for them to do. The launches, both defensive and offensive, had been effectuated. Now a president, and those in control of America's military might, waited.

While warning alarms and sirens were activated from sea to shining sea.

CHAPTER FORTY-SEVEN

Thursday, October 24
Driftwood Key

Mike wasn't able to sleep. He and Jessica had worked well into the evening, assisting Monroe County sheriff's deputies as they directed traffic in and out of the Florida Keys. At one point, in Key Largo, two drunk drivers ran into one another, triggering an all-out brawl where Atlantic Boulevard intersected with U.S. 1. It was a notoriously busy intersection where several streets came together, as well as multiple pedestrian crosswalks.

The two drunken men broke out in a fistfight. This triggered their inebriated girlfriends to join the fray. Soon other motorists, perturbed at the delay, tried to force their way past the wrecked cars in the center of the intersection. Push came to shove, literally, as bumpers were used to clear a path through. This resulted in more anger. When one of the motorists pulled a handgun and began to fire into the air, ostensibly to bring order to the mayhem, panic ensued.

The gunfire caused drivers to seek safety. They drove over curbs to race into parking lots. Some chose the median as the four-lane highway through Key Largo split. The median of the divided highway was soon filled with cars racing down the sidewalk, through parking lots of businesses, and over native plant material.

When order was finally restored, a fender bender between drunks resulted in four pedestrians being sent to the hospital, another half dozen with superficial wounds, and multiple accidents.

However, it was not news of the Key Largo madness that upset Mike the most. It was the fact he'd lost all assistance from the FDLE, and the detectives were turned into traffic cops, including himself.

That evening, as the drinks flowed, Mike and Jessica had vowed to call out sick the next day. During their entire career with the MCSO, neither had contracted the so-called *blue flu*, an act of defiance by law enforcement officers under the pretext of being ill. In this case, they simply wanted to catch a killer.

Hank raised a legitimate question. He'd asked, "In the scheme of things, wouldn't it be better to protect the living rather than worry about the dead?"

Mike disagreed with his brother and was blunt in his response. "There'll be more dead if we don't catch this guy."

The long evening stretched into the early morning hours of the next day. The group finally called it a night, with Hank going to bed first. Jessica was sound asleep as Mike stared at the ceiling, fuming over the day's events and contemplating the ramifications of bucking his superiors.

Just as he was about to doze off, both of their cell phones began to vibrate and emit an alert. The buzz and tone had the same sound as those used for Amber alerts and catastrophic weather warnings. Unlike the Amber and weather alerts, cell phone users cannot mute, silence, or turn off the presidential alert, as it was called. The message was meant to include critical lifesaving information, such as a nuclear attack.

It was 3:17 a.m. The continuous rhythmic tone shook Jessica awake and prompted Mike to jump out of bed in search of his phone. Then the computer-generated voice made the announcement.

*"Attention. Attention. This is the National Warning Center. Emergency.
This is an Attack Warning. Repeat. This is an Attack Warning."*

At that moment, across America and its territories, FEMA interrupted radio and television broadcasts. The FAA sent alerts to all airborne pilots and air traffic control centers. NOAA interrupted its weather radio network. The Coast Guard broadcast nuclear war warnings to all mariners at sea in the Atlantic, Pacific, and Gulf of Mexico.

IPAWS, the acronym for the Integrated Public Alert and Warning System, combined the Emergency Alert System used for decades with the new addition, the Wireless Emergency Alerts System. It was functioning on all cylinders.

Nine minutes after the nuclear ICBMs were launched from North Korea toward the U.S., the warnings were activated. It was estimated the incoming nukes would strike their West Coast targets within twenty-two minutes. The East Coast had two minutes beyond that.

"What did it say?" asked Jessica, who was still groggy from the drinks and the limited sleep.

"It said the shit just hit the fan," replied Mike as he searched for the light switch. The couple was staying in a guest room upstairs that they hadn't used in a while. It was located at the end of the hall on the opposite side of the house where Hank's master bedroom was located.

With the lights on, he scrambled to get his clothes on. He was desperate to get downstairs and turn on the television. Jessica stayed in bed with the sheet pulled up over her chest. She tried to read the alert on her phone with just one eye open.

Mike raced out of their room to wake up Hank. Just as he reached his door, Hank flung it open, half-dressed.

"You got it, too?" Hank asked his brother.

"Yeah."

"Do you think it's real or a false alarm like before?"

"I'm about to find out," Mike responded. Barefoot, he hustled down the wide, sweeping staircase leading to the foyer of the main house. He rushed into the bar, turned on the lights, and skipped looking for the remote. He reached up to turn on the television, which had been on CNN for days during the drama. The screen confirmed his greatest fear.

"God help us."

The voice was Phoebe's. She stood in the opening with Sonny and Jimmy. Hank and Jessica arrived behind them. All of their eyes were transfixed on the television. Their mouths were agape but couldn't speak a word.

CHAPTER FORTY-EIGHT

Thursday, October 24
Falls Church, Virginia

Peter had stayed up for hours drinking the last beers in his refrigerator and eating two frozen CPK pizzas. He couldn't recall the last time he'd been depressed and wasn't sure if that was what he was going through now. He scoured online news sources and monitored social media for any indication of what might be happening on the Korean Peninsula. His mind constantly wandered to Jenna. He missed having her to text with, or even for their occasional sleepovers. Moreover, he worried for her safety when he should've been worried about his own.

Mentally exhausted and just a little drunk, he went to bed, leaving the muted television on with BBC International playing. His cell phone had fallen between the seat cushions of his couch. The lights were on. All out of character for the man who normally kept his condo neat. Tonight, he simply wasn't interested in being responsible.

Peter bypassed the usual stages of sleep and went directly into REM sleep characterized by rapid eye movement and dreaming.

Physiologically, REM was very different from stages one through four of the sleep processes. Muscles become atonic, meaning without movement. Breathing became erratic, and the body's heart rate increased dramatically.

During REM, dreams became more vivid and were often remembered upon awakening. External stimuli, such as sounds and movements, were sometimes disregarded by the brain despite the fact they were real. Oftentimes, it was difficult to differentiate between the visions of the dream and the actual sounds surrounding the sleeper.

Peter's dream was an odd combination of his past interactions with Jenna and a nightmarish apocalyptic movie that was part *Walking Dead*, part *Thirteen Days*, the story of the Cuban Missile Crisis featuring Kevin Costner.

In his dream, he'd placed himself in the bunker with the president, visualizing the decision-making process in real time. He heard the warning signals being emitted from the myriad of computer stations in the control room filled with snappily dressed military leaders. Then his dreamy state rushed outside the safe confines of the bunker, where it witnessed a fireball followed by a mushroom cloud.

The imagery of a nuclear detonation blinded him in his sleep, causing him to roll over to bury his face in the pillow. Then, as quickly as the cloud expanded into the atmosphere, human figures appeared to walk out of the fire. They were charred and still smoldering. Skin had peeled away from their bones while muscles and organs melted before his eyes.

And there were the screams. Ghostly. Eerie. Painful. Souls in agony as they begged for help. Not help for their wounds. They sought someone to put them out of their misery.

What didn't fit into his fitful dreams were the incessant beeping sounds accompanied by an electronic, monotone voice. The wails of the dead or dying contradicted the repetition of the computer-generated monster filling his head.

Frustrated by his inability to reconcile the intrusion of the outside voice with the nightmarish scene he was visualizing in his mind, Peter opened his eyes and shot up in bed. He blinked twice in order to focus on the cheap LED clock on his nightstand. It was 3:27 a.m. He took a deep breath and listened.

The voice was muffled, as if someone was sitting on the head of the person speaking. His mind raced. Or was the voice being smothered by a pillow in an attempt to silence the warning?

Peter jumped out of bed naked, disregarding the open curtains in his first-floor bedroom that he'd failed to close when he'd passed out earlier. He rushed into his living room. The BBC International broadcast had been replaced with the IPAWS warning chyron.

He rustled through the couch and found his cell phone. Peter was fully awake now, standing in his living room unclothed and completely lucid. He noticed the time of the first text alert. He checked the time on his iPhone, which was most accurate. It had been eleven minutes.

"Dammit!" he yelled loud enough to wake his adjoining neighbors if they hadn't been awakened already. Shadows of people milling about in the hallway forced Peter to remember he was naked. He raced back to the bedroom and quickly put on a fresh set of clothes.

As he dressed, he tried to remember how long it took the IPAWS system to activate after an ICBM missile launch had been identified. How many minutes did it take to identify the launch? Who did it? Russia? China? North Korea? From where? Land-based or submarines right off our coast somewhere?

Peter gave up and rushed to the closet. He grabbed his black backpack and the tactical sling-style pack that contained his handgun, ammo, and several other items. Within two minutes, he'd filled his backpack with clothing, and he dashed out the door, leaving the lights on and the television playing. There was no time for that. In fact, he wasn't sure if there was time to escape the number one nuclear target in America, the White House, less than ten miles away.

Peter bulled his way through confused neighbors. He'd never

gotten to know them, and now was not the time to introduce himself. He hurdled the shrubs lining the sidewalk outside his building and rushed between parked cars until he reached his Ford Mustang Mach 1. In that moment, he found himself thanking God for the four-hundred-eighty horsepower the car provided him to escape what was coming.

He never slowed down to think about what he was doing. He was frenzied, intent on going as far west as possible. Hiding in a bathtub, or under a desk in a school room, or in the basement of an office building was not going to protect him from the massive firestorm generated by a direct hit on the nation's capital.

Ten miles away wasn't enough for Peter. With the gas pedal mashed to the floor, he raced west on South Washington Street, periodically passing slower vehicles by using the wrong side of the road. He risked his life by driving in excess of one hundred miles an hour as he blew past Target and into the suburbs of Falls Church.

Every radio station, both local and on satellite, was repeating the IPAWS warnings. He reached the Capital Beltway Outer Loop and took the north ramp, hoping to get on Interstate 66 for a faster getaway.

Peter glanced at the clock and performed the mental calculations. It had been about thirty-one minutes since the launch of any missiles. Whether from North Korea or the Yasny Launch Base in Dombarovsky in western Russia, Washington, DC, would be hit within five minutes.

He wheeled the Mach 1 through traffic and along the shoulder of the beltway to enter I-66. He used the five westbound lanes and the tight emergency lane against the concrete median to get as far away as possible from the capital.

Suddenly, the sky lit up in his rearview mirror. Peter resisted the urge to get a better look. He knew what it was. He gripped the steering wheel and pressed forward, driving as fast as he could without looking back.

And then, suddenly, without warning, the two-year-old Ford Mustang Mach 1 died.

CHAPTER FORTY-NINE

Thursday, October 24
Near Sacramento, California

By the time the weary travelers had reached the Eisenhower Highway, the traffic was at a standstill due to an accident at Blue Canyon some forty miles away. The hotels around the Auburn exit were packed, with many people sleeping in their cars. It was half an hour before midnight when Owen said they needed to decide if they were gonna pitch a tent or keep going. They opted to stop and set up camp.

They backtracked several miles on Highway 49, known as the Golden Chain Highway, so named to honor the 49ers, waves of immigrants and easterners who flocked to Northern California in search of gold in the mid-nineteenth century.

They pulled off into a parking lot adjacent to a walking trail built alongside the North Fork of the American River. The rocky cliffs overlooking the dark blue water would be an idyllic site to wake up to the next morning to continue their trip to Lake Tahoe.

The expert campers had retrieved only the gear necessary to set up their family tent and the extreme-cold-weather sleeping bags to snuggle into for the night. While Owen and Lacey speculated about the exodus of people and where they were going, most likely Reno or Salt Lake City, Tucker spent some time on his cell phone.

He was struggling to get a cell signal. If he held the phone a certain way, one bar would appear. When it did, he scoured the web for news. It was more of the same, so it didn't hold his interest. The long day was making him drowsy, and he was about to power down his phone when he decided to conduct one more search.

During their trial run, both he and his mom had vowed to always know where the nearest fallout shelter was located for so long as this crisis was hanging over them. His first search, *fallout shelters near me*, yielded no results.

He lost the cell signal again and put the phone away for the night. But the issue nagged at him. He tried to search a different way. He recalled his dad telling him about the elementary school near the Dumbarton Bridge. Tucker searched for schools near his location, and the first result was Placer High just a few miles away. He navigated to the school's website and began clicking on all the available links. Then he found what he was looking for, sort of.

The Placer High website touted a number of apps that were suggested to make student life better. One was the STOPit app that allowed students to anonymously report situations like bullying or sexual assaults. They also suggested the same disaster app relied upon by millions of Californians, only to be fooled by a false alarm. On that page, he found what he was looking for. The recognizable graphic comprised of three yellow triangles on a black circle.

With his eyes drooping from exhaustion, Tucker navigated to his Google Earth app and clicked on the little yellow man, as he called the Pegman found on Google map applications. He dragged and dropped Pegman onto the street in front of the school. He rotated the school into view and slowly moved down the streets to study the fronts of the various buildings. He came to Agard Street in front of the basketball gym, and he barely saw it. The fallout shelter sign was attached to the white stucco and tucked behind a large overgrown bush. It had faded from the sun hitting it from the west in the past, but it was definitely there.

Satisfied with his efforts, he powered down the phone and fell asleep.

Until seventeen minutes after midnight.

All three of their cell phones were jolted out of sleep mode simultaneously. Their initial reaction was different from most Americans from coast to coast that sounded like this:

"What's that?"

"Did somebody set the alarm?"

"Is that damn disaster app malfunctioning again?"

"Do you think we should check it out?"

"I'm going back to sleep. Let me know what you find out, will ya?"

Lacey and her family had heeded the warnings given to them by her brother. She was able to trust Peter's judgment, and they immediately sprang into action.

She found her phone and read the alert aloud. It was the same one that had wrestled her dad and uncle out of bed three time zones away, as well as Peter, who was the closest of the family to a high-profile target.

Tucker was the first to speak. "What do we do, Dad?"

Owen thought for a moment before responding, "Okay, guys. Let's stay calm and think this through. We're over a hundred miles away from San Francisco. I'm pretty sure that's beyond the blast radius."

"What if they miss?" asked Lacey. Then she clarified. "What if this is real and whoever fired the missile overshot their target?"

Owen climbed out of his sleeping bags and rested on his knees. He went to the Yahoo! News home page to see if any form of announcement had been made.

"I guess that's possible, but I don't think it's—"

"There's a fallout shelter down the street," Tucker blurted out. "It's a high school. We kinda passed it when we drove back here. I swear it's only a few miles."

"Owen, let's go there," Lacey pleaded. "Just to be safe."

Owen glanced at his watch. Remarkably, it had been several minutes. "Come on. Gather everything up and shove it in the truck."

"I've got room in the backseat," Tucker offered as he slipped out of his sleeping bag and unzipped the tent door.

Lacey began to hand him their sleeping bags and inflatable pillows through the opening. Within a minute, the three of them had cleared out the tent, and Tucker was running up the hill to the truck.

The ballistic missile warning continued. Inside the Expedition, Owen drove quickly along the winding mountainous road, being cognizant of the trailer he was towing. Lacey frantically searched the radio for information that didn't consist of the monotonous, repeated warning.

Tucker leaned forward and rested his arms on his parents' seats. He held his phone so he could follow their progress on the Google Map app.

"Turn left at the stoplight by that bicycle store over there," he began, pointing toward the intersection. "That's Lewis Street. Then take a right when the street ends."

In less than a minute, Owen had steered the truck onto Orange Street. After driving several blocks through a residential neighborhood, they began to see brake lights ahead.

"Everybody else had the same idea," said Owen calmly. "Same thing happened at Patterson Elementary the other day. There wasn't a fallout shelter anyway."

"There's one here, Dad. I saw the sign on the map. I swear."

"Park the truck, Owen," suggested Lacey.

"What?"

"We're running out of time," replied Lacey in a much firmer tone. "Park the truck. We have to beat all of these people in the door."

CHAPTER FIFTY

Thursday, October 24
Near Sacramento, California

"Follow me!" shouted Tucker as he dashed between slow-moving cars headed toward the front of the high school. He crossed Orange Street and raced across Finley Street, occasionally glancing over his shoulder to confirm his parents were keeping up. When he reached a short flight of steps leading to a sidewalk to the left of the school's main building, he waited for his parents. He caught his breath and looked around at the traffic.

Everyone was waiting in line to turn left toward the auditorium as if they were dropping their kids off for a basketball game. Follow the leader, Tucker thought to himself. Like sheep walking off a cliff.

"Where to?" Owen asked.

"Let's see if there's a back way," replied Tucker. "Come on!"

He led them down the side of the one-story administration building until they reached a courtyard filled with benches and trees. Tucker used his recollection of the high school's layout on the map to wind his way through several classroom buildings until he arrived at the two-story, white stucco auditorium.

"There are people gathered around the front of the building," observed Lacey, pointing toward the front of the gymnasium on Agard Street.

Owen started running that way when Tucker called his name.

"Dad, wait! I've got a hunch." *Like father, like son.*

Owen stopped, and Tucker ran down the back of the gym, trying all the door handles. He reached the middle of the building and found one door ajar, propped open by a gray metal wastebasket.

"Here!" He waved his arm like a third-base coach imploring his runner to head for home plate.

His parents quickly joined him, and seconds later the trio was inside the hallways. Shouts and crying could be heard echoing through the mostly empty building.

"Spread out," instructed Owen. "Tucker and I will take each end of this corridor. Lacey, you head through the gym to the front. Try to text, or meet back here once you find the entrance to the shelter."

They took off in their separate directions in search of the stairwell leading below the gymnasium floor. Once again, Tucker's instincts paid off. He reached the end of the hallway and found a door marked concessions. He opened it slightly to listen.

Hurried voices shouting instructions could be heard from the other end of the space filled with refrigeration equipment and sales counters. He moved closer to the ruckus and found people pushing and shoving toward the rear of the concession's storage area.

He turned and rushed back into the rear corridor that ran the length of the building. His parents stood in the dimly lit hall, looking in his direction.

"I found it! Hurry! There are a lot of people trying to get in."

The family was off and running again. They followed Tucker into the concession area, and then they merged with the crowd, who continued to shove their way toward a single door entrance.

The three of them held hands and then locked arms to prevent being separated by the crowd attempting to force their way inside.

"What's taking so long?" asked Owen, who glanced at his watch. It had only been sixteen minutes since the alarm was sounded.

They were being shoved from behind, but they managed to keep their balance. Babies were crying, as were their mothers. Somebody in the rear screamed women and children first. The McDowells silently disagreed as they kept their place in line.

When they finally reached the doorway, a man dressed in the green-and-gold school colors with Placer emblazoned across the sweatshirt flanked the door along with a uniformed police officer.

Owen arrived at the door first.

"ID!" the officer shouted.

"What?" asked Owen, who was genuinely confused as to what the purpose of presenting identification was.

"ID, sir! We need to confirm you're a resident. Let's go."

Owen started to reach for his wallet, and then Lacey grabbed his arm.

"We were afraid and ran out the door. We don't have it." She presumed, rightfully so, that they would try to turn back someone from outside their community.

"Where do you live?" the Placer coach asked.

"Over on Finley," replied Tucker.

His observance of his surroundings and quick thinking paid off. They were waved through, and the next group of refugees was interrogated.

Once inside, they descended two flights of concrete stairs to the bottom of the structure. Fluorescent lights flickered, causing all three of them to squint to avoid the strobe effect. They followed another group through a single thick steel door into a large room that was illuminated with more fluorescent lighting.

It was dank and smelled musty. There appeared to be little or no ventilation, causing the trio to gasp for air slightly. The excited occupants, all of whom were chatting nervously, exacerbated the problem.

"Let's ease away from the door," suggested Owen.

They grasped each other by the hand and moved through the crowd toward the concrete wall. Slowly, they made their way to the back of the space until they reached a series of corrugated roll-up doors locked closed with padlocks.

"That's it!" someone shouted.

"No more!" yelled another.

The shouts of those safely in the bunker began to explode in unison. Owen glanced at his watch. He understood why. The nuke could strike at any moment.

"Let us in!" a woman demanded from outside the protective bunker.

"There's just four of us!" argued another.

"I'm a single," shouted one woman as if she were waiting in line at a Disneyland ride.

"You can't leave us out here!" begged a woman through her sobs.

The cries for help and admittance rose to a crescendo outside the shelter. Inside, the voices were equally loud as people demanded they close the door. Eventually, the insiders won out, and the metallic sound of the nuclear-hardened blast door closing and locking shut was heard.

This final act of separating the refugees from the horrors possibly awaiting those on the outside instantly brought a hush throughout the shelter.

Everyone held their breath as they waited. They strained to listen. Some studied their watches and whispered to their loved ones. Parents tried in vain to calm their crying children. Others could be heard openly praying. Some simply closed their eyes, held hands with the person closest to them, and waited for the nightmare to be over.

They didn't have to wait long. Three minutes later, the ground shook as if a seismic wave from an earthquake had swept over them. Decades of brittle concrete and dust fell from the ceiling, coating the occupants in the grayish-white debris.

Screams filled the air as everyone found God in that moment. For those who hadn't, that all changed when the power suddenly went out, thrusting them into pitch-black darkness.

THANK YOU FOR READING NUCLEAR WINTER: FIRST STRIKE!

If you enjoyed it, I'd be grateful if you'd take a moment to write a short review (just a few words are needed) and post it on Amazon. Amazon uses complicated algorithms to determine what books are recommended to readers. Sales are, of course, a factor, but so are the quantities of reviews my books get. By taking a few seconds to leave a review, you help me out and also help new readers learn about my work.

Sign up to my email list to learn about upcoming titles, deals, contests, appearances, and more!

SIGN UP AT BOBBYAKART.COM

VISIT my feature page at Amazon.com/BobbyAkart for more information on my other action-packed thrillers, which includes over forty Amazon #1 bestsellers in forty-plus fiction and nonfiction genres.

NUCLEAR WINTER: ARMAGEDDON, book two in this epic survival thriller.

The story continues...

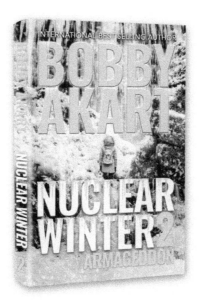

The real battle against extinction, Nuclear Winter, was just beginning.

COMING TO AMAZON

OTHER WORKS BY AMAZON CHARTS TOP 25 AUTHOR BOBBY AKART

Nuclear Winter
First Strike
Armageddon
Whiteout
Desolation

New Madrid (a standalone, disaster thriller)

Odessa (a Gunner Fox trilogy)
Odessa Reborn
Odessa Rising
Odessa Strikes

The Virus Hunters
Virus Hunters I
Virus Hunters II
Virus Hunters III

The Geostorm Series
The Shift

The Pulse
The Collapse
The Flood
The Tempest
The Pioneers

The Asteroid Series (A Gunner Fox trilogy)
Discovery
Diversion
Destruction

The Doomsday Series
Apocalypse
Haven
Anarchy
Minutemen
Civil War

The Yellowstone Series
Hellfire
Inferno
Fallout
Survival

The Lone Star Series
Axis of Evil
Beyond Borders
Lines in the Sand
Texas Strong
Fifth Column
Suicide Six

The Pandemic Series
Beginnings
The Innocents

Level 6

Quietus

The Blackout Series

36 Hours

Zero Hour

Turning Point

Shiloh Ranch

Hornet's Nest

Devil's Homecoming

The Boston Brahmin Series

The Loyal Nine

Cyber Attack

Martial Law

False Flag

The Mechanics

Choose Freedom

Patriot's Farewell (standalone novel)

Black Friday (standalone novel)

Seeds of Liberty (Companion Guide)

The Prepping for Tomorrow Series

Cyber Warfare

EMP: Electromagnetic Pulse

Economic Collapse